Embrace of the Wolf

Jack Cady & Carol Orlock

FAIRWOOD PRESS
Bonney Lake, WA

EMBRACE OF THE WOLF
A Fairwood Press Book
August 2023
Copyright © 2023 by the Estate of Jack Cady

Fairwood Press
21528 104th Street Court East
Bonney Lake, WA 98391
www.fairwoodpress.com

Series Cover Design by Jennifer Tough
Collection Editorial Direction by Mark Teppo

ISBN: 978-1-958880-06-7
First Fairwood Press Edition: August 2023
Printed in the United States of America

The first edition of this novel was published by Diamond Books in 1993.

THE CADY COLLECTION

NOVELS

The Hauntings of Hood Canal
Inagehi
The Jonah Watch
McDowell's Ghost
The Man Who Could Make Things Vanish
The Off Season
Singleton
Street

Dark Dreaming [with Carol Orlock, as Pat Franklin]
Embrace of the Wolf [with Carol Orlock, as Pat Franklin]

OTHER WRITINGS

Phantoms
Fathoms
The American Writer

Embrace of the Wolf

Chapter 1

WINTER JUMPED THE BACK OF A PACIFIC STORM THAT FIRST TUES-
day after Labor Day, and it rode the jet stream south from Alaska to
scour the Pacific Northwest coast. Winter raced from the backs of
clouds and ravaged beaches like packs of hunting wolves. Everyone
in Surfbreak felt the storm hit.

Tourists, who had foolishly planned to duck last night's traffic by leaving first thing in the morning, found themselves stung
by needles of rain. They struggled to load plastic coolers, rubber
rafts, and camping gear onto luggage racks. Soon, abandoned gear
tumbled in colorful cartwheels across grass-covered dunes.

At the Surfbreak Cafe, where locals gathered for eggs and pancakes on this first day safe from tourists, men huddled over dregs
of coffee and watched a gray view of horizontal rain. Gusts hissed
around window seams, sending shivers along plaid cafe curtains.
Later, some people would say the trouble actually started that Tues-
day morning. Other people, those with a better sense of history,
would say the trouble started eighty years before. At any rate, ugly
deaths rode that wind, deaths so horrible that stories of them would
refuse to die. Molly Snow, the center of the trouble, had barely arrived and parked her car.

A few blocks away, near the beach, Molly Snow tried to get out
of her blue Mazda. Winds pushed the door shut and shoved the

slender, dark-haired woman back inside. She shivered and fumbled the key to the Aowl cottage before bracing to fight the wind and push the door again. This time a lull freed her, but new gusts pushed her off course in a stumbling climb to the cottage door. She stabbed her key at the lock. Molly reeled inside and fought the door shut.

Inside, the Aowl cottage seemed small. It should have felt cozy, but it didn't. Set back from the road and only yards from the deserted beach, it was also isolated.

The cottage would certainly be a lonely place, but Molly hoped the solitude would feel welcome. It could provide time to achieve her goals this winter. Usually she got more attention that she wanted, and that could be distracting. At thirty-three, her slender figure and lithe movements still turned men's heads. She could not help that and occasionally even enjoyed its consequences. Nor could she help her dusky beauty, which some took for a sign of Native American ancestry.

Molly shivered and hurried to light a fire in the woodstove. The small cottage seemed to sit in the very mouth of the storm. Outside, the wind attacked like hunting wolves, and it would not be long before Molly began to imagine it precisely that way.

A few hundred yards up the beach, safe inside the thick walls of the Aowl Museum, Tess Fiddert handed a spare key to Surfbreak's one-man police force, Ed Mulling. Even inside this immense building they felt the storm. It shook the western wall and rattled Plexiglas on display cases, making the panes shimmer in pale light from the exit sign. An 1820's button blanket, hanging free above the central staircase, trembled in the air. In the Northwest nature exhibit, stiff shadows preserved by taxidermy—sea harriers, owls, and raccoons—seemed to shiver and grip claws deeper into display stands. Along the walls hung ceremonial masks from the Wolvine and other tribes. Faces of otter, cougar, and wolf took on a curious light.

Sheriff Mulling spoke above the boom of wind. "What's her name again, forgot to write it down." Mulling's fondness for pancakes in the morning, and a few beers at night, showed in the belly hanging over his belt. He did not much care for Tess Fiddert. He did not much care for anyone since he moved to Surfbreak after leaving the police force in Portland. Surfbreak was a rough town on a rough coast. Mulling felt right at home. His face was fleshy, but his eyes looked flat and impatient.

"Molly Snow. I put all her letters here by the phone. There's even a picture. She looks Indian." Tess Fiddert moved a manila folder closer to the edge of her desk. She was a heavyset woman in her late fifties. At the end of tourist season she wanted nothing more than a good long rest, and preferred getting it anywhere but in Surfbreak.

"Read through this if you want," she added. "That photo definitely looks Indian to me. And to Clint down at the hardware. And to Doc Bill, who ought to know since he has to treat them. I just happened to show the picture around." Tess thought of another picture, one resting in a photograph drawer not ten feet away. A woman in that picture looked almost exactly like this Molly Snow. After a moment's thought Tess decided not to show the old photograph to Mulling.

"The governor himself says it's okay, I go along." Mulling added the key, tagged and tested on the museum's outer lock, to the rest of his keys.

Tess took a deep breath and tried explaining for the third time that Molly Snow had only a Governor's Grant. That meant she got a key to the outer door, and permission to use the museum all she wanted while it was closed this winter. The grant did not mean that Molly knew the governor, or that the governor knew Molly. In fact, the governor probably didn't give a rip about the grant. In fact, far as Tess Fiddert was concerned, the governor and his whole bureaucracy could blow smoke just as soon as she finished certain plans she had for the Aowl Museum.

As for Molly Snow, Tess doubted the sheriff would care that she came to do research on the legendary Alford James Aowl, the first white man to walk this coast. Tess just hoped that this college girl would not go poking her nose in places where it didn't belong.

"I'll keep tabs," Mulling said. "Make sure she don't leave doors unlocked. Count on it."

"Keep close tabs," Tess said. "These college kids can get sloppy. I didn't put half a lifetime into cataloguing this place, just to see some graduate chickie mess it up."

Mulling returned his key chain to its hook on his belt. "I'd better check the beach for lost mutts any tourists left." He headed toward the door, determined not to go anywhere near that beach until the wind died. He didn't mind shooting stray dogs each fall. It was dangerous for local kids if the dogs formed a pack, but the job would go lots easier once the weather took a breather.

As he left the museum, a telephone several blocks away at the Surfbreak police station rang and rang. On the fourth ring, a recording picked up. Mulling's voice spoke a message, and after the beep a tourist's trembling voice reported that she and her husband had just been leaving town, with their kids, when they saw something strange on the beach. A man, they thought, or the body of a man. He looked dead. He lay curled over as if he had tried to protect himself from an attack. His clothes looked torn, but maybe they were just rumpled by the wind. The woman's voice said that she had to go now, but guessed she did right to call. Even her husband wasn't going anywhere near that thing. It was just too scary.

The wind chased Mulling's patrol car along Breakers Avenue. At the Surfbreak Cafe, he joined the others for coffee while the storm spread darkness southward. Winds rode the rises and rock falls up the hills at the town's eastern side. Winds howled beneath the south bridge over the Wolvine River. The old wooden structure shook.

Along the banks of that river, barely a trickle since the dam had been built, the storm headed a few hundred yards inland. It swirled over **NO TRESPASSING** signs to double back over a federal boundary. It entered the Wolvine reservation.

It tore at loose boards and corrugated plastic roofs. It rattled broken steps leading to weatherworn shacks and trailers where the last of the Wolvine tribe lived.

No one in the shacks talked much during this stormy day. At the same time everyone saw the daylight falter before a giant shadow that walked across the hills. Tourists might mistake the shadow for some local aberration in the weather, but the Wolvine knew better and they shuddered. They avoided each other's eyes, although one or two whispered the name "Storm Man" under his breath. It was an old name, and it carried an ancient curse.

In one shack, ringed by trees and cushioned by a slightly wider strip of land, Raymond Goodwillow felt the chill arrive. He tightened the ties of his slippers and wished he could ignore the coming of the wind. His feet seemed too big for his diminished frame, and his hands showed the tremble of age. He was an old man now, almost ninety. His once broad shoulders were hunched and thin beneath the blanket. His eyes seemed ageless. They were as clear as the eyes of a young child, but no child had eyes so clearly marked with experience and knowledge.

Goodwillow felt the wind rattle the door of the shack. It was possible to change the course of a wind like this, Goodwillow knew, but he hoped he would not have to do it.

He watched a feather scurry across the floor and caught a whiff of quickly chilling air. This wind was different. He knew this smell, knew it deep back in memory the way he knew (and could still hear, some nights in his sleep) every moan of men who had been brought to him. There had been men injured in the hunt, and there had been runnels of blood outlining ribs of men who had shot each other, knifed each other, or fallen from high cliffs. The smell told of children devoured by diseases that white men called typhoid, pneumonia, influenza. It was sticky sweet and spread metallic red through the air. It drew Goodwillow close and he shivered, pulled toward caves of memory and ancient power.

It was too late to do anything about memories, Goodwillow reminded himself. If memories returned, though, and turned into actual flesh, then Goodwillow would have to take action. Raymond Goodwillow felt, more than saw, the giant shadow moving across the land. That shadow would be Storm Man, and only one thing could make Storm Man return.

That thing was the return of Alford James Aowl, the white man the Wolvine knew as Man-Among-Wolves. And only one thing would have made Man-Among-Wolves return. That one thing was the woman called Birch, the woman who had once been Storm Man's wife. Goodwillow pulled the blanket around his knees. He turned toward the one small window and studied the shadowed forest outside. He had been a boy the last time this shadow walked above the hills. The Wolvine would know a bad winter. This year could be as bad as that one he had lived nearly eighty years trying to forget.

Chapter 2

MOLLY SNOW CLUMPED UP STEPS INTO THE AOWL COTTAGE. SHE shoved the last packing carton onto the kitchen table and turned to wrestle the door shut. For once the wind cooperated. Instead of fighting, it reversed direction and sucked the door back, pulling her small body along and slamming her to the jamb with a sudden thwack.

Cartons now jammed the interior of the cottage. There were two boxes of kitchen utensils, a travel bag filled with sweaters, and two suitcases of clothes and hiking gear. The five heaviest boxes contained the basis for the next eight months' work—maps drawn by Alford Aowl, or rather, photocopies of yellowing maps, biographical monographs, background material on Aowl, coastal surveys. Molly pulled up the flap of the fifth box and lifted out a thick yellow envelope.

She let herself collapse onto the room's one modern comfort— a plaid sofa with stains along its arms—before sliding the envelope's contents free. These papers would, she hoped, tell whether her grant money paid to get the lights and water turned on. Molly scanned the fine print on a legal-sized sheet.

Even in the dim light, the outline of the young woman's features revealed enough to make her look quite at home inside the rough walls of the cottage. Her straight black hair, tied with a leather thong at her neck, hung an inch below her shoulder blades. It suggested Native American ancestry, although no one in her family could ever figure out what tribe. Her mother came from a long line of Irishmen and her father swore up one limb of his family tree and down the other that no one on his side ever married an Indian. Molly had been a very little girl when her maternal grandmother died, but Molly remembered an old woman who did not seem Irish.

Molly was slight and fine-boned, with a long, graceful neck and high cheekbones. Her skin, tinged a ruddy tan without any time spent sunbathing, had begun to crease in the promise of crow's feet around intense brown eyes. She thumbed a page and brought the fine print up near enough to read in the half-darkness.

It was useless. She'd just have to pay to have the lights turned on, then figure if she could actually afford the hookup.

Before heading into town to visit the utility offices, Molly dabbed a sleeve at the water trickling from her hair. She leaned back to survey the shadowed room that would be her home for the next eight months. This was Alford James Aowl's own home, preserved on land he had personally surveyed.

It seemed to her that the storm itself attacked this cabin. She wondered how much more dark history she would discover in this place, because a lot of dark history already surrounded the name of Aowl. In the shadowed daylight, she felt a chill rise, not from the chilly air but from the inside. The tremor made her cringe, as if pulling her back from battles either waged or about to be waged, a tremor of horror.

Molly tried to laugh. She told herself that such feelings were an occupational hazard for people who studied the past, and especially people who studied this coast. If Native Americans were sometimes mystics, then the peoples of this coast were perhaps the strongest mystics of all. This was a rough coast settled by only the toughest people, the ones too practical to feel the eeriness of the place itself.

The events that brought her here felt as unreal as the wildness of the storm. By rights, she should be sitting two hundred miles away on the third floor of the Pinehaven University History and Anthropology building, typing professors' travel schedules and filing tear sheets from scholarly publications. Instead she had snagged a grant.

To her it had seemed sheer luck, but that is not what the Dean of Arts and Sciences said. When the dean congratulated her, he pointed out that Molly showed every promise of becoming a scholar. Even now Molly treasured the dean's words: "Because you have intelligence and analytic ability, but most of all you've got good common sense." She was a strong scholar, she knew, and a tough competitor, but the dean also recognized her ability to rise above the petty politics of academic life, to trust her own ideas and cut her own path.

For now, Molly thought of her present entitlement to several thousand dollars of state money, and to eight months' residence in Surfbreak, as a reward for paying her dues. It began to make up for thousands of trips to the mailroom, photocopying announcements of conferences and publication opportunities, stuffing them in mailboxes of faculty who never read them and disdained recycling to drop them into the wastebasket. Those were fat and happy professors, Molly liked to assure herself, and she was lean, hungry, and ten credits short of a Master's degree.

That was why last December, when the announcement of funds for studies to commemorate the State Centennial arrived, Molly took the time to read it. Then she passed along the six faintly printed pages in even fainter photocopies and stayed up nights for a week putting together her own application. She was one of only three applicants who met the deadline. The other two were researching North Coast settlements. Alford James Aowl, the state's most mysterious—or, as some said, notorious—explorer, had been left to Molly Snow alone.

Molly sighed and looked at the room's few furnishings. Aside from the kitchen alcove—electric stove and ancient, no doubt noisy, refrigerator—the cottage consisted of only this one room, plus a cave-dark bedroom and a small bath whose scent had made her cringe and make a mental note to pick up disinfectant.

She paused. Beneath the rage of wind came yipping sounds, like those made by dogs when they were asleep and dreaming. Yet these small cries were deep-voiced. The voice, or voices, came from large animals.

Directly across from the sofa, the black cast iron woodstove showed a line of rust along the seam of its stack. Next to the stove and its broken woodbox, a plain pinewood desk stood below empty shelves. A floor lamp, stark as a skeleton in a wild hat, rose beside the desk.

Tourists rented the cottage during the summer. The Aowl Foundation used the rent to help support the Alford James Aowl Memorial Museum which, along with twelve miles of unspoiled beach, attracted vacationers. Molly had a key to that museum, or at least was due to collect one later today. She'd never get to that, she resolved, if she didn't get the utilities fixed. The sofa released a cloud of dust as she abandoned it, a new shadow drifting in the air.

Storm winds turned to gales, and gales declined to breezes. Molly returned from town and waited for an electrician to turn on the power. She busied herself unpacking, and she thought of Aowl.

The most mysterious thing about him was his death, or the lack of it. White townspeople of his day claimed that he got lost in the forest and died. Stories from the reservation said that he ran away with wolves. One fanciful tale even claimed that he became a wolf.

It was four-fifteen by the time the man came to unlock the power box on the side of the cottage and flip the circuit breaker, taking ten minutes to do thirty seconds worth of work. When the utility truck finally pulled away, Molly grabbed her parka and headed across the dunes toward the largest shadow in the gathering dusk. That had to be the Aowl Museum, exactly where the map said it would be.

From the bedroom window, the hulking four-story shape had looked dark and abandoned. She'd written to a Miss Tess Fiddert a month ago, saying she would pick up her key yesterday, or this morning at the latest. Now she struggled to hurry, trudging through sand, and saw that even the wide black parking lot lay empty. Fading light revealed the dark building. Molly simply stared.

She'd seen pictures of this atrocity. It was a mansion built by a lumber baron for a mistress who eventually destroyed the lumberman's family and his fortune. The museum's brochures told the whole story, with color shots of the building.

Layers of spiked wooden rickrack patterned the north wall, interrupted only by swooping gables where shadows seemed to gather and ripple. Above the mutter of the surf, a stirring came from those shadows, nesting gulls perhaps. Yet, the entire building seemed to waver and pulse with a sad, dark murmuring.

And it was black. From wainscoted skirts dropping near the sand, to triangular roof peaks and towers and turrets, the mansion stood like a monument to darkness. It hovered above the land like a brooding vulture. Balusters stood like walls along widow's walks, and the house stood not like a statement of love or lust but only sorrow.

Alford Aowl himself had painted this building black, Molly knew. He started the task two years after the death of its owner. The death had been hideous. The lumberman had been mauled by an animal, either wolf or cougar. He suffered pain and delirium for three days before dying, long enough, in a place like this, to be the start of a legend.

In the months preceding his death, people said, the lumberman's body had been seen lying on the beach. It always disappeared before anyone could bury it. That winter had been the worst winter of storms ever known on this coast. Now, as legend told it, storms followed when any corpse was thrown upon the beach. Like most legends, Molly thought, there were just enough coincidental storms to make the story seem true.

Aowl and the lumberman had been longtime enemies, and painting the building black was Aowl's revenge. Even the windows looked black and impenetrable, despite vague reflections of mist flickering across them. Aowl had repaid his enemy this way, Molly recalled from her reading, by making this mansion look utterly empty.

And it probably was empty right now, she thought, shaking off a chill. No light gleamed through the windows. Tess Fiddert had surely gone home.

Two wide doors, their glistening ebony surfaces studded with brass fixtures, offered cold welcome. Both were locked tight. Molly tried knocking, then pounding. Squared inside a brass frame, a bone-white placard announced, "Open 11 A.M. to 6 P.M.—May 15 to Labor Day." Molly's knuckles struck cold wood again, more in frustration than hope, before she turned and leaned against the door. Tess Fiddert might come tomorrow to finish closing down for the winter, or else might live in town.

Overhead, murmuring from the eaves sounded louder than

it had from the dunes. Winds sobbed like dying dreams, or like predictions of a never-dying winter. Wind caught threads of sound and made them thrum like ancient murmurs. From somewhere in the darkness wind growled like an animal.

Molly guessed she should go back to the cottage, but that was the last place she felt like being. She circled the museum's southern wall instead, watching without hope for a light, then headed out across the dunes. Perhaps a walk along the beach would soothe the day's disappointments.

Chapter 3

OUT NEAR THE WOLVINE RESERVATION, ANCIENT POWER FLOWED through the forest, and other power walked through the hills. In old times, the natives believed that these forests belonged to wolf, and the hills belonged to cougar. The skies belonged to eagle and raven and rainbird.

Now the forces of wolf and cougar became running shapes of darkness. The snarl of wolf sounded through the trees. High in the hills a great shadow coalesced, sought to become a shape that looked nearly human. The shadow faltered, flowed apart, came back together. Darkness grew and the shadow took its final man-like form. Storm Man began to walk.

On the beach, Molly walked beneath moonlight as clouds blew in from the sea. The beach was in disarray after the storm. She reached the tide line. Ground mists rose along the shore, and she let her steps find their own rhythm over the bumpy surface. She edged nearer to the waves to reach the smooth surface where the last tide had packed the sand, pulled her parka close, and watched diminishing winds lift mists from the shore.

The edge of surf caught scattered moonlight, and Molly let her thoughts drift, amazed at how differently this day had gone from the way she'd imagined.

Back in Pinehaven, Surfbreak had seemed impossibly far,

some outpost within dense depths of primeval forest. Yet, driving down the main street this morning, she'd felt shocked to see a modern gas station, souvenir shops, and paved sidewalks with entirely average people walking along them.

At the same time, she told herself, the people living here could not be average. Even now, at the end of the twentieth century, this place not only felt remote; it was remote. Surfbreak had never been a large town. Now, with old forests cut, and no harbor for fishermen, the town depended on tourism. When the tourists left, it seemed that modernity went with them.

A knot of kelp lay twisted on the sand. Mist moved in clumps before her. Further along the shore, dark shapes wheeled above a cloud of mist, diving and spiraling like birds. The wind shifted, carrying back faint, screechy cries. Someone else must be walking there, scaring sea gulls into the air, although she seemed to recall that sea gulls did not fly at night. Molly paused, watching the swirling shapes swoop and complain. No figure emerged from the mist.

Molly zipped her parka up and resolved to reach the gulls before they moved further off. Wind urged the next bank of mist toward her, but she reached its far side only to enter another cloud. Faint moonglow illuminated the birds' wings, and they looked only slightly closer. They were definitely focused on something below their whirling path.

Straight ahead, the moon outlined another wall of mist. She could almost make out shapes shadowed against it. The shadows could not be people, not unless these people went on all fours.

Ahead, low-slung, swift-running shapes skimmed in circles. The shapes spun nearer, then changed direction to dissolve into invisibility. They were dogs. They had to be dogs, but if they were dogs they were all from giant breeds. Molly watched the bouncing play of the shapes, admiring their strength and grace. It would feel good to have such strength and yet to belong among others, as these dogs belonged in their pack. She felt a passing flash of primitive joy.

Or maybe the dogs actually belonged to a person. A shadow out there stood too tall for a dog. It seemed that a man walked in the middle of the pack. Molly squinted, thought of giving a friendly shout, then hesitated. She could no longer see the manlike shape, only the shapes of dogs. The closest ones looked much too large.

The largest shape, a silver-white in the backlighting of moon-glow, raced in circles as if he prowled the perimeter. His head was massive, lifting to sniff the air, then dropping to tack his immense body sideways. His turns and gyrations sent shadows spinning in all directions.

Molly recalled that Aowl's diaries rarely spoke of wolves, although he wrote about every other kind of animal. He seemed secretive. But other early settlers had often complained of wolf trouble. Those reports, though, were a century old. This many wolves could not have survived.

A gust of wind brought a faint, doggy smell of wet fur. It hung heavy and moist on the salt mist. Then the gust changed direction, pushing mist back toward the dogs. For the last few minutes Molly had merely stood in place. Now the largest silver-white shape stiffened. It turned sideways as if its attention were caught. A clear patch of moonlight fixed the animal against the sand. It stood spectral and beautiful and wild, its fur thick as a mane, a bundle of raw animal power, pure and uncontrolled.

Molly tried to hold perfectly still, trusting the mist to hide her, but sudden memory jolted her into action. Sight hardly mattered to dogs. If she could smell them, they could smell her.

She spun away. At that instant the dogs turned too, yanked from their play by one deep, low growl. The growl might have been the surf, but Molly ran, diving toward the next bank of mist, racing through it to plunge into another. She tried listening for sounds, for steps, for barks. The thudding of her own feet filled her ears. If the dogs gave chase, there was no escape. A slippery sea whip made her stumble, and her hand touched sopping sand. She pushed herself upward to run again. On an impulse, she angled toward the sound of the surf. Her steps sank deeper. Waves must be near in the deep curtain of mist. After a few sideways steps, she felt the rushing chill of surf swirl over her feet. It rose to her ankles. A receding wave pulled her seaward. She leapt and landed in the fanning of the next wave. Water might erase her scent.

Soft, flowing sand sucked at each step, adding weight. The water might conceal her, but oncoming waves were impossible to see. If she fell, a rogue wave could take her. Too dangerous, she thought, breath razoring her throat. Choking, struggling for one more gulp of air to keep accelerating, she angled landward.

The instant she broke free of the water, pressure as sudden as the closing of a trap yanked her ankle. She pulled free and spun, struggling for footing in the sand. The next bite caught her leg. Wet, solid weight thudded into her ribs.

She was going down. More weight fell on top of her, coming from the side, paws rolling her onto her back. The dogs were all over her, too many to flail at, furred shadows feinting and leaping too quickly to dodge.

Weight fell, thrusting her flat again. Now something tightened at her neck, a choking pressure as if a cord were knotted to strangle her. The parka's hood, she knew at once. Teeth here tearing it back from the jacket, yanking her head back with it. She heard nylon tear, and a new round of yipping followed. There were no growls, only the high-pitched yips, as if she were a toy they had found to play with.

Jaws snapped near her ear. She lifted her arms to shield her head and screamed, screamed again, heard her voice echo back in a deeper sound.

It was a growl, low-pitched, like a warning. The sound came from further off. Three sharp barks followed, and suddenly the pummeling stopped.

Molly risked a glimpse toward where the barks had sounded. The huge silver dog stood with its back turned, snapping at the shadows that now circled him. His low barks drove them back from her. A tongue of surf suddenly swelled under her, filling her mouth with bitter saltwater. Molly scrambled backwards, and when she looked again, the dogs were only darker patches in the mist, moving away.

She struggled to her feet. A few steps brought her to drier sand. The lights of Surfbreak winked between dunes—bright neon, paler house lights, the turning red globe above the gas station. She pushed toward them. Her shoulders heaved to clutch at breath, but once she reached the edge of the dunes she looked back.

Skimming shapes of dogs surfaced and disappeared along the white bank of mist. They were indistinct, but there. They crowded around something that had either been cast, or had fallen, at the tide line. It was a dark shape, maybe a log. A chill of terror electrified her nerve endings. The shape was also the right size for a body.

Molly felt herself shaking with relief. The dogs could have killed her. A landward breeze cooled her face and brought the faint, wet, doggy smell and a low growl of surf, or of warning. She touched the hood of her parka. It should have been torn almost full away, but her fingers found only the smooth corded line of its closure.

Her breath nearly recovered, Molly urged her steps over the last of the dunes. She took a side street to hurry past darkened summer cottages and finally emerged onto Breakers Avenue. Slowing her pace at last, she headed north along civilized blocks. She could not have imagined that attack, yet she must have. That was the only explanation. She must have tripped and fallen, passed out for a moment. Or else the parka really did have tears somewhere.

When she reached the cottage, even before getting her feet out of wet shoes and socks, Molly stripped out of the parka. She held it up to the light. Not a single rip marked it anywhere.

Chapter 4

From September to May, Surfbreak was Sheriff Edward J. Mulling's idea of a quiet town. Fights occasionally broke out at the Timberman's Cafe, between loggers too drunk to land a punch. Once in a while Mulling got a call out to the reservation at Surfbreak's boundary to settle a ruckus between Woofies. Woofies were the only real drawback to the job.

Mulling knew better than to call the Wolvine Indians "Woofies" to their faces, but he preferred that nickname. Some local whites used it because it sounded friendly and funny but pleasantly insulting. Other people were not amused. Mulling liked Surfbreak as well as he liked any place. His job was even better than the one he'd once held on the Portland police force. Surfbreak's main attitude was "Don't mess in anybody else's business."

Aside from Woofies, the biggest hassle of the job came when Hal Nickerson, owner of Nicky's Pharmacy and Soda Fountain, got fed up with kids shoplifting and insisted that Mulling park out front to nab ten-year-olds on the scamper. The system worked unless Mulling dozed off. Kids knew that Nicky's was a softer target between two and four PM.

Relief swept through town once Labor Day passed, and Mulling felt it most of all. The tourist exodus meant he could stop responding to goofy phone messages, like that stunt yesterday about a dead body on the beach. He'd looked. There was no body, and damned if he could see any washed-up logs even suggesting the shape of one. There was a town legend that was used to attract tourists—some legend about a body on the beach meaning hard times. Mulling guessed a couple tourists let the legend get the best of their imaginations.

Tourists were a never-ending pain in the neck, but the town could not do without them. They came mostly from Portland and Seattle, people romantically trying to discover some remnants of an earlier and rougher way of life. Even one old Victorian museum filled with legends was enough to bring them flocking.

Half the parking and moving violations he issued over the summer never got paid. Tourists naturally figured they wouldn't be back. Nonetheless, the sheriff spent early September days updating a special book he kept in his top desk drawer. In it he recorded each violator's license number and the date of the infraction. Many times he'd spot one of those vehicles back on Breakers Avenue a year or two later, pulling the same stunt, and he'd enjoy the pleasure of placing a red check in the margin of his book. Then he'd call the owner of Surfbreak's tow truck, and he'd chuckle. There were few enough joys in police work, and revenge was all of them.

Which was why, on that Wednesday morning, Sheriff Mulling sat at his desk when the door jangled open to admit a youngish woman he couldn't say he'd ever seen before. Mulling observed that she was of medium height, dark-haired, and pretty enough even if she wasn't white. Mulling tagged her for a Woofie and bent his head once more to concentrate on his notebook.

"With you soon as I finish," he muttered. No point interrupting pleasant work for some squaw coming in because her old man wandered off or, more likely, landed a slap.

From the corner of his eye Mulling watched the woman glance around for comfortable seating, then settle onto the church pew below the front window. She moved like a white woman, even if she did look like a Woofie. She had well-shaped legs; that was definitely a mark in her favor. Mulling fanned the stack of citations on his desk. There was a good hour's work in it.

Ten minutes passed while Sheriff Mulling continued writing and Molly Snow debated whether or not to speak up. Molly studied the bare-bones office walls empty but for official looking notices, steel desk, typewriter, fancy radio—nothing personal or human about the place. She looked at the shining crown of the seated man's bald head. Something about him repelled her. The problem was that Sheriff Mulling, if the paunchy man in khaki was Mulling, might have to be persuaded to give out the information she wanted. If he got annoyed she'd lose her last option. He looked like the easily annoyed type.

Kept awake half the night as wind returned and rattled the bedroom window, Molly had set out early to locate breakfast and a telephone directory. The breakfast was not half-bad, eggs over-easy in the company of a drowsy waitress and several plaid-shirted men. The directory in the phone booth outside the restaurant was only slightly thicker than a pamphlet, and Tess Fiddert's name was nowhere in it. Molly returned to the museum, but found the parking lot still empty. A small notice posted below the placard on the front door gave a phone number to call in case of emergency.

Unfortunately, when she dialed, a man's gruff voice answered, "Sheriff's Office, Ed Mulling speaking." The man sounded offended at being disturbed. Molly took a deep breath, then chickened out. She hung up. She would return to the cottage to watch from the window. If no car pulled up at the museum before noon, she'd go personally to ask for Miss Fiddert's number.

Meanwhile, Molly had tried to wedge the cottage's bedroom window tighter into its frame, a task which quickly proved hopeless. Dry rot had weakened the wood, and every scrap of newspaper she stuffed along its side only widened the gap. The next good wind might take the window out, or shove the whole thing inward to smash on the bedroom floor. When she went to get the Aowl Museum key, she would stop for wood and nails.

Tess Fiddert clearly was not coming to work. It was nearly noon, so Molly headed out for the sheriff's office, a square concrete building at the head of Breakers Avenue.

The hard bench was beginning to hurt. Molly got up and crossed the waiting area to examine the bulletin board. She paged through the list of job openings for county government, then riffled them loudly.

From his desk, Ed Mulling could tell the woman wanted attention. He applied himself more diligently. When she spoke up at last, her tone mixed exasperation with politeness.

"Maybe I should run some errands and then come back?"

Mulling ignored her. The woman's voice didn't sound Woofie, despite his earlier guess. She talked like a white person.

"If you'll just tell me what time?"

"Keep your pants on," Mulling said. "I'm just finishing up."

Molly returned to the church pew, then chose to pace.

She remembered that small-town people often liked to size up strangers with idle talk before getting down to business.

"Wind sure got going last night," she tried.

"Uh-huh."

"It tried chewing one of my windows right out of the frame."

Mulling gave no answer.

"Which reminds me," Molly tried again. "You don't have any big dogs around here, do you? I mean huge ones, running on the beach?"

Sheriff Mulling sat bolt upright. He examined the woman's face. She'd clearly seen something. If enough tourist strays had collected over the summer to make a pack, he'd be all week shooting and trapping them.

"Probably just heard the surf," he answered slowly. "New folks think it yaps and growls like old dogs."

"No, I saw them."

Mulling's heart fell.

"I was walking by the surf and it was misty." She hesitated, as if unsure of whether to say more, then shrugged. "I'm sure they must have been there."

"Nothing to worry about." Mulling closed his notebook and flattened his hands on the desktop to push himself up. "Now what was it you wanted? You didn't come interrupting to talk about dogs."

The woman smiled, turning on the charm. She extended her hand. "I'm Molly Snow. I'm here working at the museum"—she paused, searching for words—"on a job. I'm staying out by the beach, at the Aowl cottage. Except I can't get started at the museum because I was supposed to meet a Miss Tess Fiddert."

Sheriff Mulling gave no response.

"She has a key for me. I have letters, permission to go in. If you'd like to see them?"

"She said something about that."

"I thought since you were the sheriff," Molly went on, "and your number's listed on the museum door, you could tell me where to find Miss Fiddert."

Mulling supposed he could. Mulling also supposed he could shrug and say nothing. Fiddert would raise holy hell if she heard about that. Giving this half-breed his own key, on the other hand, or letting her in, was out of the question.

"I could give her a call," Mulling said slowly. Molly said she'd be happy to make the call herself.

"I'll take care of it. You just go on about your business." Glad that he'd found the right attitude, Mulling stepped around the desk to usher Molly Snow out the door. "I'll tell her to come by that place you're living, tonight."

"But what if you can't reach her?"

Mulling stiffened. "I'll reach her. You just go along." If she planned on living here all winter, he thought, this college type might as well learn who was in charge. He began closing the door before she had completely backed out of it. Outside Molly paused to zip her jacket. What was his problem, she wondered, aside from being overweight with skin that looked as unhealthy as the gray-green of his uniform? She felt thankful she had stopped herself from trying to explain everything that had happened when she saw those dogs last night. Today the memory felt as unreal as a dream.

She pulled her list from her jacket pocket. There were groceries to buy, if she wasn't planning to go broke eating in restaurants, plus nails and wood for that window.

The encounter with Sheriff Mulling continued to rankle as Molly ran errands along Breakers Avenue. Surfbreak's sheriff was unpleasant, but people in town seemed only slightly better; tired, but distantly friendly. Some of them seemed intimidated, but not by her. A group of men stood at a street corner looking toward the hills. They talked in low tones.

The hardware clerk silently helped her cut several wooden shims and select an assortment of nails. The clerk at the pharmacy was courteous but quiet.

Molly guessed her orange hiking jacket and denim skirt set her apart. Around here, only men wore denim; work-worn overalls and jackets torn at the elbows. Their counterparts, to a woman, wore pastel dresses. Molly guessed that she looked like a tourist.

The grocery store beside the gas station had a wooden floor and an imitation brass fan turning lazily just inside the door. The selection of exotic lunchmeats in the cooler, and the lack of a straightforward loaf of white bread on the bakery shelf, confirmed that this store catered to a motel kitchenette and picnic-basket trade. At the checkout, Molly asked if they carried bread without raisins, walnuts, or sugar swirls.

The overweight checker turned her back before letting out a yell. "Pam, honey!"

From behind a curtain at the back, a slightly built girl, her straight black hair tied with a beaded leather thong, darted out. Her tawny skin and dark eyes showed her to be Native American. Molly recalled a section toward the end of Aowl's diary indicating that he'd become friendly with a tribe living around here, the Wolvine.

"Show this lady that reservation bread."

Molly followed the girl past the understocked meat counter into a cul-de-sac beside the crackers and dog food. "This is all we sell except that other," she said, her voice tinged with the soft nasality Molly recognized as distinctively Native American. Up close, it was clear the girl was out of her teenage years but not by long.

"It's cheaper. My grandfather says he likes it." The girl shrugged and stared down at the wooden floor, strangely shy.

"Well, he must know what's good."

A flickering glance caught Molly's smile. The girl's awkwardness seemed to soften.

It would help, Molly suggested, to get to know someone from the local tribe. Natives' oral histories were occasionally more accurate than scholarly, white research.

"Are you from around here?" she asked.

The girl nodded but would not look up. Molly took a loaf, whose poorly printed label announced that it was "Native Hearth Bread—Produced as a Special Project to Assist Local Economies." The loaf felt hard and too heavy for its size. Opaque white paper surrounded it, and it was dated a week ago.

Molly hoped to stall long enough to set Pam at ease. "So local people bake this bread. Do you help?"

The girl nodded and seemed to smile. "Not me. But my two sisters. A lot of years ago my grandfather wrote out papers and got the money."

"Sounds like a good project." Molly struggled to keep her praise from sounding false. "A good way for people to make money."

The girl nodded, and Molly felt encouraged. "I know the name of one tribe around here."

"Wolvine." Pam's head lifted at last and her dark eyes held a quiet ferocity. "My grandfather is a"—Pam paused as if selecting a word that would serve—"sort of a chief."

The word "chief" could mean anything, Molly knew, or nothing. She held out her hand. "My name's Molly Snow. I'm here to find out about history. I like to hear about the way things used to be."

"Sure."

"Maybe I could meet your grandfather sometime."

The girl moved away toward the front of the store. "I better get back to work. Look, if you don't like the bread, just bring it back. I'll pay your money back."

With a quick turn, Pam disappeared behind the curtain. Molly heard the sound of boxes being moved and stamped flat. She added the hard loaf to her pile of purchases on the counter.

The checker surveyed the collection of staples and cleaning supplies. "Looks like you plan to stay a while." She punched cash register buttons. "New around here?"

"I'm staying out at the Aowl place. By the beach. I'll be doing work in the museum."

"Honey, be careful," the woman said. "That Aowl place is close to the reservation." The woman took Molly's check and identification.

"What's wrong with the reservation?" Molly momentarily thought she was being insulted.

"Nothing, dear," the woman said, "but there's something wrong with that particular part of the reservation. Even the Indians don't hang out around the Aowl cottage. And they sure don't go anywhere near the museum."

Chapter 5

MOLLY PATCHED TOGETHER A LUNCH OF PIMENTO SLICE ON RAI-
sin bread, then stepped outside to feed Native Hearth Bread to the
sea gulls. The loaf was impossibly hard, but the birds swooped and
dove for it gladly.

She looked forward to Tess Fiddert coming by tonight. At least
they'd share a common interest in Alford Aowl. For now, she needed to get that window fixed.

For the first half-hour the job looked easy. Molly tapped shims
around the window frame on the outside, then went inside to add
more shims. The pressure split the wooden frame. Nails did no
good. There was too much dry rot. As she worked, she distinctly
felt that someone was watching. Molly leaned the hammer on the
sill and scanned the view. Beyond the rises of the dunes the lacy
edge of the surf rose and fell, but no figures walked along the sand.
To either side, sand hills rose, motionless but for the occasional
blade of eel grass twisting in a breeze. Molly went back to work,
hoping for at least one sturdy corner that might hold a nail.

The watched feeling persisted, raising prickles along the back
of her neck. Molly paused to walk a short distance into the dunes.
If she actually looked behind the near ones, the feeling might
pass. The hills of sand rose high enough to conceal anyone who
might crouch behind one, but no man-sized footsteps marred
their smoothness. Bird tracks showed webbed patterns of three
spoked cuts, and the wind had twirled long grasses, scraping out

26

pinwheels. The only big marks were the prints of a passing dog.

It must have been a big dog, and it had apparently gone this way more than once, and in both directions. Molly stepped beside a print and stretched her arm toward the next one to estimate the animal's size. The prints looked too wide apart for the usual pet's stride, but she guessed that if the dog were running its gait would lengthen. Reassured, she headed back to the cottage to look for a new approach to securing the window.

She found one but it didn't work. Nor did the eerie sense of an unseen presence pass. It grew stronger as she fought to ignore the prickling along the back of her neck. At last a cool breeze brought goose bumps and a strangely familiar scent. Molly spun, hoping to spot the dog she smelled. She faced a man.

"Ahh—" Sand slid beneath her backward step.

The stranger stared.

He was a handsome man in his mid-forties with weathered skin and surprisingly silver, shoulder-length hair. Dark, penetrating eyes met her gaze and held it, almost too calmly, and certainly too long. He seemed unconcerned at her surprise.

"You scared me." Molly caught her balance on the cottage wall. "Why'd you sneak up?"

"I'm sorry. I didn't mean to." His voice sounded husky, as if from long disuse.

To cover her nervousness, Molly brushed sand from her jacket. The man simply stood, watching. He was over six feet tall, his worn denim jeans and a faded flannel shirt well fitted to his muscular frame. The prematurely silver hair, framing his rugged features, actually added to his attractiveness. For no reason at all, Molly felt that she already knew this man, and that she liked him.

"That will never work." He spoke at last, nodding toward the window.

Molly wanted to resent the typically male assumption, but the impulse to like him won out. And besides, he was right. Nothing she'd tried worked.

"So I'm finding." Molly shrugged. "It's going to cost a fortune to replace it once it blows out. Which it will."

She paused. The man said nothing.

"Don't tell me. You've been watching me make a fool myself on this for the last hour, right? I knew someone was watching."

Her words, it appeared, brought only confusion. The tanned wrinkles along the man's brow deepened and his gaze clouded.

"Not really. No. I just got here. Just now." He spoke as if the words were somehow surprising, even to him. "But would you like me to fix it?"

"I guess." Molly sacrificed the small shred of pride she'd held out. "If it's not too much trouble."

"No trouble."

He took the hammer, but only turned it slowly between sure, strong fingers, examining its head before setting it down on the sand. With grace rare for a man so tall, as if reluctant to disturb the sand underfoot, he stepped to the window and pushed it inward. He drew it back by its ledge.

"Mind if I take a look inside?"

"Sure." Molly felt an urge to accompany him, but her city-sense took over. "I'll wait in the sun."

Without a word, he turned to circle the wall that would bring him nearest the door. So he had been watching, Molly thought. Otherwise the opposite way would look like fewer steps to the front.

Through the glass, Molly watched him probe at the window, shifting it gently in its frame. He disappeared for what seemed too long a time, then reappeared from the wrong side of the cottage. With smooth strides, he moved toward her from the direction of the small shed to the left of the building.

"I thought there was one of these around." His broad palm held a rusty piece of metal that looked like a long corkscrew. "It isn't much of an auger, but it will do."

Molly doubted she'd ever seen an auger, whatever that was. It certainly looked old-fashioned. She watched him select bits of wood and examine them, poking the rusty metal bit at one, then another. She resigned herself to relaxing on the sand, contributing a comment now and then in case he wanted conversation.

Apparently he did not. He did live around here—a nod response to her question—but when she probed further merely tossed his head in the direction of the forest out past town.

He was wealthy, Molly guessed, since he merely shrugged

when she asked about a job. "I don't work anymore. Mostly I used to work for myself."

He remained quiet, intent on using a pocketknife to whittle pieces of wood into smooth pegs. When he had a half dozen pegs, he set them on the windowsill and went to work on the frame.

His large hand looked awkward turning the small tip of the auger, but soon shavings spun away beneath it. He worked smoothly, careful not to crack the fragile wood.

"Looks like you've done this sort of work before," Molly offered.

"This place," he said, glancing up at the roof, "this place always did want a lot of work."

"You worked on the rebuilding?" It had been twenty years, Molly recalled, at least twenty since the Aowl cottage was rebuilt. "You probably even remember what it was like before."

"I remember a good deal of it," he said and picked up a peg. He turned his back and spit into the palm of his hand. Then he rolled the saliva along the peg. "I could use that hammer now."

Molly provided it quickly and obeyed when he directed her to go inside and push the frame out. She watched soft taps drive the peg home, joining the frame securely to the ridge of the wood.

"We got it," she called through the glass. For the first time, he smiled. His smile was quiet and slow, accompanied by a satisfied nod.

The remaining pegs seated quickly. She could see how they actually supplied points of support and took up stress that could not be borne by the rotted wood. By the time she got outside again, the man was walking away, looking back over his shoulder once more to examine the cottage, or maybe to look at her. "That should do it," he said with a wave.

"Wait a minute," Molly called. "Can't I pay you? After all, I did take up your time."

The man stopped, confused. "I don't think so," he said. "People do things for each other. We know we must. That's how we all get by."

The words seemed strangely old-fashioned, but Molly acknowledged them with a smile. "Well at least let me know your name. I'm Molly Snow, by the way. I'm here researching the man who first built this cottage you just put back together." Molly stepped across the distance, her hand extended.

His big, rough hand accepted it. The grip was firm, but felt almost tender. "I see," he said. "Then you wouldn't by any chance be from the Goodwillows. Goodwillow family of Wolvine by the river."

"No, no." Molly laughed. She explained about her ancestry, adding that she had in fact met a Wolvine named Pam this morning. "Any way, thank you for your help. And do stop by sometime for a coffee if you like. But what was your name?"

The man paused. "Call me Al. I always kept that for my friends."

Molly watched him stride away across the sand, enjoying the lithe grace of his movements. Only when he was too far off to call out did she wonder at the oddness in the way he talked. For a man who couldn't yet be forty, he sure had an antique way of putting things. Molly Snow also wondered why watching him go brought a stab of loneliness.

Chapter 6

"IF IT'S THE RAW PAST YOU WANT, THAT KEY WILL OPEN THE DOOR to it." Seated on the couch, Tess Fiddert touched the key lying on the kitchen table. "I've got lists of everything in there. Haven't catalogued it all. You won't need anything that's not out—help yourself to the map drawers and document files. I put out keys for the important ones. The ones you'll need."

Tess Fiddert had arrived just as Molly finished up the dinner dishes. Tess was more than willing to stop for coffee and one-way conversation. She was a portly woman, imposing in bulk and style. She too quickly made herself at home on the couch.

"There's old tools and a couple carvings. Supposedly whittled by the man himself. Ducks and ground squirrels mostly. And maps. Maps, maps, maps. And the original letters, they're on display. I unlocked those. But you probably read all those already in books."

Tess Fiddert paused for a sip of coffee. The contents of her cup had gone cold, Molly guessed, because since her arrival an hour ago Miss Fiddert had done considerably more talking than sipping. The woman was trying to be friendly, but she resented Molly, that was certain.

"I read true copies, of course," Molly put in. She brought the pot from the stove and refilled both their cups. "But there's nothing like seeing originals, the actual page and the author's handwriting."

"Oh, sure," Tess said. "Except his handwriting's worse than Dr.

Bill's. That's the young doctor that took over old Marsh Hazlett's practice. Can't cure a cold but everyone says he knows his rashes."

Tess's voice held the enthusiasm of a small-town gossip. Her flowered house dress made her seem even more bulky than she was, and while she slumped in a way that tried to look relaxed, Molly couldn't help feeling that Tess Fiddert did not like being here, or perhaps did not like her.

"Toward retiring, Hazlett killed more than he cured," Tess went on. "Got sort of disorganized, but those that died went feeling safe. Hazlett had that way."

Molly kept moving the conversation back to Alford Aowl and his explorations, but Miss Fiddert had a way of shifting her chatter over to contemporary Surfbreak. Molly now knew more than she cared to about which farms were going bankrupt, whose son had stolen whose car, and how a plague of real estate agents was spreading northward up the coast from California.

"Those real estate people have their uses," Tess said. "I've picked up a little property here and there. Prices are starting to rise." Her voice made it clear that she expected to make a tidy profit.

"And the originals of the maps, are those catalogued?" Molly tried again.

"Oh, those." Tess's wide shoulders gave a dismissive shrug. "Now, I know they're history, and I'm the first to appreciate that. I got my degree in history just like you. In California, more years ago than I'd like to mention. Let's leave it at that."

"Then they aren't catalogued?"

Tess smiled, tight-lipped. She sipped the fresh coffee. "Don't get me started." But Tess was already started. "Let me give you some history, dear. You, Molly Snow, can go for a Master's degree. You, Molly Snow, can even go for a Ph.D." She sounded angry.

"Yes."

"Tess Fiddert couldn't," Tess said. "In my day women could not get into graduate schools in history or anthropology or classics. If they did get in, it was only for a Master's." Tess sipped again, but her hand shook. She set the cup down. "I'll tell you something else, young lady. You can get in and bust yourself trying to preserve records and protect history, and you know what happens?"

Molly felt defensive. "What happens?"

"The very people you try to protect don't give a damn," Tess said. "The damn Indians don't care any more for their history than the whites. The only thing you get are complaints. And I've found just one answer. Build yourself a nest egg, and let the whole bunch of them grow fur or rot." Tess fell silent, her gaze gone hard and a glint of steel flashing in her eyes. Then, a quick shake of her head and a shrug, and she was back, almost as if she thought she had said too much.

"So you want to know about maps," she said. "They're screwy. Of course, Aowl was screwy." All at once, her outburst past, Tess was back to gossiping. "When Aowl was good he was very good, I give him that. And when he got lost, he was hopeless. It's like he was mapping two different worlds. Any of these new backpacker kids tried following one of those maps, they 'd go right off a cliff."

"That's what I've read," Molly put in quickly. "And seen myself. I studied a few."

Actually, as Molly wished she could get a word in edgewise to explain, she had personally tried to reconcile the discrepancies on several Alford Aowl maps. Aowl, the region's first explorer, had either deliberately invented false landforms, gotten lazy and filled in unexplored spots as impassable wilds, or gotten lost, regularly, and always in the same spots. It was one of the puzzles Molly had come here to solve. If she could crack that, and perhaps also the uncertainty surrounding Aowl's final years, she'd have enough material to move straight out of her M.A. into a solid Ph.D.

So far, her answers were no better than the guesses historians had made over the years, or Tess's guess about two worlds. That theory was as good as any, but now Tess was chatting away about a family called the Woofies, it seemed, whoever they were.

"Maybe Aowl really thought he was mapping two different worlds," Molly put in tentatively. "He lived with the Wolvine. They have a very certain belief about power. They wouldn't be surprised by two separate worlds."

"That Great Changer business?" Tess Fiddert looked at Molly as if she thought her deranged. "Girl," she said, "don't take this too seriously. Aowl just did a lousy job."

Tess veered into explaining how Surfbreak visitors had changed over the years. Apparently backpackers filled up the parking lots downtown. "Then they walk right off. Won't spend a penny in town. Like to see one of them try sleeping outside around here some winter. Wind and rain would drown them first, then blow them back to California."

Tess obviously thought she had revealed too much. Molly saw that it would be even more difficult to keep the conversation pointed toward Aowl. She decided on a direct approach. "That reminds me, Aowl disappeared in winter. Do you have anything in the storage drawers dated after 1910? November, I think."

"No, but I'm not surprised. Aowl had already moved up the hills by then. Didn't like the idea of them cutting the trees. Then the mansion really put him out." Tess rambled on, recalling Aowl's feud with the lumber company as if it were last week's gossip.

"Any chance that one of the lumbermen killed Aowl?" Molly interrupted. It had always seemed odd that Aowl made his loudest complaints over the cutting of trees for the mansion. That timber came from one of the plots he'd mistakenly mapped as rocky grassland.

"If one killed him, wasn't the owner. There was bad blood there, but that one was dead two years before Aowl went off. You've heard that bit about the body on the beach, I bet."

Molly nodded, recalling a tourist brochure.

"Pure rubbish. And remember, Aowl was the one that painted the whole building black after the old guy died. Volunteered for the job. And now we have to keep it that way. Historic preservation people say so, the skunks. Every five years I have to put up with all that black paint again. Or else we don't get any money."

Molly gave up. "You have to paint every five years? Of course salt air would be hard on paint."

"Wait until November." Tess launched into details of the worst Thanksgiving storms of recent years. "I go to California next week. If you've seen twenty, thirty-foot waves once, that's plenty."

Molly suppressed a yawn. Miss Fiddert rambled on about the weather, so Molly mentioned the window that had kept her awake.

"I fixed it, though," she explained. Technically, at least, the museum also owned the cottage. Tess Fiddert might worry about upkeep this winter. "Actually, I didn't fix it. A nice neighbor happened along the heach. He fixed it for me."

"Big man? White hair?" Molly nodded.

"Probably John Dill." Tess's interest returned. "Chubby fellow with just this sprout of white hair left? Lots of freckles?"

Molly shook her head and stood up. "I'll show you. It's the bedroom. He did a fine job." Getting this biddy on her feet might be the first step to moving her out the door.

"Well now, that was an old-timer, wasn't it?" Tess said when they reached the bedroom. She tried wiggling the window. It held. "Museum's got some work on it like that, but they don't do it around here anymore. Anyway John Dill won't do it, he's the carpentry shop down on Breakers? He'll build new every time. How old you say this guy was?"

"Not that old. Maybe forty, I guess. He said his name was Al."

"Then he learned from an old-timer."

Tess continued talking as Molly led her toward the cabin door. "See, they used to do it like that, with the pegs. When it's windy and wet, why that piece of wood'll swell up. You won't hear a click out of that window all winter."

Even on the way out the door, Tess Fiddert chattered. "You have any trouble, call Mulling. He won't win prizes for friendly, or for I.Q. either, but he takes care of property. Give him that."

"He frightens me," Molly said.

"He scares the bejesus out of a lot of people," Tess said. "He got fired in the big city. The big city couldn't handle him." She looked at Molly, and tried to be cordial. "Mulling tried to be a decent cop once. At least so I suppose. Now, he's just okay. But don't cross him." The hint of threat in Tess's voice seemed to echo even after she had turned away and headed for her car.

Molly waved a farewell. She guessed the winter months would get fairly lonely once the storms moved in, but she wouldn't be tempted to invite that woman back. Or Sheriff Mulling either.

Chapter 7

MOLLY SNOW SLEPT PEACEFULLY, UNAWARE OF THE WIND RAGING outside. It picked up around midnight when the tide turned from its ebb and began doubling backward, rushing wide ivory combers further and further into shore. As the roar of surf rose, the cries of beasts also rose from the forest. Wolves howled amid the hiss of cougars. The elements seemed to skirmish, preparing for battle.

Pam Goodwillow slept too, but restlessly, in her grandfather's cabin. High tide would not come for many hours, so most of the coastline lay safe from flooding until daybreak. She dozed, dimly aware that her grandfather sat listening at the window.

When settlers first arrived on this coast, the Wolvine tribe, to the white way of thinking, was an inconvenience. The tribe hunted the deer, elk, and beaver, so numerous in the rolling hills. They wore clothing cut from the skins of these creatures. When they hunted at sea in cedar canoes, they wore sealskin. During salmon runs they dried fish along the Wolvine River's banks.

For as far back as stories told, wolf and salmon shared this coast with the Wolvine. Stories told how wolves once were men, and before The Great Changer turned them into wolves, a wise man among them was the first to fashion arrowheads. The oldest dances told how wolf and cougar came from the mountain. Wolf held power in the low forests, liking the easy hunting for deer and mice, liking the open places of grazing elk, and of course befriending the Wolvine. Wolf was their totem animal and their power.

Wolf's skin was scraped and smoothed to make robes and to cover drums used during sacred ceremonies. Wolf skins shrouded the medicine man's shoulders as he invoked the power spirit, the tamahnous of war or peace. And always, in the sky or the forest, The Great Changer lived. That One could change anything to anything; change a fish into a tree, a man into wolf, or the wind into a star.

Only one white man came at first. That pale stranger, Aowl, understood about wolf. He walked with the wolves. Stories spread rapidly of a man who sat among a circle of wolves and how they stayed with him, unafraid of his campfire. Stories told of a hunting wolf pack that left its dens and its young in the care of this stranger. And this man came to know the wolf 's people, the Wolvine. He became as one among them.

But, in the end, he had betrayed them. Aowl had taken only one thing, but that thing was the treasure belonging to Storm Man, the medicine man in those days. The first white man had taken Storm Man's wife. For that he suffered a fate which even grown men trembled to think about. Storm Man laid a curse. Sometimes the Wolvine still suffered from floods because of that curse.

In the spring the river usually flooded and the Wolvine were used to that. It was the autumn floods that brought real fear. Then the river raged with great muddy swirls pushed from the ocean to mix salt water with fresh . . .

Raymond Goodwillow thought of these things as he listened to the roar of the wind. In his bones he felt wind shake the tops of the cedars, then swirl downward to fling lower boughs like dogs shaking water. He listened for the sound of waves and wondered if this would be a night when the water would come.

Being old was a good thing. An old man was supposed to sit and think. An old man was supposed to tell the old stories to children, although these days the children thought of the stories in the same way they thought about television stories of guns and cars. Goodwillow remembered how carefully he had taught the stories to his granddaughter, Pam, who now lay sleeping.

Pam had wanted to stay with him tonight. She usually stayed with one of her married sisters, but on this night of wind and water perhaps she had noticed how he was becoming thoughtful. She was a quiet young woman, foolish about grown-up things but oddly wise in her own way. She would notice him listening more closely to the wind and the waves. She was right to stay, Goodwillow admitted. Even if she did not really understand why.

Great power rode in the wind. Power dwelt upon the surface of vast waters. It lived in the forest, and power muttered along the dunes and through the mountains. *It is the first power*, Goodwillow thought, *the strongest. It is the power that created the world, the power the white people know only a little about and still call their god.*

Back when he was younger, he had learned of this power and how to make his powers enter the flow of power that covered this land. Now he believed, as he became older and fewer children heard the old stories, that his power wasted away while the mountains and sea and forest withdrew from him.

Of course Pam would think that he was acting strangely. The great powers of the world were acting strangely. In Goodwillow's visions The Great Changer danced in the smiling eyes and the smiling mouth of Wolf. Goodwillow felt power rising about him and knew that all he needed to do was sit in quiet acceptance. The old powers had never left, after all. He could, if he must, call up the old powers and turn back a flood.

But other powers hovered also. Wolf still lived in the hills although his tribe was small. Yet Wolf was strong with cunning. It might be that The Great Changer himself ran through the forest at night in the shape of Wolf.

Visions and dreams—but mostly visions—came. Out there cougar ran too, spilling his swift shadow through the hills. Cougar, and Goodwillow's grandfather, Storm Man, sometimes visited in the visions and dreams. His grandfather stood laughing beside the laughing wolf that was The Great Changer. His grandfather's tamahnous was cougar, a tamahnous of the mountains. His grandfather came as a laughing cougar.

Wind swept the sea as Goodwillow felt power surround him. An old man needs little sleep, he thought. He sat at the window and watched the forest and the night. Later, it might be necessary for him to stretch forth power and turn back the flood.

Chapter 8

It was the damnedest thing, Mulling thought as he pulled his squad car onto the beach. Last night around midnight, the very hour when every man, woman, and child in Surfbreak braced for a real howler, the storm died and the tide ran in low breakers. It was like someone had drawn a line around Surfbreak, and the storm could not cross the line.

The weather on this coast was so changeable that nothing should surprise him, he guessed. This morning of sun and temperatures in the 50's looked tailor-made for shooting dogs. Generally speaking, if you got the pack leader, the pack dispersed or ran to some other town's beach.

Mulling drove from the access road onto the hard sand below the tide line. Litter from the last storm lay tossed at the tide line—sea whips and ship's timbers and broken trees. A dead seal and a handful of dead fish soured in the sandy muck. Mulling idly wondered how the Woofies had made out in the storm, then guessed they'd done okay. He figured the only thing that killed Indians came in a bottle, or a Sterno can.

The thought of Indians reminded him of Molly Snow. Tess Fiddert wasn't happy about Miss Snow's fooling around in the museum, but Mulling knew that Tess had covered her tracks. By the looks of her, Molly Snow was no accountant.

Mulling idled down the beach at 10 m.p.h. If a pack was running, he'd come across it sooner or later.

Tess Fiddert definitely skimmed admission money from the museum. Otherwise, as Mulling had it figured, she couldn't go to California each winter. Mulling envied her. Tess Fiddert was sitting on a gold mine.

Tess was clever, though. She never took too much, not so's it showed. Mulling understood her resenting some stranger coming onto her turf, the tough old bat, but Tess could take care of herself.

And, if the truth be told, everybody skimmed somewhere. He had learned that on the police force back in Portland, back in the days when he still believed that having a badge was important. Then he discovered that if you refused to play the payoff game they set you up. In his case he was allowed to resign, rather than face a charge of stealing evidence.

Mulling scanned the beach ahead, halfway expecting to see a corpse. By all reports, the beach should be littered with corpses. The phone rang at least once a day. Half the town seemed to be hallucinating.

Sheriff Mulling prided himself on out-guessing the town neurotics, and knowing who was shacking up, and which ones were downright drunks. So far, at least, no *normal* citizen had seen a corpse; only wackos.

High in the dunes, as if looking out to sea, the silhouette of a dog showed black against the blue sky. At that distance Mulling could not tell the breed. He allowed his car to drift to a stop and reached for his rifle, a reliable old 30.06 with a scope. More modern rifles might be slightly higher-powered, but their mechanisms were complex. You couldn't depend on them.

He patted his holster, home to a .45 Army Colt, another straightforward piece of work and all any police officer needed. Mulling set the parking brake and eased the car door open. Sal Baker's place was right beyond those dunes, directly in the line of fire. Beyond Baker's place was the Aowl cottage. Mulling grinned and told himself he sure wouldn't want to shoot a pretty lady like Molly Snow, especially since he had hopes for some fun with her. He ducked low, eased to the back of the car, then slowly rose to rest his elbows on the trunk. Maybe he couldn't get off a shot yet, but he could take a good look.

The rifle pointed, then steadied, and then the barrel began to tremble as Mulling gasped. He lowered the rifle, checked the beach at his back to make certain it was clear. Then he raised the rifle and looked again.

That was a wolf. That was damnedest wolf he had ever seen—gray-maned, with a heavier muzzle than most of the breed. The cock of the head looked almost insulting. It stared straight at the rifle, then sat on its haunches and yawned. The scope picked up fangs too long for any dog. The head was broader than many wolves', the hindquarters strong and powerful. The sunlight made the wolf shine silver.

Mulling lowered the rifle, shaking. Wolves ran in packs. Any animal this size would lead that pack. Which meant that more wolves hid around here someplace. But wolf packs belonged in crazy places like Alaska or upper Canada. There had not been wolves in this area for thirty or forty years. He raised the rifle once more.

The wolf caught his movement and shifted. Now it seemed playful. It stuck its front paws forward, lowered its head, and sort of bounced, taunting. It looked like a pup trying to convince somebody to throw a ball. Then the wolf jumped high, like it was snapping at an invisible bird. It began to run toward the beach.

"Gotcha," Mulling whispered. He scanned the shore. He had a clear field of fire. The rifle led the wolf, and Mulling squeezed off a round; the kick of the butt threw a satisfying punch into his shoulder. The wolf leapt high as a dog after a Frisbee. It came back to the sand in long loping strides, a serious run.

It was not headed back to the dunes. The wolf ran with the smooth stretching that could carry a pack over miles and miles of forest in a single night. In Mulling's eyes, it grew larger with each stride. He quickly got off two more rounds; the rifle punch, punching hard, then the butt hitting the sand as Mulling raced for his patrol car. The door slammed as the wolf arrived, leaping high toward the closing door, crashing onto it.

The wolf turned and made a full, quick circle of the car; paused to sniff Mulling's prints in the sand, then glided casually toward the hood.

Along the tops of the dunes other wolves appeared. They circled, making elaborate patterns as they played.

Mulling sat in the car and told himself this could not be happening. He eased the .45 from his holster, worked the slide, and rolled the window just enough to aim. For the best angle, he had to kneel on the seat. When that wolf circled the car one more time, it was going to be one damn dead wolf.

Mulling flicked his gaze from hood to trunk and back again, watching for that huge silver shape to show itself. Meanwhile he reached for his radio. There was no one at the station, but Joan Frazer kept a radio on standby. Her husband, Jim, headed the volunteer fire department.

"Tell Jim to get his tail down here," Mulling hissed into the radio. "On the beach, half a mile north of town. Bring some guys. Bring rifles."

The wolf had stopped circling. It stood in front of the car as if deciding what to do next. Mulling felt the silliness of his position; a grown man, butt in the air, sticking a .45 out a car window. And yelling for help.

"Let's have a little more to go on, Sheriff." Joan Frazer had a reputation for being practical. "You starting a war?"

"If I told you, you wouldn't believe it," Mulling said. "Move it, Joan."

The wolf sat in sunlight ten yards from the hood. No chance of running the car over it. Even on compact sand, you had to ease into motion or your wheels dug in.

And, Mulling told himself, there wasn't a chance that his shot had missed. He had nailed this big bastard at least twice, but no blood marked the silver fur. The gray mane changed. Hackles rose, and points of fur glowed with sunlight. No wolf acted this way, not even a wolf with distemper. Wolves avoided men.

Then the wolf jumped. It leapt onto the hood as easily a bird lighting on a wire. The car shuddered. The broad silver-and-black nose pressed right up to the windshield, lips curled back to bare fangs. White foam dripped from the jaws, bubbling as a growl sounded. Mulling turned, raised the automatic, and fired just as the wolf jumped away. It loped easily into the dunes as Mulling stared through where the windshield had once protected him. His ears rang with the heavy boom. He thought he might pass out, or have a heart attack.

Then he thought that he had better get away. He got the car moving, turned it, and headed for town. Wind blew chill air through what was left of the windshield. At the head of the access road, Jim Frazer's jeep and a posse of pickups were circled.

Four men with rifles listened as Sheriff Mulling told what had happened. The men looked at each other and grinned. With Frazer in the lead, they drove down the beach. They found no prints, but did find broken glass and Mulling's rifle. The men nudged each other, smirked like schoolboys, and gunned their engines to get back to town. The story was just too good to keep. By nightfall all of Surfbreak knew that Mulling went out to shoot dogs, got attacked by something—probably a tourist lady's poodle—and blew hell out of his own patrol car. Mulling was never going to live it down; and sure as anything this story would make folks feel fine through what looked to be a long, dark winter.

Chapter 9

MOLLY SNOW SLID THE SHINY NEW KEY INTO THE DEADBOLT LOCK, and the black door swung wide to release a cold cloud of darkness. Morning sunshine did not reach here. There were only whispers of darkness, creaking of antique timbers, and small scurryings; mice, or squirrels, or rats. Molly felt her way along the wall and reached the switch. Fluorescence leapt to life inside a glass cubicle and showed a small office, an old wooden desk, and file cabinets. Molly let the door swing shut, then shot the bolt.

She'd brought tablets, pens, file cards, and her own portable typewriter. She unceremoniously deposited everything on the desk and then flipped light switches. Corners, doorways, arches and exhibits jumped from the shadows. Today she hoped to get a good start, but first she would explore the Aowl Museum, four stories of architecture originally designed for a sumptuous late nineteenth century mansion. A central archway led into the parlor, a huge hall of shadows watched over by a curved ceiling. Standing out in relief on that ceiling, plaster cupids danced with nymphs. Walls were long panels of gleaming wood holding tall, slender windows. Dusty green velvet drapes hid the windows. Molly thought of opening one, but decided against it. Sunlight might damage the exhibits.

From the ceiling hung a replica of the canoe Aowl had used to navigate the Wolvine River. Like the original, the replica was fashioned from a single cedar log. A rusty bailing bucket with a chain handle lay in the bottom. Aside from the boat, the room was filled with photographs, sepia-toned prints of Aowl's cabin, a native fishing party, and the mansion itself when it was first built. Glass topped cases held yellowed maps and the original commission Alford James Aowl received, signed by the territorial governor. Wide drawers below the display cases held more maps.

Molly checked the photos, but doubted she'd find one of Aowl. He had always declined to have his picture taken, preferring that traveling photographers spend their expensive film on pictures of tree-furred hills and pristine shores. Aowl had come west before the transcontinental railroad arrived in 1888. He was among the first to notice the scar those tracks cut through the deep forests.

Molly shivered at the irony of this mansion carrying Aowl's name. The ground floor celebrated everything Aowl had fought to prevent, the cutting of old growth trees and the taming of wilderness into clever patterns on flowered wallpaper. Even the building itself, a black tomb decked out with turrets and cupolas, had been plunked down on a shore that Aowl's diary called, if she remembered correctly, "as immaculate a vista as God ever spread before us."

Molly climbed the wide central staircase. It continued the theme of its builder's waste, ornately carved banisters showing forest scenes, tree trunks and vines permanently contorted to match the grains of lighter woods inlaid as leaves and flower buds. The second floor was, if anything, more grotesque. These exhibits focused on native traditions, mostly Wolvine. A button blanket, identified as having been made in 1823, hung from the beams above the staircase. Small rooms held glass cases displaying baskets for carrying water, fishing hooks made from yellowing bone, bentwood boxes, and a replica of a Wolvine ceremonial drum.

The replica was clearly inferior, one metal staple showing where the imitator haphazardly tacked on a line of feathers, but Molly admired its size and the skill of its design. Such a drum would be used to speak to those ancient powers that tribes believed went back to their very beginnings. She felt ashamed. A sacred object, even a replica, looked obscene here.

Glancing into the room devoted to native animals, she had a momentary sense that there were spirits in there, or dark shadows of sorrow. She did not want to meet the museum's otters, wolves and panthers, their glass eyes glinting back pinkish light.

She decided not to explore the third and fourth floors. Molly knew that she would have to work in this building all winter, but she hated it. Maybe Aowl's records were here, but this place violated everything Aowl had fought to protect. For all its ornate excess, its waste of talent and irreplaceable materials, the building was finally ugly. Its builder had pillaged this land, deliberately, arrogantly, knowing what he was doing. She would work here, but would never—she vowed—never feel at home in this place.

Chapter 10

SEPTEMBER DAYS PASSED RAPIDLY AS MOLLY WORKED, AND AS HER uneasiness in the Aowl Museum grew. It was a month of storms, of windblown tides, and of shadows running through the forest when she returned to the cabin at dusk. During the nights dogs howled. She looked out, but saw only shadows. As she passed townspeople on the street, they seemed uncomfortable around her. They hunched into their raingear, peering out only to cast fearful glances toward the threatening skies. Molly found herself avoiding them.

She arrived at the museum most mornings before nine and settled to work. After a noon break back at the cabin, she returned for two or three hours, studying maps and missionary reports. When she paused over a map or diary passage, she sensed that memories moved inside the walls and sifted like dust from the rafters. The huge wooden building creaked when wind whipped the western wall. Rain lashed the windows. Eerie presences filled the air.

Molly avoided the second floor. She'd read enough while at Pinehaven to get some idea of the region's Native Americans, and the museum's books and documents supplied the rest. The Wolvine were a deeply spiritual people. Their dark, beautiful beliefs still drifted in the air.

According to missionaries' reports, the Wolvine believed in a universe where every object and act dwelt beside ancient, primal power. Cedar trees held power to become anything: timbers, roofs, baskets, arrows, boats, even shoes and clothing. Fire held power to warm and restore. Power could cause evil, or it could cause good. That was because each and every being was a part of a greater being. Apparently The Great Changer, the name the natives gave to this primal power, didn't make much distinction.

Molly wondered if any Wolvine still believed in such power. The older generation might carry on tribal beliefs, and it would be interesting to learn what practices went on during Aowl's time. She returned to the grocery store twice, trying to locate Pam to arrange an appointment to meet her grandfather. Apparently the girl only worked a few days a month.

Molly wished she knew more of the native stories, if only to imagine herself communicating with the mute, spirit-like breathings that hovered in this old building. Tracking down native stories might be useful, too, in solving the mysteries surrounding Alford Aowl, especially the question of his death. Odd clues kept turning up in his diaries.

"Storm Man brewing," Aowl's crabbed handwriting noted on September 8, 1900. "Has young men watching me from a distance, I feel it, but when I double back it's nothing but crushed pine needles and a broken twig."

At first Molly took the repeated mention of Storm Man references to the coast's changeable weather, since Aowl had adopted many of the Wolvine ways of speaking. More reading made her doubt that. One diary page, a month earlier, remarked on a week of balmy, cloudless days, then commented,

> Storm Man pulls up a flower long before it comes to bloom. He's more like the white man than the red in that. The young men do as he tells them, his power's secure. If her own people come to steal that flower back, young men's blood will soak the ground.

Molly tried to fathom the meaning. "Storm Man pulls a flower—" Aowl might be recounting some native myth of natural calamity, wind tearing flowers from their stems or battering boats against sea rocks. The interpretation felt strained and unsatisfactory. Or he might be using the language of his time, an extravagant Victorian way of putting things. In that case, a "flower" would mean a woman.

Finally, a missionary's account of the Wolvine's sinful ways mentioned Storm Man. "He is grown fat as a barrel," the missionary wrote, "made round by consequence of overindulgence in his tribe's meager fare, leaving others to starve." Apparently Storm Man was a human, and a very unpleasant human at that. "Of all his sins, gluttony and theft among them, his adultery is most foul. He has three wives already, quick to do his bidding and fearful of his hand. He talks openly in my presence about taking a fourth wife from people who live to the north." Storm Man appeared to be the shaman or medicine man of the tribe in the 1890's, perhaps later.

Could this Storm Man have been the one Aowl knew? The dates tallied, but Molly doubted that Aowl would bother criticizing the local shaman merely for collecting flowers or herbs, pulling them up before they bloomed. Herb-collecting was part of a medicine man's work.

"Storm Man," she spoke the name aloud. Its sound broke the silence of the past few hours. She tried concentrating on the page again, but the sound rang in her ears. "Storm Man," she said again, "shaman of the Wolvine," and all at once she sensed a change in the air. A chill had gathered. She had been sitting for hours, unaware of the coolness, but now that chill intensified. Through her heavy wool socks she felt a breeze sweep along the floor.

Molly stood, determined to stretch the kinks out and warm up, but now the cool wind eddied around her shoulders. It lifted pages on the desk and laid them flat again. She felt her hair ruffled. Could the wind have worked the door open? She remembered closing the bolt.

Crossing the hallway toward the front door, she assumed the creaking noises she heard must be the wind testing the door's edges. By the time she reached it, the sound seemed to have moved. Now the breeze blew steadily on every side, as if uncertain of direction, but the sounds were definitely coming from the large parlor. Molly hurried back to the office and flipped light switches. Even before she reached the doorway, she saw the shadow. It moved across the floor, swinging into view, then slid sideways from sight.

She stepped inside. An inky black stain glided along the floor toward the wall, then paused and turned back, heading her way. The creaking sighed with its shadow's turning. Molly looked up.

The canoe. The ropes holding the old cedar canoe were sighing. The canoe swung from side to side with the gusts of cool air that rushed past like currents in a river. Molly reached to steady it, but the canoe swung far out of reach. It jostled as if fighting a wave, and the rusty bailing bucket at the bottom clanked onto its side. The bow lifted, then lowered.

Her heart thudded. What could make a heavy log-boat roll and sway like that? She thought of the spirits hovering so near in this place, then recognized a better explanation. There must have been a small earthquake. Maybe she hadn't felt it. Perhaps a window had slipped open upstairs, which would account for the breeze.

"Nearly made a believer out of me," she told the silent walls. The canoe heaved from side to side in the air, the bailing bucket clanking. "Clank all you want," she laughed, turning her back. The thing would settle down on its own after a while. If she remembered it before she left today, she'd check the second-floor windows.

"I'm a believer all right," she chuckled, speaking aloud dispel the frightening darkness. "I believe in the solemn power of a Ph.D. committee," she recited, "and I believe only Alford James Aowl can help me with that."

The breeze seemed to fall off as she stepped back into the office. She straightened the papers the wind had disturbed and decided to let the question of Storm Man rest for a while. It was only a puzzle-piece that might eventually fall into place. As the sighing of the canoe's swinging settled toward silence again, she concentrated on matching up several of Aowl's maps with later explorers' surveys.

Here, too, she met frustration. Either Aowl was a terrible surveyor, which he was not, or his occasional bad days made him blind, stupid, and geographically incompetent. Aowl had twice placed steep cliffs in places where rolling hills now lay. He had drawn impassable swampland where other surveyors found rich meadows. All versions of his maps showed these nonexistent cliffs, swamps, and impassable chasms; yet quick sketches of the same areas, recorded in his diary during early treks, made no mention of difficulty passing there.

Frustrated, Molly returned to the fragile pages of the diary. Days, weeks, months of the nineteenth century slipped beneath her fingers—November 1899, December, and then the coming of the New Year.

Suddenly, in the spring of 1900, Aowl's handwriting grew darker. His spidery script thickened and ink drips splotched the curves of capitals. "Young men went north four days," he wrote, "and returned with the prize ripped from its root. Storm Man insisted I come to the first night feasting."

Storm Man, that name again. Molly stifled a shiver. Details of some ceremony followed on the next page. Aowl's pen strokes raced. Further down, the script pressed hard into the inferior paper and tore holes.

> *He set that blossom closest to the fire, ahead of his many wives, and all their faces looked sallow. His old eyes, small as the eyes of a fattened pig, glistened with hunger. The young men tell me he will wait a year to consume this newest food. They laugh among themselves, watching his wives' misery, and especially that of his newest one. She weeps and will not look at him. In one year his next meal will be ripe.*

The entry broke off, whether from fury or due to some interruption, Molly could not tell. This time Aowl's Victorian doubletalk obviously spoke of a young woman.

Molly made a note of the entry's date and promised herself she'd come back to it. It was late afternoon and the shadows signaled the end of a frustrating day. Perhaps she should check at the grocery store again for Pam. She set her papers in order for the morning.

On most afternoons Molly left lights burning in the office, preferring not to cross the front hall in the dark. She knew the way well enough, so today she flipped all the light switches off and paused a moment.

The spirits of this building were there all right. They murmured sadness among the rafters' creaks and low toned settlings.

Shadowed presences seemed to circle close, bringing the distinct feeling of many eyes watching, ears listening, shapes that refused to confront her. Behind those sounds of hopelessness, a deeper silence watched and waited.

Opening the door and stepping into gathering dusk of this last day of September, Molly stopped herself from speaking her good night out loud.

Chapter 11

"She seems like a nice lady. She bought our bread."

Pam Goodwillow stood at the woodstove in her grandfather's house. She shifted the frying pan toward the corner and put the metal pot filled with corn mash in the center.

Raymond Goodwillow watched his granddaughter work. He appreciated her company, especially when old memories haunted his days.

"Why does she want to come here?" he asked gruffly. If Pam was going to go meeting white people and inviting them home, she should have better reasons than merely liking them.

"She's a college lady. They gave her money to come and find out about the old days here."

"White people's history."

"Both, maybe." Pam knew her grandfather would give in. After all, it was her request. Whenever her sisters wanted a favor, they always arranged for her to do the asking. "She asked about the old stories."

Raymond Goodwillow remained silent. He knew his granddaughter was too kind and trusting, but at least she was generous to an old man. That was the way children used to be. In the old days all the young men and women would have served him, because he was their shaman, but back then he would have given his tribe more than they gave him. Those times were gone now. He had managed to provide a few jobs by starting the bakery, but half the young men drank, anyway, and did not show up to do the heavy work.

Pam waited out a respectful silence, then went on. "She wants to know about some man who used to live here, a white man who drew pictures of places. She has a key to the black building."

"The place is cursed." Goodwillow spat the words. He wished Pam remembered the Wolvine word, which said it more clearly, but despite his efforts to teach her the old tongue, she was not always as quick as her sisters. Her mother drank too much before she was born and Pam had not cried correctly until she was six weeks old.

"You know that is a bad place, don't you?" he went on. "Even if you work at the store, you should not go there."

"Yes, Grandfather." The old man's silence insisted she tell why. "A bad man lived there, right?"

Goodwillow nodded.

"He sent his young men to take trees," she went on, "and they left all the branches to clog the river so the fish didn't come that year." Pam hoped she was not getting this story mixed up with the others about the years when fish did not come. "Then the great shaman—"

"Storm Man, your great-great-grandfather before me."

"He wanted to burn down the building. But the white man who lived among wolves"—Pam paused, trying to remember—"Man-Among-Wolves, he said no. They were friends then, but later Storm Man made a curse." Pam thought she was getting it right, but something felt missing. She fell silent to wait for her grandfather's help.

"That is partly true," he said quietly. "Remember the building now. Remember how the spirits of sacred things send all dying shadows to that building? That is why Man-Among-Wolves painted it black, remember?"

Pam nodded. "When the shadows of trees and men disappear, they go there to live."

"Yes. You know now." Raymond Goodwillow watched wonder cross his granddaughter's face as she fully remembered the story.

Pam had not remembered, however, the metal pot on top of the stove. Goodwillow nodded toward it and watched her spin to discover corn mash burning. She pulled it from the hot spot, burning her fingers, then went looking for plates and some leaves for his tea.

Pam thought about only one thing at a time, Goodwillow reflected, but at least she thought of that one thing deeply. Even before she could talk, Pam understood animal ways and how to play so that animals never turned on her. When she grew old enough to walk, she often spent hours alone in the forest, and when she came back, her young eyes always looked wiser.

Raymond Goodwillow hoped that this strange, slow girl might be special, her mind an unusual home for The Great Changer. Pam was not quick in school, but that made little difference. Restless winds calmed in her presence. When her toy floats spun beyond reach in the Wolvine River's currents, new eddies urged them back to her small hands.

Raymond Goodwillow was nearly seventy when Pam was born. His own daughter, almost too old to have more children, had come home pregnant again. She already had two children, left with their grandfather while she lived in town with white men. White men bought her drinks, and she seemed to like those better than her children.

The baby came too soon and too small. This baby could not laugh, but she could find things with her eyes almost from the moment of birth. Her mother left, back to the white men or into the hills.

Maybe growing up without a mother meant this child could not be quick or smart in the usual ways. Goodwillow taught her as well as he could, and since no young man had come forward to understand what a shaman must know, he supposed The Great Changer must have made things different again. Perhaps The Great Changer brought a strange girl to be the tribe's new shaman.

For ten years he worked to teach her their language, the old stories, the names of plants which were safe and those that brought sickness. Pam tried hard, but she still made mistakes on some songs. She explained her mistakes by saying that the songs now went 'this way,' that the songs had changed.

"I gave you the pretty plate." Pam set the blue and white plate in front of him and took the cracked white one for herself. The corn still smelled slightly scorched, but the salmon was baked a bright russet. Raymond Goodwillow smiled and watched Pam's eyes shine with pride. "So, will you let me bring the lady?"

"This lady looks at maps and goes into the black building," Goodwillow repeated, taking up his fork. "What does she look like?"

"Like a Wolvine," Pam said. Her grandfather gave her a startled glance. "I thought she was Wolvine the first day. But she talks like a white person."

Some Wolvine had gone to live with the white people, and they must have had children. Goodwillow did not like the idea that such a woman would come during this season of fierce storms and early floods.

"This lady came to see you two times. What was the first one?"

"She came today. Before that, she came right after the bad storm. Back when the extra white people went home." Raymond Goodwillow let his fork settle to his plate. He tried to recall everything he must already know about this stranger.

This might be the woman with long black hair and dark eyes, the vision he had seen rushing along the surface of the floodwaters. So this was the woman The Great Changer had spoken of with the wind. She had appeared time and again in his dreams, and another creature came with her, a half-wolf and half-human thing. The shaman felt certain now, The Great Changer had made some business with this woman.

Goodwillow took up his fork and forced another bite to his lips. He wished he could tell Pam. He needed help now, more strength than an old man's body could give.

"Yes. I will meet her," he said at last.

Hearing the sadness in his voice, Pam looked up. Her grandfather appeared too tired for only dinnertime. Lately he seemed to worry much of the time, but he never said why.

"Next time when you go to the store, if she comes, you tell her a day when she can come. I will meet her then." Raymond Goodwillow hoped a week might pass before this woman arrived. It would be good to have time, he thought, but no delay would be long enough to help him prepare for the danger she would bring.

Chapter 12

WHEN MOLLY SNOW GOT READY FOR BED THE FOLLOWING THURSday night, she felt glad that she had accomplished one of her goals. Work on the Aowl diaries remained slow. Whatever spirits haunted the museum had grown no friendlier, but at least she had an appointment to interview a Wolvine elder.

She had finally managed to contact Pam, and they set a time for Saturday. Pam claimed that her grandfather must be almost ninety. If Pam was right, the old man might actually have been alive before Aowl disappeared.

Too excited to sleep, Molly turned the light out and went to stand by the bedroom window. It was an unusually warm night, and she had pulled the pegs to open the window. With a shiver caused only partly by the breeze, Molly realized that she had grown lonely. Wolvine ghosts and a dead man's diary were poor substitutes for flesh and blood human company. The only local she had spoken to at length was that handsome stranger, Al. The man seemed interesting enough, but was probably married. Molly told herself she was thinking romantically of some married man, when she was too busy for romance.

She left the window open and crawled into bed. If only she could get her mind off plans for meeting Raymond Goodwillow, the sound of the surf might lull her to sleep. It was too much to hope that Goodwillow had actually met Alford Aowl.

Within moments of falling asleep, the dreams began. At first she dreamed of meeting an old man who was obviously an Indian chief. His face appeared unspeakably old and lined. Then she saw the bright fan of feathers crowning his hair, a headdress so out-of-place it could only come from the prop room for a cowboy and Indian movie. He spoke, at first in a voice that sounded like some Hollywood director's idea of how Indians talked, and then the dream began to change.

Now, instead of seeing his headdress, she saw his hair, which was long and gray. The old man spoke clearly, but he did not speak English. This was an old language, probably older than English, and she was supposed to understand it.

"Yea waa te ya wea."

The words sounded like a poem. They seemed to come from deep inside, as if his chest were a drum.

"Yea waa te ya wea," he said again, staring at her eyes.

He waited for her to respond.

"I don't know what that means," Molly heard herself answer. Questions formed in the old man's eyes, but he only repeated the sounds a third time.

This time she knew what they meant, but the words would not make sense when she tried to turn them into English. They told about something older than the language itself, about a feeling for which there was no English word.

"Yea waa te ya wea nanee," Molly tried repeating, then realized she had added an extra sound. The old man's eyes brightened. She had chosen the right word.

"Yea waa te ya wea nanee," Molly said again, and now she saw that the old man wore a robe made from the skin of some huge animal. When he stood, it unfolded toward the forest floor. He stepped backward to reveal what lay on the ground.

Stretched on its side, nearly six feet long with silver-white fur, lay a large dog. Too big a dog for an old man, Molly thought. Then the man spoke a name and shame washed over her. That word he spoke meant "wolf."

Molly repeated it, a glide of syllables slipping over her tongue, and the shape of the shimmering fur stiffened. The wolf tucked its forepaws beneath its huge chest and levered its body up.

"Nanee yea waa te ya wea," the wolf said. Its open mouth did not move, its tongue lolled, yet it spoke. The wolf's bright triangular head rose nearly as high as Molly's hip. It moved toward her with cautious gliding, so silent that not a pine needle on the forest floor stirred.

The silvery muzzle approached, bringing a new smell. Mixed into the scents of pine and oily smoke from a fire that the old man now tended, Molly sensed the swampy smell of wet fur, thick and heavy. It swelled like a cloud around her.

The wolf sniffed her thigh. Her hand hung near it, and he sniffed that too, one long whisker touching and sending a prickle up her arm. Molly tried to turn away, but something held the back of her head. She felt pressure tug at her shoulder, as if it too were bound in cloth that would stretch only so far and no farther. She pushed against it.

It felt like a sheet. Molly shoved herself up from the pillow and stared at the darkened room.

It was all a dream, she realized. The white noise of surf still came from the open window. A smell drifted in the air.

It resembled wet fur, but as she relaxed onto the pillow Molly realized that mist would bring smells from the shore. The dream was typical of how the unconscious worked. The mind turned Saturday's meeting with a Wolvine chief into a meeting with a wolf.

As she drifted to sleep the dream returned, but the old man no longer stood in the clearing. The fire still burned, and the wolf remained, its dark eyes staring. Molly remembered feeling afraid only moments ago, but now this huge creature appeared friendly. The animal lifted up on its haunches, stretching its long shining body, then came erect on all fours. As it glided closer, Molly tried to remain still, determined not to frighten it off again.

The swamp smell increased. The wolf was near and now she could also smell the fertile warmth of its breath. The wide wedge of its head moved toward her face, which seemed impossible since the wolf's head should be lower than her own. Then Molly realized she was lying down.

A soft form supported her head, a pillow it seemed, but the dream she was in a forest staring into two bright eyes. The wolf's muzzle approached. A cool wet nose brushed her cheek. Molly turned and opened her eyes. Ahead of her eyes the shape hesitated but held its ground. Molly rolled sideways.

She screamed. Her knee hit the floor and she scrambled across cold wood toward the window. She gripped its ledge to pull herself up.

A large triangular shadow stood watch by the bed.

The room was growing light with the beginnings of dawn, and Molly could clearly make out the silver shape. It was a wolf. Or a dog. It had to be a dog. Perhaps, half conscious, she had seen the dog and incorporated it into her dream, like the buzz of an alarm clock, or the ring of a phone. It stood watch and it did not move. It did not even look dangerous.

It was the wolf of her dream, but surely not a real wolf. Molly gripped the windowsill, willing her heart to slow. The great, silver-maned head turned to watch.

Wolf. A rush of adrenalin made her want to leap out the window and run, but she held still. If it was a wolf, then running would do no good. This must surely be only a dog that had come in the window, an incredibly big dog. It must have gotten lost on the beach and found the open window, hoping this was home. The shape across the bed remained alert and frozen. Settled on its haunches, the animal did not look vicious.

"Are you a dog?" she said at last. Its ears stiffened. It wouldn't answer, of course. Giddy with relief, Molly half wondered if this creature might understand the Indian words from her dream better than English.

She hesitated, stunned by a mad impulse to touch the dog, to pull its head close to her cheek and bury her face into the warm scent of its fur. That was dangerous, she told herself, stupid and dangerous. She took a deep breath. She would have to pass near him to get to the bedroom door. If she could go out that door and leave the window open, he might leave. Maybe it would be best to find out if he was domesticated.

"Lie down," she tried.

The animal remained still.

She tried to convince herself that it was only a lost dog, and untrained at that. It would be helpless if left to roam. It would not even know enough to come to someone who offered help. The dog was probably hungry, and by the looks of it, soaking wet.

Her mind made up, Molly reached behind her and lowered the window so the poor thing would not run away again.

"I'm going to leave you in the bedroom," she said, then felt foolish for speaking aloud. He could not understand. "Stay," she added, and took a step around the side of the bed. Just in case, it felt better to keep talking. "I'll have to go to the store when it opens. I'll buy you some food."

The dog's eyes followed her. This thing was truly huge, Molly realized, even bigger than in the dream. Yet he sat calmly as she approached.

Molly reached to touch the doorknob. Suddenly the animal's eyes went wide. She heard a low, guttural sound. The sound came again, subdued and sad, as if he feared she was leaving.

Molly kept one hand on the knob and stretched the other to touch his head. The fur was soft and slightly damp. "I'll be back," she said, and his eyes seemed to understand. Molly slipped out the door and closed it softly behind her. The grocery store would not open for another hour. She could use the time to shower and make Found Dog signs. Molly perked a pot of coffee and felt the knot deep in her stomach loosen. She paused occasionally to peer through the crack of the bedroom door.

The dog remained beside the unmade bed, his gaze fixed on the door. Molly guessed she could let him out into the rest of the cabin, unless of course he was the type to destroy things while she was gone. Safer to leave him there; she decided, and felt a twinge of regret. She finished up the notice to go on the bulletin board at the laundromat. In a way it would be better if no one claimed him. A big dog would definitely improve a social life limited to dead men and Wolvine ghosts.

Chapter 13

SHERIFF MULLING PARKED HIS PATROL CAR IN FRONT OF THE Surfbreak Grocery. People passed with barely concealed smiles, looking as if they wanted to compliment him on his new windshield. Mulling knew the entire town was laughing at his expense, but he steeled himself to endure it. Time was on his side, he knew. Sooner or later a wolf pack would start taking somebody's cattle. When that happened, these damned fools would laugh out the other side of their faces. Mulling turned off the engine and eased down in the seat.

A few minutes earlier he'd seen Molly Snow walk into the grocery. He meant to be ready when she walked back out. Ed Mulling had a professional interest in what the half-breed was up to today. A legitimate interest, he told himself. He'd kept tabs on her comings and goings from the museum. It was fine and dandy for Tess Fiddert to think Miss Snow was from a college, but Tess could be real innocent when it came to the criminal mind.

On the other hand, Tess had made his job easier. Tess had spread rumors that Molly was a Woofie. Or, for those in Surfbreak who could tolerate Woofies, Tess implied that Little Miss Snow's research might end up closing the museum. Tess claimed that only the mansion would be left, but no exhibits. That would mean an end to the tourist trade. Tess guaranteed that no one in Surfbreak was going to get friendly with Miss Molly Snow.

Maybe Woofie-looking girls did come from colleges, but Ed

Mulling knew his Indians. Maybe Tess was right for the wrong reason. It wasn't research they had to worry about, it was Indians. Damn Indians all over the country were complaining about museums stealing their sacred stuff. As if it mattered to anybody but Indians.

Mulling leaned sideways to block the sun. He wished he could see through the store window, but the sun blasted back from it.

Indians could be slick. With just a few days' planning, Little Miss Snow could clean out this town's best tourist attraction. Or Molly Snow might invite all her friends and hold a sit-in thing, call the newspaper, start a real mess. Mulling had read about places where that happened.

So far, for a month, Molly Snow went back and forth from the old black building alone, just like she was supposed to. That would be the natural way of course, nothing suspicious at first. Each night Mulling used his own key to check the building. So far, nothing important looked moved. But this morning Molly Snow changed her routine. She left the shack earlier than usual and started making stops. She stuck a piece of paper in the library mailbox, went into the laundromat right when it opened—spent two minutes in there—then made another stop at the newspaper to stuff paper into that mailbox. Now she was in the grocery. She arrived early and waited out front, lounging around on the steps but visible from behind the post office. This college girl had a pretty good body for a Woofie.

Stretched out on the grocery store's wooden steps waiting for the doors to open, she looked all tan and lean. Most Woofie women got fat, and the ones living in town drank too much. If he hadn't known the physical type, Mulling might have thought the half-breed just had a good tan, skinny and sexy like that. Woofie women knew how to have a good time, as every white man in town knew, although only the lowest would admit to sleeping with a redskin. Besides, Woofie women were easy. With Miss Snow it wouldn't take much. Stop in the museum, have a little chat to warm her up.

"Sheriff Mulling."

He must have been drifting. Molly Snow, in the flesh, stood beside his car. Mulling snapped alert. She carried a five-pound bag of dog food. No other packages.

Mulling nodded good morning.

"Just who I'm looking for," Molly Snow rushed on. "Did anybody report a lost dog? I found one. This morning—" The woman paused as if trying to get her story straight. "Sort of last night actually."

Lost dogs, Mulling thought. What did she think he was, dogcatcher?

"So which was it?" Mulling kept his voice level. "Last night or this morning?"

The woman hesitated, her face all innocence. "It's just a big dog that wandered into my cabin. Anyway I kept it inside and I put up posters." Her voice had begun to get defensive, a sure sign of hiding something. "I was going by your office right now."

Sure she was. And sure she found a dog. There was one easy way to check that.

"Better have a look." Mulling turned the key in the ignition. "You go ahead, I'll follow you out."

"That's really not necessary." Molly Snow shifted the dog food bag to the other arm. "It's just big and sort of silver, like a shepherd. I wouldn't want to take your time."

"No problem." Mulling rolled up the patrol car window.

Molly Snow stared at him for a moment, bold enough to look annoyed, then walked back to her car, a beat-up foreign ricegrinder. As it pulled into the street Mulling fell in right behind.

The car moved at a careful 25 miles per hour, and Mulling trailed it, reviewing the clues. The bag of dog food was a good cover, except she could have seen him and gone back to pick it up. He shouldn't have drifted off, his first mistake. It was just that lately, thanks to the wackos, he was coming up short on sleep. As if a probable Indian agitator weren't enough, Surfbreak was developing nut cases. They called at all hours and kept him running.

The month after the tourists left was supposed to put this town to sleep, but last month had lit a firecracker under its butt. First there was the old mission church. The church was abandoned, and if the damn missionaries hadn't built it of stone it would have thoughtfully fallen down. These days historic-preservation nuts were ranting to the city council that it should be resurrected, or whatever they did to churches. Somebody was breaking in there like clockwork, ten AM every Sunday morning, and ringing the tower bell. As soon as the bell rang, his phone started ringing. He'd have to traipse out there. But not a soul was hanging around, not even last Sunday when he dragged himself out of bed at six AM to stake it out. Every door was boarded over, staked coffin-tight.

Then there was that mess with the Gimetta kids, and the mom too. One of the kids got sick and her husband was off someplace being a salesman. She called the sheriff to get the kid to the hospital. The kid looked feverish, Mulling granted that, but not so bad a little aspirin wouldn't fix it. Then the hospital called two days later and said Mulling had to come in for a shot.

But first he was supposed to play county health superintendent, since he was already exposed. Smallpox my foot, Mulling thought, watching the car take the turnoff toward the beach. There hadn't been a case of smallpox in this county for going on fifty-five years. But naturally he'd had to go out and quarantine the whole Gimetta family.

Mulling took the turnoff to the Aowl cabin and noted how the half-breed's car needed new shocks. Smallpox, and ghosts in the churches, he thought; he really needed that. Plus there had been two more calls, a week apart, people claiming they saw bodies on the beach. The fools in this town were beginning to fall for their own press releases about that body. Except that the latest callers began adding details to the legend. Same description both times.

If some fiftyish fat slob wanted to get himself drowned, he could at least stick around to get collected. Not a chance, no body in sight. And that second caller, a widow living up by the point, even said the corpse looked chewed up as if some kind of animal had got to it.

Nut cases, all over. What he wouldn't give for some nice quiet twentieth-century problem—dopers or a tourist kiting checks at the pharmacy. Mulling tried to put the nut cases out of his mind. After all, now it looked like Miss Snow was up to new tricks.

At the Aowl cabin the sheriff pulled his car in next to Molly Snow's, opened the door, and levered his body from the seat. The Aowl cabin looked quiet and kept up okay, as unsuspicious in the daylight as it looked when he drove past at night.

"I left him, or left it, in the bedroom," Molly Snow called over her shoulder, "so it couldn't mess up the house."

Mulling climbed the two porch steps and followed her inside. Molly Snow gestured toward the closed door. "It's in here." She looked afraid to turn the knob.

Mulling drew his gun.

"You don 't need that," she said skittishly. "It's a really quiet dog."

"Just a precaution." Mulling doubted there was any dog, but guns had a way of impressing women. He nudged the door open.

So this was where the skinny Miss Snow slept, Mulling thought, entering the bedroom. The bed was a real mess. She must have spent the night tossing and turning, poor lonely woman. The bedroom window was shut tight. He stepped around the bed, hearing her move behind him, and scanning the floor on that side. No dog. No wolf. No pee spot either, just like he expected.

"But he was here!" Her protest sounded high with disbelief. "How could he have gotten out?" She stared at the closed window.

"Beats me." Mulling pushed the gun back into his holster. "Unless of course he never got in."

Molly Snow stood at the foot of the bed, going redder by the second. She leaned over and looked under the bed. Long, pretty legs.

With a flash of insight, Mulling saw how the whole drill finally made sense. He'd walked right into her trap, driving all the way out here to protect her from some big dog. Naturally the dog would be in the bedroom, where he now stood facing the pretty Miss Snow. The horny Miss Snow in fact, directly across the bedcovers. She was damn smart, luring him out here and into the bedroom.

"But he came in the window last night. A big animal. Just like those dogs I saw on the beach." She stepped past him to the room's one window and opened it. "Honest, I don't know how he got out, but there must be tracks out here." She leaned over and looked, her neat, tight butt bent over the sill.

Tempting, Mulling thought, but not the way he'd imagined it. He did appreciate how she'd got the same idea he did, about them getting together, but this was a small town, and a dozen people probably saw him heading this way. It was one thing to get it on with a Woofie. It was quite another thing to get caught. He had enough trouble with people laughing already. They would get a real howl if he shacked up with an Indian.

Besides, he was the man. He liked his women when he was ready for them. Ed Mulling might get around to Miss Molly in his own sweet time, some night when no one knew. Then he would have the advantage. Mulling moved to the window and leaned out too, nudging her hip to give her a thrill.

"No tracks," he said as Molly Snow pulled back inside. "Unless your dog is a man. I'd say maybe six feet tall, medium build."

There were boot prints out there, coming and going from the window. One set led up to it, Mulling saw, but the cleaner ones, pressing in since last night's fog dampened the surface, led into the dunes. Unless her wolf wore size twelves, this was a tall man's gait.

The woman craned her head beside him. She stared at the prints, her eyes as wide as if she were seeing a ghost. Her body strained back from the window. She must have picked up his signals, Mulling guessed. She wasn't going to get what she wanted from him today. He gave her a long look.

"How about if I check in on you from time to time?" he said solicitously. "Might make you feel better."

Molly Snow hurried toward the front door, swishing her butt with quick little steps. "There's no need for that. I just don't understand." She held the door open, embarrassed that her trick had failed. "Sorry for your trouble, Sheriff. But a dog got in, I swear it did. Last night."

"Sure, sure." Mulling settled a hand on her shoulder. "I'll stop by every so often. It can be pretty scary being out here by yourself."

That did the trick. Mulling snapped his holster closed. Women were best kept a little scared and a little hungry. He took the porch steps in one stride and walked to his car, then turned to give her a wink. The door was already closed.

On the other side, Molly Snow leaned against the rough wood and took a deep breath. She felt dirty. She'd taken a shower, but this felt like dirt on the inside.

Damn Sheriff Mulling. She could have sworn he was rubbing

against her when he leaned out the window.

And the dog was there this morning. It was. Big as life. Molly shivered. Mulling had seen those footprints too, she thought. They had to belong to Al. Al would have left prints when he fixed the window, but that was nearly a month ago. None of her own prints had remained, only his.

Chapter 14

RAYMOND GOODWILLOW OPENED THE DOOR OF THE WOODSTOVE and returned as quietly as he could to his shack's one upholstered chair. He settled into it slowly, willing it not to make a sound. Inside the stove's firebox, embers glowed orange and red.

It was Friday evening, after midnight, but Goodwillow would not sleep. Pam had insisted on staying with him, as she had stayed every night this week. He told her many times that he was all right. Old men did not need to sleep. Old men slept best in a chair by the stove. Pam was afraid to leave him now, he saw. Perhaps she sensed the end of their time together approaching.

Raymond settled deeper into his chair, thinking that he would not mind if death came. These days he often received visions of wolves. Rushing floods combined with the sound of church bells ringing as they rang very long ago. It seemed the forces of the white world, and the forces of the Indian world, were once more going to do battle. Goodwillow stared into the dying fire, facing his sorrow that such things happened.

From a few feet away he heard a whimper. Pam tossed between the covers, lifting her head from time to time and punching the pillow before falling back into it. Occasionally soft outcries came, mixed and scattered with words in the old language. Her dreams must be making her speak in her sleep. Goodwillow felt glad his granddaughter remembered those old words. It felt good to hear that tongue spoken again.

Ever since I was half her age, Goodwillow thought, *I have stayed away from white men's troubles. I have tried to take care of my people. I have told the stories that should be told. I have kept secret the stories only a shaman should know. Now, if Raymond Goodwillow must die, this story should not die inside of him.*

Pam muttered again. One of the noises sounded like the word for love. She said the word that meant "to wait." Pam rolled over on the bed again. The stirrings from the other side of the room sounded wakeful now.

"Grandfather?" Her voice thick with sleep, Pam slid upward on the bed. Dark arms angled out as she rubbed her eyes. "Are you awake?"

Goodwillow grunted. If she needed him to be awake, he would admit it. If she could fall back to the pillow, that was better.

"Grandfather?" A whisper again. Pam's small silhouette rose from the mattress, and she pulled a blanket up over her shoulders before coming toward him.

"I'm here," he said softly. "Are you too cold?"

Pam settled onto a wooden chair. "You opened up the stove."

"It helps me sleep," he said. "It will help you too. You should be tired."

"I kept having funny dreams."

Pam gathered the blanket more closely around her shoulders, burrowing in the way the old people once did to warm themselves on long nights. Once Pam got comfortable, she began to speak. She used the old name to speak of the wolf.

"I dreamed of him. He ran down by the water. His friends ran with him," she said softly. "Then he came to me. I was bigger than I am now, and sleeping. I looked into his eyes."

Raymond Goodwillow thought of the wolf's teeth, which The Great Changer always showed to him in his own sleep. Shining black lips drew back when the wolf grinned, and his fat pink tongue lolled lower than his whiskers. For many weeks now, the wolf had run through his dreams, clouds of sand bursting behind his fast paws.

"Did he speak to you?"

"No, not me." Pam sounded wide awake now. "But someone spoke to him. And you were there, except you weren't you. You wore the old robes, like when you used to teach me stories."

So her dream made him wear the storyteller's robe. It was another sign. Goodwillow knew what he must do. This story must not die with an old man.

Pam could not understand this story, of course, nor grasp why the dreams wanted her to know it. She had a different wisdom, a deeper wisdom perhaps. Yet the woman named Molly Snow would come tomorrow. Pam must know this story before then.

"Would you like me to tell you a story?" he said at last. Her blue shadow shifted against the darker lines of the chair. "Could you make it a fairy story?" Pam nestled deeper into her blanket. "Once upon a time," she recited. "That's how they start."

"Once upon a time," Goodwillow repeated, and began telling the events he had always believed he would reveal only to a true shaman.

Chapter 15

"IT HAPPENED A LONG TIME AGO," GOODWILLOW SAID ALOUD TO the darkness. "I was ten years old. Storm Man was the friend of a white man. Then Storm Man took a new wife." Goodwillow made his voice full and strong, a storyteller's voice. He remembered little of the beginnings of the trouble between his grandfather and the white man, Alford Aowl, but Storm Man had repeated the details on his deathbed.

This white man, Aowl, came long before the others like him. He was not a trapper or one who cut down trees. He told Storm Man about the dangers of new white men coming. This white man lived as the Wolvine did, but not among Wolf 's people. He lived in the hills and drew pictures of places he saw. After a time, the white man learned all the names of the hills and the rivers. He learned the places where water came and places where all the animals lived. He did not kill the animals except to eat, which was good.

"Then in those days," Goodwillow said, his voice calm and strong, "he even learned the places of wolves. He followed their trails between the trees. He saw where the wolves brought their young out of caves."

The white man told the Wolvine people that they must protect their sacred places, yet now he had found the secret homes of the most sacred animals. Still he did no bad killing. Instead, this white man earned his Wolvine name, which Storm Man gave to him. Man-Among-Wolves gave up calling himself Alford Aowl and went to live among wolves.

"Wolf loved this man. If the man made a soft noise, Wolf came to him."

The Wolvine people had always talked with wolves, both the wolves that ran in the forest and the bigger wolves, those that grew out of the smoke of ritual fires or came to visit when a man slept. Storm Man talked to the wolf in the old language, but Man-Among-Wolves understood wolves' own speaking. Man-Among-Wolves made whimpers and wuffing noises. The pack listened and obeyed. He slept with wolves curled around him.

The white man drew pictures of places where wolves lived, but he did not draw them correctly. "To keep other white men from coming there, the man drew lies," the old shaman told Pam. "When Man-Among-Wolves explained this, Storm Man said it was good."

Those had been happy days, Goodwillow remembered. He was his grandfather's favorite child, picked to be the next shaman of the Wolvine. Before Goodwillow was six years old his grandfather began teaching him dances and songs. The year he turned ten his grandfather took him to the great cave, the secret place no one went except the shaman. There Raymond learned the names of sacred objects—the feathered stick, the talking seed, and other things he would be allowed to touch when he was older. Then those happy days ended.

He knew, even as a boy, that the trouble was about women. His grandfather had three wives, strong, fat Wolvine women who took care of him. Then around that time the younger men, those who followed the seal and the deer to bring back food, told Storm Man of a tribe that lived to the north. This tribe's daughters were more beautiful than Wolvine women.

Storm Man was old but he wanted a wife from these people with beautiful daughters. He sent the young men, telling them to bring back the best one.

"Our young men were gone for many days." Goodwillow spoke to the pale light remaining among the embers. "Storm Man told his wives to make everything ready and to make a great feast."

When the young men returned, they carried a slender girl tied with cedar rope. Even though still a girl, she was taller than

Wolvine women. Her face looked as delicate as the finest carving any man could make. When they reached the river, she looked too tired to fight against the ropes, but her arms showed stripes from fighting them. Her name sounded like the word for the birch tree, so Storm Man called her Birch. He set her by the fire and invited everyone to come and celebrate.

Even tonight, eighty or more years later, Raymond remembered the frightened feeling in his stomach. He watched his grandfather examine the girl. He could tell that Storm Man liked her. If Birch made another son for him, no matter how old Storm Man was, the new son might be chosen over Raymond to become the shaman. Raymond wanted to chase this girl away.

"Man-Among-Wolves also came for that feast," Goodwillow said.

The white man arrived late. Raymond could see that he was angry. He wore skins like the Wolvine did and he ate their food, but Raymond sensed that his anger was a white man's anger.

"Man-Among-Wolves came to ask me about this new wife. I told him Storm Man would take her to his bed when spring came again. Everyone knew that."

Man-Among-Wolves went away. Goodwillow could no longer remember when the real trouble had happened, but he guessed it was during winter. Nights were darkest then, and animals and men slept most soundly. He heard his grandfather and Man-Among-Wolves argue many times. He spent much time with his grandfather and heard Man Among-Wolves saying that Birch was too young. Man-Among-Wolves wanted Storm Man to send her back to the north.

"Then Man-Among-Wolves came in the night and stole that girl."

Raymond Goodwillow fell silent. He felt awed, even so many years later, at the memory of Storm Man's anger. He had awakened to the sight of the old man's shouting face. Storm Man dragged Raymond from the blankets. His anger came like a bright stick picked up from the fire and it tore through the places where all the young men slept. Storm Man could not find his new wife.

Everyone knew where Birch had been taken. Storm Man could not go himself, but he sent young men to the sacred places where wolves lived and raised their young. They went each night, but came back each morning without the girl.

Then Storm Man told Raymond to come into the sacred cave. Storm Man covered his shoulders with skins, picked up the feathered stick, and lifted it high in the air. His song began as a wordless rumble. It got louder and louder, until Raymond's head pounded hearing it go up and down, up and down. Storm Man said unknown words. Raymond only learned their meaning when the rains began to fall.

Storm Man attacked Man-Among-Wolves with a storm that became a flood before its drops touched the ground. It swelled along gullies and ravines, sweeping into valleys where Wolf lived. It flooded caves in Wolf's denning places, and some of Wolf's children were killed.

"Man-Among-Wolves talked in snarls to those around him," Goodwillow explained. "He made wolves turn against their own people. Wolves would not let the young men come near. They stayed in the hills and protected Man-Among-Wolves. After many nights, Storm Man began to teach me new chants."

Goodwillow was young and had difficulty learning all the new words, but even today he could hear them in his mind. The words squealed and howled and hurt Raymond's throat. Storm Man had taken out the old drum, the drum nearly as big as Raymond himself, and carried it deep into the cave at the back of this very shack. Storm Man could not do this chanting alone. He needed the drum to speak and help the new words do their work.

The drum roared. Raymond threw cedar shavings on the fire when he was told. He brought water and poured it slowly on the rocks. He spoke the words on the third night while Storm Man danced, no longer Storm Man; no longer even a grandfather, but some pounding, twirling, hot-breathed thing that wrapped itself in smoke and mixed itself into fire.

At last the fire burned down. Storm Man rested. Raymond watched and waited, his heart making the sound of the drum all night inside that huge cave. Then Storm Man awakened and looked at his grandson.

"'They have become wolves,' my grandfather said. 'Both of them.' The old man's eyes looked black in the light left from the fire. 'He will always be a wolf. If she comes back, I will make her human again.'"

And it was true. In the years when he was growing up Raymond heard stories of two wolves running as mates, running so fast they could outdistance the pack. He even saw them once. One was a great, gray-maned wolf, and the she-wolf was lean, light gray, moving like the spirit of wind.

Goodwillow paused and listened for the sound of his granddaughter's breathing. In the stove, beside the gleaming black door, a log seethed and hissed in its underside. Perhaps Pam was asleep. Perhaps The Great Changer only wanted this part of the story told. That would be a better way for things to happen. He heard a stirring from the darkness near Pam's chair and felt hope die.

"That's what happened," he went on. "Birch finally came back, a skinny wolf slinking close to the trees. Storm Man said some words and danced alone in the cave. She appeared—a girl again. But Man-Among-Wolves did not come back for a long time. When he came he was a man, but during that other time he walked as a wolf."

Everyone knew which wolf he was. He stood taller and rounder than the others in the pack, and he ran among them just as he always had. But wolves grow old, wolves die. This wolf never did. Because of Storm Man's curse, he would live forever.

For several years after that, Birch lived with Storm Man and obeyed him quietly. She was silent and quick because she did not want to be turned back into a wolf. During those years Storm Man spent many days in the cave with his grandson teaching him the most difficult songs and dances. Raymond learned how to handle sacred things.

But Storm Man's new wife learned things, too. Birch crept into the mouth of the cave after Raymond and his grandfather went there. She watched and listened.

"My grandfather might have made a mistake," Goodwillow said. "He forgot he had once made her a wolf. That girl learned what the wolf knows. A wolf is silent and cunning."

A wolf could wait a long time until its prey tired. A pretty girl from the north could grow into a woman in those years, never fat like Wolvine women, but healthy and strong. She could wait while

Storm Man got old. The day he died, she threw the blanket over his face and turned her back on the body.

"Then she came to me." The old shaman still remembered his horror. "She wanted me to go into the cave with her, but I would not go. I was a young man by then and it made me ashamed. I had to say no to this woman who pretended to be my grandmother."

Birch argued with him. She had listened in the cave, she told him, and she knew the sacred songs. She had practiced secretly. If the new shaman would help her, she could turn that wolf back into a man.

Raymond Goodwillow commanded her to stop speaking, but she did not listen. He told her he would not go with her, but he did not stop her from going. To this day a place still burned inside of him for that shame. Storm Man, his own grandfather, had made the curse. It was a bad curse and it should not have been made, but Storm Man's grandson, a shaman himself now, would be wrong to change it. Raymond Goodwillow walked away to sleep alone between the trees for three days.

Birch went into the cave, and she took the great drum with her. She sang the songs and drummed and danced.

She cursed the spirit of Storm Man. Out in the forest—which should hold only rustlings and the shrieks of night things—Raymond felt the pulse of that drum pound his chest. The shadows around him grew darker. He thought he smelled the smell of his grandfather—the seal oil Storm Man used to slick his hair, the dry, feathery smell of the skins Storm Man died in.

Raymond searched among the dark trees, but the smell of Storm Man drifted everywhere. He lay down to sleep in the scent, and when he awoke he understood what had happened. The forest had changed. It felt darker and more quietly dangerous than ever before. Storm Man's spirit curled into every hiding hole and tree stump and mossy curve of the ground. Birch had driven that spirit out, but she could not destroy it. Storm Man's spirit became trapped in the hills, and it walked there as a great shadow that could not die.

Again that night, Birch sang the songs and drummed and danced. She said the chants that she knew, trying to make a wolf into a man.

On the fourth morning, Goodwillow came back from the forest. A white man stood in front of their house. He looked like Man-Among-Wolves, but no older than he used to when he walked as a man.

"Because he was a wolf, he did not age. But I listened there at the door and learned what Birch told him."

Because she said the songs alone, she could not make the curse go away. She had only changed it. If the white man lived as a man, all the sorrows of the white man would come to live among his own people and the Wolvine. He would grow older and age as men aged. Eventually he would die. Yet if he chose, he could live as a wolf. Then white men's troubles would be fewer. And Man-Among Wolves would never die.

Raymond Goodwillow moved sideways and studied the dying embers in the firebox. He found words to tell Pam the last things that had happened in those days.

"She told the white man he must go away. He must not live as a man because his coming had brought these terrible things. Whenever he lived as a man, The Great Changer would bring death to people."

As a young man, the new shaman of his tribe, Raymond Goodwillow saw that this slender woman spoke the truth. She knew the ways of The Great Changer too, but she could not fix things.

"Very soon our people grew sick with fevers. Storms came and smashed our boats. Fire burned down many of the white men's houses because a wolf walked as a man." That winter was the most terrible ever sent to the Wolvine. The white people suffered a great sickness, and soon it killed many. As long as Man-Among-Wolves walked on two legs, sickness and death came as fevers that white men called smallpox.

As Storm Man walked the hills, he became stronger at commanding the winds and rain. His spirit was trapped in those hills, and the curse caused its own hate.

"To make Man-Among-Wolves leave, that woman who had once been a wolf went away from us. No one knew where she went. Later everybody said Birch went to live among white men. She never came back. After she went, the wolf walked away on two legs to look for her. Then he walked on four. He returned to life as a wolf." Goodwillow paused, counting Pam's breaths in the darkness. "Then things got better."

He listened as the silence asked his granddaughter's question. He hoped Pam was not still awake to ask it herself. Perhaps even as he spoke, good dreams were making pictures in her mind.

"Man-Among-Wolves always looked for Birch. He could choose to walk as a man or as a wolf. Stories said he kept himself furred, living out lives beyond the other wolves that died beside him."

Goodwillow felt his voice growing weak. He was tired, that was true, but sadness drained the strength from his veins. In his mind's darkness he could still see Birch, her aging, crying face the last time he saw her. She had slipped away when it was late at night, but he had looked out the door and seen her go.

"They had lived together as mates, and he loved her," Goodwillow said aloud to the dark. "He will always look for her, and no bullet will kill him to end his sorrow. Only words that I know can do that."

The last of the fire glowed dimly in the black cave of the stove. Pam's breathing beside him sounded low and even. It had finally become sleep. Then a voice spoke.

"Molly Snow is the granddaughter of Birch. Now she is here, and in Molly Snow's body. Birch's spirit has returned. Molly Snow is the woman he loves."

The old man turned to see his granddaughter's eyes, but he could not be sure. Reflecting the last gleam of the fire, two embers—like the eyes of a wolf—met his own.

Chapter 16

SATURDAY MORNING ARRIVED SHEETED WITH WIND AND RAIN. Molly found her parka beneath a pile of papers, where it had fallen when the weather turned warm. Pam Goodwillow had given her directions to the Wolvine reservation.

During the night, puddles on the cottage's road had swelled to minor lakes. Molly steered around them, reaching Breakers Avenue after only a few splashing jolts. At the turn onto the highway, wind whipped rain in great blurs down the windshield.

Today did not feel promising for an expedition. She had slept badly for two nights. First the lost dog had awakened her. Then her dreams had grown even more strange. In an odd way, the dream last night felt like a good one, Molly thought, scanning the highway's margins for the marker Pam had said would be there.

The dog had returned in last night's dream. It came straight toward her, running playfully. It rolled and scratched on the ground, nudging her sideways so she too would fall onto all fours. For a long time she and the dog played like two animals—chasing each other around trees, rolling and tumbling on pine-needled ground. *This is fun*, Molly realized, but with that thought the dream turned strange.

Memories of running at great speed mixed with memories of savagery, of deer pulled down from behind, of the strong animal smell of dens. She began to feel wolfish, or doglike, but certainly feral.

The dog had not changed; she had. Barrel-rolling over onto all fours, Molly decided to stand up before falling again. She pushed backward, but the stretch for uprightness felt impossible. Her body would not go that way. Her hands were no longer hands. When Molly sniffed them, she knew at once that they were paws. Webs joined her fingers, which were only short, furry knuckles. She felt the fur on her neck stiffen as panic gripped her. Molly pushed herself upward, screaming a sound that came out like a howl, and found herself in bed on her stomach. She was pushing against blankets, shoving her back into the air, and crying.

She crawled from bed and stood at the window. The first gusts of wind blasted drops against the glass. She found herself suddenly lonely, as if the dog had actually been close and run off at the sound of that scream.

Up ahead a sign took shape, identifying Wolvine Reservation Land. Two smaller signs hung below—a triangle advertising "Native Hearth Bread" and another, smaller and crudely lettered on a broken plank, offering beaded leather goods for sale. Molly pulled onto a bare patch of ground beside the sign. A few yards in, where the state highway system apparently left off, an unevenly cut ribbon of rough road began.

Molly collected notebook, pens, and tape recorder from the back seat, then decided to skip the recorder. It might make the old man nervous. Besides, this land seemed so primitive that modem technology would feel out of place. She pulled the parka's cords tight.

Wind carried rain into the tops of pines, then shook water from the boughs. With her first steps, Molly felt as if two storms raged around her. Water struck her back and also fell straight down from rain-starred branches. The terrain looked alien and utterly wild, yet within a few yards the rain-blackened trees and soggy ground gained a pleasant familiarity.

In Aowl's day people walked through weather like this wearing little more than deerskin capes. Given time, people could acclimate to almost anything, she guessed. Molly tried to imagine herself living in this mossy landscape and finding her way in the near-dark by smells of cedar and pine, by sounds underfoot and ancient knowledge deep in memory. The task felt surprisingly simple. If she was, in fact, related back to Indian blood, her own ancestors could have lived in a place like this.

Boxy shapes gathered form by the roadside, man-made intrusions flickering between trees. Raymond Goodwillow lived in a house beyond this road of tumbledown cottages. In the dim light, the houses appeared abandoned to hopelessness, yet carved sticks stood planted upright before several.

The sticks carried traces of old red and black paint. Tamahnous sticks, Molly recalled from her reading. Like miniature totem poles, they were there for luck or defense or even as a record of a family's history. The houses near those sticks were hardly more than shacks, roofs swaybacked, porches crumbling to the forest floor. In a few, electric lights glowed their little suns in the early gloom. Televisions flickered ghost-dancing light. No one came to a doorway to wave. Perhaps they were afraid. Despair tainted the dusky light and seemed to harry this place, like a hound running back and forth over her footprints.

When Goodwillow's house finally appeared, Molly wondered at first if it was even a house. Its dark shape grew out of a cliff side like a natural landform. On first sight it was little more than a long roof resting on thick poles. No walls, no windows distinguished it until two walls finally began farther back. Their ends met the cliff. At the far end of the open structure, a wall held a door, and another small roof rose beyond the roof of the shelter.

Molly hesitated. She looked back and realized she had taken a turn through the trees, then another hairpin cutback, without giving direction a thought. It felt natural to come this way, even though the road had left off and the other structures slipped from view several hundred yards back. She examined the building.

The basic shape must have been added to for more than a century. Someone of great power and creativity had designed it. She felt darkness in its hunched shape, and a flicker of familiarity as if she had come to a place like this some time before.

Molly stepped beneath the roof and was surprised to feel its shelter cut out the rain completely. The roof was wide. Perhaps thirty people could live beneath it. They could cook and the smoke would blow away.

Smells of old cooking fires mixed with the smells of a newly scraped animal skin stretched for drying. At the end of the open shelter, pine needles and cedar shavings lay dry before the doorway. The house had a short roof, she realized, because it was only a hut with its back built into the cliff. The design saved the trouble of building one wall. You could make your own cave in the earth, for defense or escape; could dig tunnels and storage areas.

Over the house's window, a flimsy-looking curtain hung. If what she had heard about Goodwillow was true, then someone was taking care of both him and his place. He was far too old to fix roofs or scrape deerskin.

The eerie echo of familiarity persisted. Molly listened. No sounds escaped except the sighing of wind and the wash of rain. Ready at last to see the inside, Molly turned to push the door open.

She caught herself at the last instant. She was supposed to knock, not jump right into someone's house as if she lived there. It was one thing to imagine yourself as a native living in this place, but quite another to make yourself right at home. Her knuckles struck sturdy wood.

"You came." Pam opened the door instantly. "Grandfather knows you 're coming. He's glad."

Molly smiled and stepped through the low opening. She let Pam peel the dripping parka from her shoulders.

At first it seemed that there was not much to the low-ceilinged room. A wooden table and three ladder-back chairs stood near the sink. Shelves along one wall held clothing and skins, and beside the sink a length of cracked linoleum provided a counter. The other wall lay hidden for several feet by a curtain, probably shielding a bed, then ran straight back to a doorway draped with a long skin.

Molly tried to estimate the distance. The cliff should lie not far beyond that doorway, yet the door looked as if it led to another room. That room could be a small storage space, a large cave, anything. Along the far wall stood a woodstove, the lamp beside it giving the room its only light. Nearby, a large upholstered chair sat with its back to the door.

"He's over here, by the stove."

Molly had a quick moment to admire the hangings on the walls, feathered shapes and carved poles, baskets that looked old but well-made, and clumps of dried plants. Pam pulled her around the side of the big chair and urged her toward a fourth ladder-back chair, obviously pulled close to the stove for conversation.

Molly paused and extended her hand. "I'm pleased to meet you, Mr. Goodwil—" The man's head lifted. Dark brown eyes looked into her own.

This was the Indian chief. Here was the ancient, lined face that had been typecast for her dream. Now it sat in front of her, and without any feathered Hollywood headdress. The old man's hair was long and gray. His eyes were the darkly intelligent eyes of the dream, eyes that had waited for her to speak words she did not understand.

The old man's hand touched hers and his lips opened to speak. Molly readied herself to answer, at a loss to remember words of the old language.

"My granddaughter said you would come."

His voice was rough with the gravel of age and less strong than it sounded in the dream.

"Your name is Molly Snow. And you have come." Molly found herself suppressing a shiver. The resemblance was too strong. The old man's gaze softened, as if he understood her confusion. He gestured toward the chair.

"Coming here makes you cold. The fire will warm you. My granddaughter will bring us tea."

Molly fumbled backward to steady herself on the chair back. She sat. Beneath her hand she felt her notebook and distantly recalled that it held dozens of prepared questions. She could not imagine asking the old man one of them.

"I got a chill," she managed. "I'm sorry."

"I understand that," the old man said. "Of course you would."

His eyes closed. Pam hurried away to pull cups from the sink.

Chapter 17

WHILE PAM MADE TEA, THE OLD MAN APPEARED TO REST. HIS large easy chair dwarfed his frame, making him look shrunken inside his pale blue shirt and faded denims. Shadows carved hollows beneath his high cheekbones.

Molly felt thankful that his eyes were closed. She did not want to look into them again, at least not until she calmed down. She examined her surroundings and tried to quell the panic icing her flesh. For a minute there, half-remembered dreams had felt more real than the work she had come to do.

A quick survey confirmed that Raymond Goodwillow lived entirely in this one room. Cans of food filled several shelves, and a frying pan hung on the wall alongside two dented pots. Other walls held skins and an occasional length of animal fur. The wall leading to the back doorway held the most unusual objects, a length of carved and polished wood shaped like a canoe paddle, a strand of feathers and beads cascading down a rawhide cord, and a broad deerskin cape, buttons and feathers marking a spoked circle on its back. Below the hangings, and a few feet out from the wall, solitary and venerable, stood a drum. As her eyes adjusted to the light, Molly tried to gauge how big the drum actually was.

Even as she stared, the dim shape seemed to expand and grow more imposing. Its sides were of bent cedar, fastened with pegs. The cedar glowed dully red, the skin of the drumhead light brown, and fur cut from a pelt trailed down one side. A very large man

LACK CADY & CAROL ORLOCK

could probably hold it between his knees, but he would surely have to play it with sticks the size of small clubs. A drum this big would have a deep voice, one strong enough to call over miles. Molly imagined herself going over to the drum and touching the skin to release that sound. She immediately knew she should not. The act felt taboo, terribly wrong behavior, perhaps because she was a visitor, or a white woman, or a woman at all. Nonetheless, beneath the crackle of the woodstove and Pam's clatterings at the sink, it seemed that great thuddings sounded, the roar this drum would have made when it was pounded with every ounce of her strength.

Or maybe I'm just hearing my own heart pounding, Molly corrected herself. She would mention none of this to Raymond Goodwillow. Even though a shaman must be accustomed to beliefs about spirits and ghostly memories, Goodwillow might not take kindly to a white woman walking in his door and telling him she felt she'd once lived here and struck that drum. *Strictly bad manners*, Molly thought.

Pam placed a chipped cup on the floor beside Molly and put a second cup on the arm of her grandfather's chair. With that, the old man's eyes opened. Apparently he had not been dozing, but listening.

"I can answer your questions. You have come a long way." He spoke far too solemnly, each statement a separate pronouncement.

Molly quickly explained her work at Pinehaven and the grant that had brought her to Surfbreak. "I work every day at the museum on the shore," she said. "At that big black building with all the cake decorations on it."

She smiled, but a flicker of distaste crossed the old man 's face. "I know that place."

"I study maps and old books, going back to find out what it was like then."

Raymond Goodwillow assessed her with his gaze. He seemed doubtful whether she was lying or really interested in talking about history.

"I'm especially interested in a man named Alford James Aowl. He was the first white man here, at least that's what everyone thinks."

At the mention of Aowl's name, Goodwillow's eyes brightened, as if finally hearing news he recognized. Yet their intensity faded, watchful and waiting, as Molly laid out her first question.

"I thought maybe, since Alford Aowl knew the Wolvine people, maybe in your lifetime, you might have heard of him. Does the name sound familiar?"

"I knew this man."

"You knew him?" Molly's heart leapt.

Raymond Goodwillow nodded. "I was a boy. There was a time when he was a friend of my grandfather. My grandfather's name was Storm Man."

Molly could hardly believe her ears. She slid forward on her chair. "Storm Man? That name Alford Aowl mentioned that name in his diary. Storm Man."

"Storm Man was the shaman of our people in those days. As I am the shaman now."

Molly struggled to quell her excitement. Raymond Goodwillow was the shaman, she reminded herself, and it would not do to pummel him with questions. Which was exactly what she felt like doing.

On her lap, the notebook lay open to her planned questions. "What can you tell me about him?" She abandoned the list. "Anything, anything you can tell me. I want to know everything."

Saying Storm Man's name with a seriousness that approached reverence, Goodwillow pulled himself erect in the creaking upholstered chair. Now Molly saw that he was actually much larger, and possibly stronger, than he'd first appeared. The care in each of his movements betrayed age, but it also told of great power, as if this body held forces much larger than its shrunken shape.

"An old man knows many things," Goodwillow said slowly. "He does not know everything." A disarming smile crossed the pale lips. Goodwillow paused, thinking.

"Of the many things I know, you wish to know perhaps a few, perhaps more than that. You must tell me which."

Like a memory from her dream, Goodwillow's alert brown eyes met her own. He expected her to say something, Molly realized, to give some answer that felt as precise as the words of the old language.

"I think I understand," she said when she could no longer

stand his scrutiny. "I should narrow my question?"

"Perhaps."

"You said you were a boy, but you met him. Maybe you could tell me what he looked like? Or anything about the work he did, drawing maps. Did he talk very much, or was he a quiet man?"

Goodwillow's penetrating stare continued, as if at any moment she might make a wrong move, or a right one. "Does that help?"

Goodwillow's gaze softened. "You wish to know what I saw with my own eyes, those things I heard with my own ears. You have come to me as a witness to those events you read about in books?"

The question seemed an odd one, but Molly nodded. "If you don't mind. I'd like to know about Alford Aowl, anything I can."

Goodwillow relaxed deeper into the chair, and his knobby hands, which had tied a pale knot in his lap, separated to slide down to his sides.

"This is not difficult." The words carried a sigh of relief. "About the man, Alford Aowl, I can tell you many things." And he began to speak.

During the next two hours, while the old man's voice mesmerized her, Molly raced to spread words across the lines of her notebook. She often fell behind and could note only key phrases, catching up in the pauses when Goodwillow rested. He closed his eyes occasionally, but did not sleep. Then he resumed his story.

Goodwillow described Aowl's clothing in great detail, naming the locations of the animals he had hunted and skinned, and naming the names of Wolvine women who had sewn the skins. He told what the Wolvine ate, and said that Aowl ate many of the same foods, along with other things that came in boxes, tins, and kegs when visitors traveled here to see him. Goodwillow spoke of the house that Aowl had built on the shore, and seemed pleased to learn that Molly lived in it now. Along with memories of feasts, hunts, and conversations he had personally held with Aowl, talking about animals and their ways, Goodwillow supplied remarkable detail about Aowl's opinion of white men.

As he spoke, Goodwillow stared straight ahead, or occasionally glanced past Molly to let his gaze rest on the great drum. In those moments his voice would fade, as if his mind chased a memory. Then he paused, took a sip of tea, and continued.

Pam withdrew to the sink, washing two plates over and over, and obviously listening. She turned once, as her grandfather described a feast Aowl had attended on the occasion of Storm Man's fourth marriage, and the overly washed plate in her hands dripped suds onto her shoes.

"The man who built the black building, the building that's now a museum," Molly said, taking advantage of a pause, "I understand that he and Alford Aowl disliked each other."

"I did not see this myself, but people believe it," Goodwillow answered. "Your -Man-Among-Wol—" Goodwillow paused to clear his throat. "This man among other white men did not like those who took trees without thanking the earth. The black building took many trees." Molly hoped she was not tiring Goodwillow too much, but at last she sighted an opening where one of her questions might fit. "Some people, in books I read, said Aowl might have been killed because he fought with the man who built it." The old man's hands shifted from his sides to knot once more in his lap. "I know that can't be," Molly went on. "Aowl was alive after the builder died. But nobody knows how Aowl himself died. Did you hear of his death?"

The answer came back quick as a ricochet. "I know nothing of Alford Aowl's death."

The words sounded truthful, yet the tightening in the old man's knuckles said he knew more.

"Perhaps someone else did?" Molly probed. "Maybe a member of your tribe found his body?"

Goodwillow measured his words. "No one came to tell me this. No stories speak of the death of this white man." Goodwillow took a sip of tea and set the cup carefully back on the arm of his chair. Confronted by a stone wall of silence, Molly hesitated. Goodwillow obviously did not want to answer. At least there were other questions she could ask.

"What about the maps? There's something not right about some maps, and everybody's been trying to figure it out." Molly tested words, wondering how to explain the errors. "In some places, always the same places, Aowl made mistakes. He put cliffs all wrong. Marshes weren't where he drew them."

"I can explain about that," the old man answered, and then simply, elegantly, Raymond Goodwillow laid out the answer Molly had expected to spend a year chasing.

"Your Alford Aowl was a good friend of Wolf. Perhaps you know that Wolf is a sacred animal of my people."

Molly nodded.

"Alford Aowl did not want other white men to come to places where the wolf is a child. Denning places," Goodwillow added uncertainly. "I think that's what your people call them. He drew the maps wrong."

"He lied?" Molly could hardly believe she held the explanation in her hand.

"He mixed places together. As The Great Changer, who makes the earth shake sometimes, can do," Goodwillow answered. "However I did not see these maps myself. Storm Man told me this."

Goodwillow smiled, bestowing the secondhand report like an apology for his unwillingness to answer earlier. "Are there more things of this kind you would like to know?"

Molly paused. Already her mind spun with facts and impressions. She could keep asking questions, but that might tire him. She had one answer, an answer she could confirm by studies of the region's wildlife. That answer alone would justify her thesis.

"I could listen to you all day," she said, hoping the compliment sounded as sincere as it felt. "But I should sort these notes, then come back with better-targeted questions." She paused. "If I may come back?"

The old man's eyes closed and he leaned against the worn cushion. "You will always be welcome in this house," he said simply.

Pam came to pick up her grandfather's cup and refresh the tea leaves. She left Molly's beside her chair. That might be an oversight, Molly supposed, but the air of calm finality in the old man's words was not.

She closed her notebook and stood. The instant she imagined herself passing out that door, however, she felt deeply sad. The fire was cozy and warm. Yet as the sadness swelled, she knew the real reason lay deeper. She turned to stare at the drum.

The memory of its sound, the illusion of having struck it, beaten it, thrown her whole weight into calling up its voice, issued only a faint throbbing now. This place held sweetness and safety, but that throbbing also pulsed with darker soundings. There were hammerings of fear. There were blows of anguish. This place held power that felt more real than the weight dropping onto her shoulders. Pam helped her shrug into her parka.

"You'll come back?" Pam asked when they stood by the door.

"When she is ready, Pam," Goodwillow answered. He leaned around the side of his chair to wish Molly farewell. Still Molly did not want to leave. It felt too painful to pull herself from this place, even though she had come here only hours ago. At last a delaying question came to mind.

"This might sound kind of silly," she began, "but if you don't mind one more question? That museum I work in, you said you knew it. I got the feeling you didn't like it?"

"That is a bad place," Pam said quietly, glancing at her grandfather.

"That's what I thought, in my own way of course. When I'm there, I feel like all the Native American, the Wolvine parts, are—well, I'd call it haunted if I didn't know better."

"It is cursed."

The words seemed to rise from the earth below his feet. Raymond Goodwillow pushed himself up from his chair. For the first time, Molly saw his startling strength. Beyond frailty, this was a man of imposing stature, emanating a quiet power that mixed strength with a thrumming alertness and control.

"Cursed." Molly felt small and stupid facing him. "It feels like that. I don't feel good in there. I feel—well, memories."

Goodwillow reached to the back of his chair to steady himself. It was only a touch. "They do not want you there. Especially you. They know who you are."

"I'm a researcher, that's all. And who doesn't want me?" Suddenly she was trembling and did not know why. The safety of this cabin made her wish never to leave. The darkness of the Aowl museum might reach anywhere but here. "I'm just there researching."

"They are shadows. They know you not as yourself. Not as you know yourself. But as another being you are. Or may yet become."

Goodwillow paused, then nodded toward his granddaughter. "The Great Changer is at work, and he has some business with you.

You will ask about these things next time you come." He turned away.

Pam opened the door. Molly whispered a hurried apology, hoping too much talk had not tired her grandfather. It was all right, Pam said. She helped Molly pull up her hood before letting her step into the rain.

It was nearly dark, but Molly struck out without hesitation. Surprisingly confident of the way, she strode surely through shadowy glades toward the lights of the houses.

By the time Molly emerged onto the highway, Pam Goodwillow had made her grandfather a fresh cup of tea and begun fixing dinner. Raymond Goodwillow sat comfortably in the soft chair, silently thanking Pam for her kindness. He also thanked the trees that gave wood to warm his house, and the earth for the bittersweet favor of the leaves that made strong tea. Then he let his memory drift. He thought about the young woman who had sat next to him all afternoon.

A girl from a tribe to the north had married a shaman of the Wolvine. She had no children, but later, when she was the age of this white woman, she went away to live among white men. She had a child, and that child had another child. There was no doubt of that now. Goodwillow let the memory of Molly Snow's face fill his vision. It was the same face . . . but the last time Goodwillow had seen her, Birch had looked haggard and drawn. Birch's face had been turning away as she escaped, running from the love of a wolf into the night.

Chapter 18

OCTOBER WIND AND RAIN SWEPT THE NORTHWEST COAST, AND the hills disappeared under mist. Mist shrouded the turrets of the Aowl Museum and blew like lonely ghosts along the streets of Surfbreak. People on the outskirts of town reported the howling of a dog pack, although one old-timer insisted these were no dogs. To some of the older people it seemed that a contest of wills went on between the hills and the forest.

In Surfbreak too much trouble happened too quickly. A new logging truck lost its brakes and rammed into cabins at a motel. No one died, but an ambulance carried three people to the hospital. Ten cases of scarlet fever appeared at the school, baffling doctors who had never seen the disease. Two ugly bar fights broke out between men too drunk to care what they did. Fire erupted at City Hall, and before it was contained it burned records of land plats. A storm swept in, riding a high tide, and took a large section of the boardwalk. The people of Surfbreak felt under siege.

Molly Snow awoke Sunday morning to the sound of church bells. She yawned and stretched, enjoying the bells' song above the grumble of the surf. She got a fire going in the woodstove and put the teakettle on. She could almost believe that she had lived in this rugged cottage during Aowl's own time, an early settler on the windswept coast.

After breakfast, she cut and pasted her notes onto cards and cross-referenced bits that overlapped. Then came the difficult part, checking where details differed, and highlighting items she would need new sources to confirm. The work felt pleasant and satisfying. Her energies were calmed by a day at home instead of frayed by the eeriness of the museum.

Molly thought often of Goodwillow's comment on that building, his belief that the place was cursed. A curse gave as good an explanation as any for the haunted feeling. She decided to spend a few more days working at home.

By midweek she had exhausted the possibilities for avoiding the museum. She resolutely set out across the dunes. When she opened the museum door, she paused a moment in the dark and listened.

The presences were as real as phantoms could be. She switched on the office light, wishing that driving away darkness could banish all shadows. The ghostly rustlings merely withdrew to drift with faint murmurings along the walls.

Despite the museum's distractions, the work went well. First, Molly skimmed missionary reports, early settlers' accounts, and Aowl's diary, flagging every reference to Storm Man. Now that she knew who he was, Storm Man turned up all over the place. He didn't sound like a man anyone but his grandson admired.

At last she located one of the clues she'd been looking for. The diary entry for November 12, 1908 listed members of the Wolvine tribe Alford Aowl personally knew. There, halfway down the page, lay the name Raymond Goodwillow. "Son of Wandering Dove by Good Willow, grandson of Tsi'lan and Storm Man. Favored prospect for leading the Wolvine in years to come, much beloved of Storm Man." The list continued with more names, but Molly let her finger rest beside this one.

She felt tempted to jump into the car and race out to the reservation to show this to Goodwillow. This link carried thrilling certainty. Interviews with Raymond Goodwillow, a survivor who knew Aowl, guaranteed not only her degree but a big jump on an academic reputation.

Part of her mind enjoyed the triumph. Deeper down, down where loneliness nestled alongside unreasoned hatred of this building, this perfect fit felt less satisfying. She could get her degree—yes, that was certain—but a degree now felt like a miniature toy beside the prize she had come for. And what prize was that? Molly shook her head. The intuition grew no more solid. Well then, she decided, the degree—and fleeting fame guaranteed for a few years in scholarly journals—would have to fill the bill.

She glanced at her watch. It was too late to drive to the reservation, and besides, Raymond Good willow would laugh at the thought that she needed a piece of paper to prove who he was. Molly sighed and tucked the file card into the mounting pile. She was not looking forward to a walk across the dunes in the dark. Rain and wind had been hitting the windows for hours.

Wind walloped the windows, and the surf sounded close and angry. Gradually, Molly noticed a series of sounds filtered from the background of rain.

Creaking noises came from the floorboards above, not unusual in weather like this, but these creaks held a regular rhythm. She left her chair and moved quietly toward the office doorway. The front door was locked tight.

Then the sounds returned. A faint tread passed overhead, then paused before fading toward the far wall. A second-floor stairway lay in that direction, probably up to an attic, although she had not bothered exploring that far. Now footsteps were climbing the stairs, or coming down. Molly moved from the office, walking lightly, and stepped into the darkened parlor. She would be safer if she stayed hidden. Whatever it was—man or phantom—it would step from the shadows where she could see it. Molly waited. Footsteps scuffed each step, apparently climbing, yet some trick of sound in the old building made them seem to approach.

She could race for the door, or run to it quietly. That would put her outside in the storm, her parka still hanging in the office. Retrieving it meant crossing in front of the staircase again, risking being seen.

Or she could follow the sounds. Except that the sounds had stopped. Wind landed two broad slams on the western wall. Heavy surf muttered. Inside these walls nothing moved but the quickness of her own breathing.

If the footsteps had been there—and perhaps she had only

imagined them—someone else was in the building. She was responsible if she had let someone get in. If she left now, the intruder could vandalize the exhibits. Precious objects might be stolen.

A chill washed over her, but she shook it off. If the ghosts in this place wanted to take shape and make noises, she wasn't going to buy it. Either way, a human intruder or a disembodied troublemaker, she was going to have to climb those stairs and confront it.

But it was human. It had to be human, she decided, gliding close to the wall to reach the staircase. She took the edges of the treads, placing each step stealthily and gripping the wooden rail to pull her weight up. Overhead, a squeal sounded. She froze. It shrieked again, like the sound of a nail being pulled. A dull thud followed. Whatever, whoever, it was, had gone up to the attic and come down. The door had squealed.

Above her, an immense black cloud floated. It moved with stirrings in the air, swaying now nearer, now further away. The button blanket. The button blanket formed that shadow.

The sounds were fainter now. They grew indistinguishable from the rattle of the rain and the intermittent lashings of wind. Yet they came. She stepped into a room and glanced around. Dots of light looked back. Two by two, unmoving eyes stared from the darkness. Molly felt a fit grip her heart, and stifled a scream. They were the animals, that was all. Sea green light reflected from their glass eyes. Gradually it outlined their shapes. Every hair on those bodies seemed to prickle upward as she watched. A floorboard squeaked. Another. Closer. Then a different sound arrived, a soft clunk, and the sigh of a stair tread. Another clunk. It was moving down the stairs.

Molly gripped the doorjamb and peered outward. Beneath the floating blackness of the button blanket, a shadow skimmed around the turning of the staircase. It moved lower. Molly hugged the wall, leaving the darker room and slipping toward the landing. No shadows moved below its height now.

Nor did any sounds come from the first floor. Yet if something was down there, it had the advantage. It could hide and watch her move into the light.

Molly crept low in a crouch, taking the first step. Her hands gripped the banister. With each step, she peered between the carved posts. Nothing moved below. No footsteps. No whispers. And then a long, sleepy creak sounded and the rattling of the rain grew louder.

A cool breeze arrived, carrying the smell of the ocean. The front door was open. That was the creak. With another sigh, it closed and clicked shut, a sound she had heard every morning and night since she came here.

Whatever came in must have gone out, but her fingers would not loosen their grip on the banister.

Molly settled onto a stair tread and let out a long breath. The cool scent of ocean and rain washed over her, then faded. The intruder was gone.

At last, when the muscles deep in her thighs began to shoot sparks, Molly stood. She moved down the stairs, staying close to the walls until she reached the office. She quickly opened the light panel.

When every switch was thrown for the downstairs, she made herself walk to each doorway and look in. All was silent, unmoving except for the gentle swaying of the button blanket.

That settled it. Molly walked back to the office, her fear congealing into anger. She would not work in this place another day. She would take the books she needed and would come back only to exchange them. If this place was cursed, it had won.

She collected notecards and stuffed them into her bag. Two volumes of Aowl's diaries went on top of them. They would be safe and dry if she carried the bag under her parka. Nevertheless, a pang of guilt caught her. These things should stay in the museum. If something happened to them, if fire destroyed the cottage or someone broke in, these objects could not be replaced.

Fire could easily start at the museum. And as for theft, they might be safer at home. Into her parka's inside pocket, she tucked three pamphlets containing settlers' reports, and coiled two of Aowl's maps around them. That was enough for three days. When she came back, it would be in broad daylight and with a friend if she could find one. Perhaps Pam would be willing to come.

She switched off the first floor lights, but left the office light on as she crossed to the front door. She tested it. The lock was still tight. She slipped the key in and turned, but as her fingers reached for the light switch, a scrape sounded.

The cloakroom. Molly whirled as she remembered it. There was a cloakroom back there.

Its door began to open. It swung wider and a huge shadow filled the gap. Molly pulled in breath to scream. She grabbed for the door handle. A voice spoke.

"Good evening, Miss Snow. Mind if I see what you put your bag?"

Chapter 19

He had her now.

Edward J. Mulling took his time, studying the white look of fear on the woman's pretty face. She stood against the wall. He had her red-handed. Pretty funny, catching a redskin red-handed. When Molly Snow had screamed, her bag slipped from her shoulder, and now it lay on the floor. When he reached it, he paused, wondering if she would pick it up and hand it to him. The woman just leaned against the wall, gasping. He picked it up himself.

Of course he knew what was in it. Sheriff Mulling had watched through the cracked cloakroom door while Molly Snow stuffed papers and books inside. Those books looked old enough to belong to the museum.

Mulling pulled two books from the bag and glanced at the bindings. They held dates, and sure enough, there was Tess Fiddert's handwriting, numbers printed in white ink. The edge of the pages showed a red stamp—Alford James Aowl Memorial Museum. Just as he'd expected.

"You nearly scared me to death," Molly Snow whispered. She was still gasping.

"I check the museum every night."

Mulling examined the books, savoring how well everything had come together. Molly Snow need not know that he'd come by earlier than usual tonight. He riffled the pages and took his time studying the bindings.

He'd considered skipping his usual stop tonight. The weather was raw and he'd spent half the day traipsing over the beach, the other half listening to loonies on the phone. Nevertheless, he'd pulled into the parking lot and come in for his usual check.

The light had been on in the office and there sat Molly Snow, so wrapped up in her work she didn't hear a thing. Mulling had eased the door shut and paused a moment to congratulate himself. He'd strike up that conversation, soften her up a bit by driving her home, and finally give her what she'd been looking for last week.

Then another idea had struck him. He'd stepped back from the light near the entrance and decided to go with it. No sense letting Molly Snow see how carefully he checked all the rooms, upstairs and down. He'd just go about his business, maybe making a little extra noise upstairs to give her the willies. Frightened ladies had a way of being much more friendly when a big, strong man showed up.

The problem was, Molly Snow disappeared. She'd been the office when he crept upstairs, but by the time he got back down only her coat and papers remained. It took a few minutes to figure out. When he did catch on, Mulling thought he would fall over laughing.

She'd heard the noises and gone into hiding somewhere, scared as a bunny in front of headlights. Mulling checked the cloakroom, the likeliest cubbyhole, but it was empty. He opened the front door and closed it loud enough for her to hear. Then he settled into the cloakroom himself. As soon as she crept out, he'd be there to save her.

Except that the show she put on was almost too much. She was damn funny. She came down the steps like some kind of spy, sneaky-creeping on her tiptoes. It had been hard not to jump out and yell "Boo!"

The two books he'd seen go into the bag now lay on the table beside the museum' s front door. Molly Snow, her color coming back, stood staring. Mulling dug deeper into the bag. Piles of white cards lay at the bottom, probably hers. He pulled them out and let the rubber bands slip as he added them to the table.

"Please be careful with those." She was beginning to look annoyed. "They're all organized."

"Those books are museum property," Mulling pointed out levelly. "It looks like they were on their way out the door."

"I do research at home," Molly Snow said. "They're for my work."

"Sure."

Mulling considered his options. If she was telling the truth, he might act generous and forgive her. That would put her in the mood to give him a good time. And he could play nice guy, coming in to save her from spooky noises. She'd be grateful.

"And that stuff you've got inside your coat?" he said, letting a hint of threat ride the words. "I guess that's for working at home, too?"

"Sheriff Mulling, I don't appreciate—" Molly Snow paused and met his eye squarely. "It's really none of your business."

"Anything inside this place stays here. That's why Tess Fiddert gave me a key. Now, I wouldn't want to say you were exactly stealing."

Mulling let the word hang in the air, glad to see the woman open her coat. She removed two large sheets of paper, wrapped around a few other books. Mulling set them beside the others on the table.

"I'm sure Miss Fiddert wouldn't have minded," Molly Snow said snappishly. "Thank you for stopping by, Sheriff. And good night." She picked up her scattered file cards, pulled her parka tight, and opened the door.

"Mighty rough out tonight."

A blast of wind hit. It pushed the girl backward, but Mulling grabbed the door as the wind swung it. He pulled it shut, then fell into step beside her.

"I'll give you a ride," he yelled across sheeting rain. Her mouth moved and she spoke, but the wind carried away the sound. She was headed out of the parking lot. Once Mulling caught up, she repeated the words in a yell.

Mulling caught the word "walk" as Molly Snow plunged ahead toward the dunes.

"I'll keep you company," he yelled back, then added, "It can get dangerous out here." She kept going. Mulling pulled his flashlight from his hip pocket and cast its beam on the sand ahead of them.

Wind coming off the water drove needles of rain he could feel through his leather jacket. Molly Snow ducked her head into her hood. Either a lot of rain was hitting her face or she was crying. He'd get her settled down once they reached her place.

The sheriff took the ocean side, blocking the wind before they crested another dune. Miss Snow seemed to appreciate that. Mulling leaned into his steps, and considered how good it was going to feel to get out of wet clothes, and to help her out of hers. He'd calm her down, talk her out of her scared mood, and show her a good time.

Mulling swung the flashlight in arcs ahead of their steps. Out of habit he scanned the shore for motion. Nothing moved out there except weather. Today had been shot to hell, but at least it got him away from the phone.

The whole week had brought nothing but problems. Hal Nickerson called about wolves. Hal claimed to have seen a whole pack, and that made Mulling glad. It was about time the town got past its jokes. When people saw real wolves, they'd quit the sarcasm about blown-out windshields.

And it had been a real, by-damn pleasure to tell Hal Nickerson that wolves were outside of Mulling's jurisdiction. Mulling had suggested that Nickerson round up a few hunters—if, of course, the conservationists didn't step in and start yelling about endangered species.

Maybe, the sheriff thought, he should deputize the whole town and set them loose looking for dead bodies. Mulling caught himself on a loose slope of sand. He reached over to steady Molly Snow. She moved ahead.

Two more calls had come in about the body, same description both times, but the calls tended to turn up at any hour of the day. The body, of course, did not.

Thanks to the last caller, Mulling was beginning to feel a personal grudge against that now-you-see it, now-you-don't corpse. The call came from Eleanor Carson, a woman with an uncanny knack for getting to the point, but not politely. The thing she had seen, Eleanor explained, most resembled what Mulling himself would look like—overweight, balding, and about his age—after he'd wandered through a tiger cage around feeding time.

The problem, as Mulling saw it, was that all of the other reports had come from people who were not exactly reliable. Eleanor Carson was no looney. Mulling decided to press any future callers for better details. Of course if he could just nail down that body, there could be no future calls.

All of which was why Mulling had spent several hours along the shore today. Besides, as if wolves and dead bodies weren't enough, weird stuff was popping up all over. First, old Wilson Montgomery's antique cap-and-ball rifle, safe on the wall for a good twenty years, decided to go off. The gun let rip a blast that knocked it to the floor, gave the dog diarrhea and the wife a fit of conniptions. Wilson swore he hadn't even cleaned the gun in years. Dust on the barrel backed him up.

Then some drugged-up hiker checked into the county hospital raving about seeing ghost Indians in the woods. He tested positive for the whole medicine chest, but county health hardly bothered reporting that before they sent Mulling to investigate. Even after the kid got coherent, he swore he'd seen a pack of foggy-looking redskins on Wolvine Ridge.

They'd been dressed in animal skins, like in the old days, and were dragging some Woofie girl along with bark ropes. The hiker's footprints were there all right, waffle-stompers, but no other prints, no rope, no girl. Just a wasted afternoon. The kid was out of the county before Mulling got a medical report to back up his drug suspicions.

And Mulling was beginning to mistrust anything that doctors said. Every doctor in the county claimed to have seen at least one case of scarlet fever. Any fool knew that nobody got scarlet fever these days.

To top it all off, the church bell kept up its shenanigans. One more week and Mulling was going to call the preservationists and tell them to knock the place down. It was disturbing the peace.

Mulling looked toward Molly Snow. Her face was ducked under her hood, but it looked like she'd stopped crying. He lifted her elbow to help her over a clump of dune grass and held on while they climbed the next rise. To escape the phone, Mulling had spent the morning in the patrol car, facing up to the fact that a dog pack must have formed. Badly savaged small animals were showing up by the highway. They were too chewed up to be road kills. Mulling resigned himself to tracking whatever it was, went back to the station for his rifle, then cruised the beach.

Bad weather had come in around mid-afternoon. He had turned the patrol car back right away, but rain fell hard and the sand went soft. He drove nervously for the best part of an hour, fearing the moment his back tires began to dig in.

And the wind had been blowing ever since. Now, walking beside Molly Snow, Mulling pulled his wet hat down against a swat of wind and surveyed the distance. The square shadow ahead had to be her cabin. Maybe she'd make him some hot chocolate.

Mulling reached to encircle her back, going for a light hugging walk as they came down off a dune. Molly Snow lost her footing, overbalancing them both and shaking his arm off. Mulling went for the elbow again, but held on tighter.

At last they rounded the side of the cabin. At the sudden turning of the corner, the building cut the wind and dropped them into near silence. Mulling followed the back of Molly Snow's parka up the steps. She dug for a key.

In the glow from the flashlight, her face was soaked. Straggles of black hair hung over her cheeks. It was going to feel good to grab hold of that hair, Mulling thought, and feel even better to pull her close.

"Thank you, Sheriff," she said. "You really didn't have walk me home. I was okay." Her hand ran along the doorframe, feeling in the darkness for the lock.

"Pretty lady shouldn't be all by herself out there," Mulling said softly. He closed his hand over hers, helping her fit the key into the lock.

"Yes. Thank you. I'm fine now." Her shoulders were pushing back at him. "Thank you again."

"Better go inside and get warmed up. We'll be lots more comfortable." He felt the lock turn, but the door did not open.

"I'll start up your fire," Mulling emphasized. With that, she finally caught on.

Molly turned, both hands pushing his chest. When he pushed

back he could feel her breasts slide against him under the wet parka.

"The fire in the fireplace first, of course," Mulling added. "Then maybe you'll make me some hot chocolate."

It was not a question. Molly turned away and her voice sounded hard. "I don't have any hot chocolate. You'll have to go. Sorry. And thank you again."

Mulling could hardly believe it. The little Woofie bitch, he thought. She figured it was funny to drag him all the way back here in the rain and then start acting cute.

He braced his arm against the doorframe to keep her still, and to steady his own anger. Who did she think she was, anyway? He'd gone easy on her about taking that museum stuff. He'd gone to no end of trouble over her lost dog. A man tried to do a job, got set up, and the next thing he got was the old heave-ho. See you around, and thanks, pal.

Molly Snow had better understand that the time came when flirting was over and she had to deliver the goods. Her arm, when his hand clamped around it, felt small and easy to twist.

"I bet you feel more grateful than just saying thanks," he grunted and pulled her close. He might have to take crap from tax-paying white folks, but he was damned if he'd swallow it from a Woofie. "Let's go inside and find out."

Then the bitch started fighting. Her head came up and caught him under the jaw, clacking his teeth hard. Her skinny arm was as weak as a pipe cleaner in his grip. Red rage burned at the back of his throat. She would find out how easy he was to dump. He had her hard against the door, grabbing both arms to pin her wrists. Her shove to push him backward was like a joke. She screamed, and pain shot along the side of his head. She had bit him. Bitch. Right in the ear.

Then she was on top of him, or something was. It came down on his back. Not her. She squirmed between him and the door. She couldn't be on both sides.

Weight fell on his shoulders and now he remembered the noise. There had been a sizzle in the brush, like steps leaping over slick weeds. A growl leapt with it. He was falling sideways and it was on top of him. Something alive and clawing, and it wasn't her.

Mulling hit the ground flat on his back, but got his arms over his face. Only his leather jacket saved him. The snarling wetness pushed lower, tearing at his collar, tearing at his skin. Mulling pushed his arms down. The animal, whatever it was, wanted his neck. He rolled sideways, out from under the weight, but fur and claws scrabbled after him to pin him again.

The weight was heavy, wet from the mouth and wet fur; heavy and snarling. It smelled foul, smelled of wet and hate. His hands found sand, fur, bone, and hit that gnashing mouth. He took a rip on the wrist and yanked upward to smash something rough, something hard. Tree bark. The weight seemed to explode, convulsing in guttural snarls writhing upward with him as he got another arm around a tree trunk.

Then he was on his feet. Underbrush slurred as the creature rolled to its feet. Something was screaming. Molly Snow, damn bitch. Mulling slid sideways. When the shadow sprang again it snapped at his shoulder. The clashing of teeth sounded like death, and Mulling struggled to work the slide of his pistol.

Teeth snapped beside his ear. Thudding weight hit again. This time Mulling caught himself and came up fast, came up shooting and running. Molly Snow could keep on screaming, tell the animal right where she was, but he was getting the hell out.

Mulling dodged between trees. With every few steps he caught a pocket of sand and fell, pushing up again, expecting the slick, whizzing sound to find his back.

It ran with him. He fired at the sound, and the boom of the heavy pistol was lost in the wet forest. A few yards back, the animal ran with a hiss that slithered over wet leaves, with huffing breaths and a low growl each time Mulling fell. He struggled to his feet again and again, tensed for the weight that would come down on him if he did not keep running. He pushed himself through the trees, edging sideways toward the museum. Molly Snow's screams were gone by the time he could make out the patrol car. It gleamed beautifully below the museum's entrance light.

Mulling fell onto pavement and clawed across it on all fours. He reached the car and pulled himself up, but his legs went to jelly. He slid sideways, grabbing for the door handle. He fell to his knees and let the wind push him all the way down.

He could roll under the car, he thought, but first he listened. Rain pinged in puddles. Wind whined along the ground. Mulling turned and looked.

An unbroken border of trees swayed in the wind. There was nothing back there.

He should reload the pistol. In a minute he could pull himself up and do it. He could open the door from the ground, but it was already too late. There would be nothing back there to kill.

Chapter 20

MOLLY REALIZED SHE WAS NO LONGER SCREAMING. SHE LEANED against the cabin's firm wall. Rain flowed from the roof and dropped a veil a few inches from her face. It trickled from leaves to the ground. Surf muttered, but those other sounds—the sounds of the sheriff shrieking, the snarling, grunting, clawing explosion of madness, and the heavy explosion of a pistol—those were gone.

She dug under her parka for cloth dry enough to wipe her tears. She found her shirttail and swabbed her face.

Something had attacked Sheriff Mulling. Molly tried to remember exactly how it happened, but everything had gone crazy at once. Sheriff Mulling was pushing her against the door. She remembered his weight, remembered knowing she would not be strong enough to fight him off. Her only chance had been to get around him, to get away. Once he got her inside, there would be no point in fighting. Then suddenly, beyond his shoulder, a deeper blackness swelled. A shadow rose from the ground.

Molly tucked her shirttail back under her parka and wiped her face with her hands. The tears were hot and the drops of rain felt cold. She reached for the doorknob, but her hand stopped.

Mulling might come back.

If the sheriff came back, he could get through the cabin door easily. If she headed for the highway, he might find her. She could watch for him. She could listen. She could hide.

A woodpile stood in a dry corner of the porch. Molly felt her way along the wall until her hip found it. She was wet and cold, but crouching down and pulling her hands up into the parka's sleeves helped. She tried to imagine what his footsteps would sound like.

Rain made a steady music without rhythm. To seaward a low thrum spoke of approaching storm. Rain ticked on the leaves and whispered down the tree trunks. Wind shivered the branches, spattering drops intermittently. Out on the cabin road, one puddle plonked even measures, and there was a higher sound too, a plink-plink-plinking as water hit something metal.

The car, Molly remembered suddenly. The car was out there and she could get inside. If he came back, she'd start it up and get away.

Taking a deep breath, she threaded across the yard in a crouching run. The door handle was slick, but she pulled at it and felt it open. She fell inside, easing the door shut. Before she sat up, she dug in her pocket for the key. She pushed down the door lock and eased the driver's window open a crack. She listened.

The big puddle ticked evenly. Rain sluiced from the side the roof with a washing sound. The memory of those screams came back, unsettling in the quiet air.

Sheriff Mulling was a crude, cruel, manipulative bastard. He might have been making those noises upstairs in the museum. He knew she wasn't stealing, but he'd made her feel like a thief. He wanted to make her feel ashamed. Then he thought she was going to sleep with him. Or acted like he thought it. He'd been pushing too hard, as if it could turn into rape any second. Maybe he was already thinking rape. Of course he was. She wasn't going to talk herself out of knowing what he'd tried.

But she had no evidence. If she went to the police, any cop would—but dammit, Mulling was the police. The next step up might be the county, and she had no proof. Mulling would say she was stealing. Mulling would twist the whole thing around. Damn him and his key to the museum.

Something was moving out there—a swish of leaves, a rustle focused in one area. Molly slipped lower in the seat. The sounds of the rain were there, and wind sighed high the trees. On lower branches leaves moved with a wet, sliding sound. That sound could be anything. Animals lived back in here, but they would be in their nests, safe and dry for the night. Molly pushed up to see over the sill. A shadow moved. It formed the shape of a man, but too tall for Mulling, and it moved differently. Two clear, steady footsteps climbed the porch steps. An arm lifted and sharp knocks rang on wood. "Miss Snow?"

Not Mulling's voice, but a familiar one. It sounded calm and sure. Molly searched her memory.

Knuckles rapped again. "Excuse me, Miss Snow?"

It was that stranger from the beach, it was Al. A cry of relief escaped before Molly could stifle it. The shadow spun and peered toward the car.

"Miss Snow, are you out there?"

Molly grabbed the cold handle of the window and rolled it up. Her other hand was turning the key, and the engine came up just as she reached for the headlights' knob. Two beams cut through black, and the porch leapt into brightness.

Al, thank God. Al stood at the edge of the porch, wet and bedraggled in a faded denim jacket. He threw one arm up to shield his eyes.

"Miss Snow?"

Molly punched the headlights off, cut the engine, and opened the door. "I'm sorry," she called out, and stepped toward him. "Yes, it's me. I just—I didn't know who you were."

"I stopped by to check—" The man paused and pushed wet hair from his forehead. "One of my dogs ran off and I thought maybe you saw him."

Molly crossed the yard and stepped onto the porch. The key still hung in the lock. Once she had turned the knob and flicked on the porch light, she turned to get a good look at Al.

He was even more handsome than she remembered him. And he was also even wetter than she was. Two soaked epaulets draped the shoulders of his jacket. Long strands of silver-gray hair trailed raindrops down his jaw. Despite all that, he was the most beautiful sight she could imagine. Al studied her face, his eyes sweet and concerned. Standing beside him she felt safe.

"Sorry, no. I didn't see any dog." Molly wondered how explain sitting in her car in the dark. She decided to ignore it. "I just got home. I didn't pass any animals." Then she remembered. Al's dog probably leapt on Mulling's back. Al's lost dog must have saved her.

"Wait, there was a dog. But it wasn't, it came—" There would be no easy way to explain this.

"Let's get you inside. You can tell me later." Al's voice was calm, but his look betrayed tension. "There's a storm coming, and it will be worse than anything seen around here in over seventy years."

She would have to tell him the whole story, Molly realized; someone would have to be told. With that knowledge, a clot filled her throat. Tears hit like a dam bursting.

Chapter 21

RESIDENTS OF SURFBREAK KNEW THEY WERE LIVING THROUGH a night that would become legend. Winter storms rolled from the sea, and even greater storms crashed from the hills. As thunder followed lightning, the skies looked framed in the harsh light of artillery. The sea storm blew down acres of hundred-year-old cedar. Salt water invaded the Wolvine River, and was met by torrents of fresh water rushing from the hills. As people huddled in their cabins, floodwaters began to spread toward the Wolvine reservation. The Wolvine feared the flood, but they were even more afraid of the power that walked across those hills with steps of thunder.

While the Wolvine people muttered fearfully, saying that Storm Man had returned, the residents of Surfbreak had neither fact nor religion to explain what was happening. If they thought about it, as some of them later did think, it seemed the bombardment of lightning was directed only at their town.

Lightning took out the tower of the old missionary church, stopping the bells forever. Lightning danced as the wooden roof burned. Sea wind blew flames sideways like a mighty candle that tried to ignite the wet forest. Rain extinguished the dying fire, but not before supporting beams crashed and the bells tumbled from the tower with dead clanks.

And lightning hit one turret of the Aowl Museum. Volunteer firemen fought smoke and wind, thinking that they would surely lose the museum. Flames rose around the turret, and then rain squalls hit and helped bring the flames under control. It seemed that Sheriff Mulling was everywhere, and that he must have taken desperate chances. His leather jacket was torn, his face scratched with marks like claws. Mulling helped the firefighters, and he saved the exhibits. It was his idea to chop holes in the side of the burned turret, lay canvas on the floor, and funnel the incoming rain harmlessly down the outside of the building. People told each other that they were seeing the good side of Sheriff Mulling, and not the idiot side that shot windshields out of patrol cars.

And, as the citizens of Surfbreak agreed, everyone behaved very well considering the circumstances. All electricity was out, except for a few portable generators. Wind continued to rise as the tide also rose, and surf broke higher and higher. Salt water ran along Breakers Avenue, so people turned out to help store owners move merchandise to second stories.

The Woofie reservation was another matter, of course. Everyone figured that the Woofies were goners. Either that, or they had taken off for the hills. No one in Surfbreak saw Raymond Goodwillow leave his cabin to stand near the head of the river. Nor did they see the water begin to divide, or how the windblown tide split from the river to spend its force among the dunes. No one saw the flood hesitate, then retreat from reservation boundaries. The people of Surfbreak were too busy to worry about Woofies, and none of them worried two snips about the newcomer, Molly Snow, either.

Molly had not been held by anyone for a long, long time, and she had never been held by arms this strong and gentle. It seemed she would never stop sobbing. At first she clung to Al, so relieved she had no time to feel awkward. Her nose ran, her eyes ran, her hair was a wet sponge, and she couldn't speak because of the sobbing. He held her and waited.

The room finally came into focus. After the icy wind the room felt warm, and Al had reached over to turn on the floor lamp. With him here, and the door closed, her fears gradually began to slip away. Then she realized that she was in the arms of a stranger. She remembered Al's courtesy, and his earlier words, "People do things for each other. That's how we all get by." Her city instincts relaxed. Both of them were wetter than drowned cats, she realized, and managed to choke back a final sob. She moved a step backward. When his arms let go she felt lonesome.

"I'll tell you about it in a minute," she said. "Sheriff Mulling attacked me, but it's more than that. Right now we have to get dry or we'll catch our death." She motioned toward the woodstove, and he turned to gather kindling from the woodbox. His wet hair made a silver cape around his shoulders, and his denim jacket and shirt were nearly black with rain. She hurried to the bathroom for towels.

"Dry off," she said when she returned. "I'll be right back." In the bedroom, she dried herself and changed into dry shirt and jeans. When she came back, Al stood beside the stove, his sleeves rolled back as he toweled his arms.

"Take the shirt off. You can dry it by the stove."

Al looked startled at the suggestion. His cheeks were pale with cold but he actually seemed about to blush.

"It's all right," he said softly. "I've dried out standing clothed on many a night."

He was shy. Either that, or there was something old-fashioned about his thinking. Molly went to the bedroom for a blanket. "Hang this around you," she said, "and get the shirt dry. I'll make coffee."

She tried not to watch from the comer of her eye, but it was a small cabin. He stripped away his soaked shirt, then his boots and socks. The man had the broad chest of a runner, with a chevron of fine golden hairs spread across it. Once he wrapped the blanket around him Indian-fashion, he showed no embarrassment about taking off his jeans. He seemed as comfortable in the blanket as he did in clothing.

Outside, the storm raged. Thunder boomed from the hills, and wind swept over the dunes. Wind circled the cabin, tore at cedar shakes on the roof, and caused drafts so large that the stove drew and turned orange with heat. Al adjusted the draft, then sat calmly, waiting.

"It will hold," he said quietly, glancing at the cabin's walls. "This place was built simple but true." Molly handed him coffee and he sipped it with more pleasure, she knew, than it deserved.

"The sheriff attacked you?" His voice was low. The dim light left shadows on his face, but his eyes looked furious. His muscular forearms tensed, and she was glad that Sheriff Mulling was nowhere in sight. "There are ways of dealing with problems like that." Al took another sip of coffee.

"I wouldn't want him dealt with." Molly found herself nearly whispering. She spoke more firmly. "I just wish he'd stay away. I wish someone in this town would be friendly . . ." She realized that she was on the verge of spilling her troubles.

And then her sorrows began to come out. She told Al of it—the loneliness, the frustration of trying to do a good job when everybody, including the sheriff, seemed against you. She confessed that she could not stand the darkness of the museum, the whisperings, the sense that evil lurked in every balcony and turret.

"An evil man built it," Al said, "and the place is cursed. It won't hurt you, though. Anything trapped in that building is just that—it's trapped. There are shadows in there, but those shadows are helpless." It was a long speech for him, and he fell silent. Molly remembered Goodwillow's words. Goodwillow had also said something about the museum's shadows knowing her as someone else.

Al sat listening to the storm, then continued. "The Wolvine believe that the shadows of dead things go there. There are the shadows of trees and animals and men. But remember, they are not the spirits of trees and animals and men. Only the shadows."

"Do you believe that?" she asked, surprised.

"Do you know Raymond Goodwillow?"

"I've met him once."

"If Ray Goodwillow says the shadows go there, then you can bet they do." He glanced toward the stove, where steam rose from the drying clothing. "Nothing lasts forever. Someday that place will come down. The shadows will be freed. They will cause no harm, but they'll be happy to be free."

Listening to Al was a lot like listening to Raymond Goodwillow. Al said things that he knew to be true, but did not explain why he knew. If some other man talked that way, she would think he was only opinionated, but like Goodwillow, Al spoke with such authority that she hardly thought to question what he said.

"You can work there," Al told her. "I'll post one of my dogs outside. If the sheriff comes anywhere near you, the only thing he'll find is teeth."

"One already did run him off," she said. "Something attacked him. It could only have been one of your dogs."

Al seemed unsurprised. He reached to feel the cloth of his shirt and jeans. His boots sat away from the fire, glistening but not discolored by the rain. Molly supposed they must be well worked with mink oil or animal fat.

He saw her looking. "You never roast a pair of boots. It just ruins them."

Al glanced around the room. Obviously he wanted to talk about something besides boots and dogs, but he probably didn't know how to go about it. More of his old-fashioned shyness, Molly guessed.

She considered her feelings. She had never met a man like Al. She knew how to deal with college men. She knew the little games everyone played, knew most college men's lines before they were delivered. She knew how to fend off a pass, or let the man know that she was interested. Now nothing she knew felt like the least help with Al.

She didn't even know why she was attracted to him. True, he was more mature and far more manly than those well-scrubbed college men, and this was somehow comforting. But, she decided, the most comforting thing of all was his courtesy. If asked, she would have said that he was a gentleman in the best sense of the word. She had met a lot of highly intelligent men, and quite a few whiz kids, but she could not remember ever having met a true gentleman.

He sat silent and shy. One of them had to speak.

"I've been meaning to walk in the forest," she said at last. "Sometimes it helps to get the feel of where and how people lived. I got some of that feeling visiting Mr. Goodwillow."

"Not by yourself." He looked immediately alarmed. "The forest only looks safe from the road. If you get even a quarter-mile away from the road, the forest turns dangerous. Unless you are experienced."

Outside the wind pounded as unremitting as surf. A distant

crack sounded, as if a tree had snapped like a toothpick. "If a storm came up," he said, "you would not stand much of a chance." Wind rattled the door in its frame. "I expect a storm would come up." He thought a moment, but did not explain. At last he spoke almost shyly. "I would come if you wanted. I know the forest like townfolk know their main street."

It was what she hoped to hear. She did not know whether her attraction to Al could lead to something deeper, but at least he would be a friend in an otherwise grim place.

"I should go," he said suddenly. "You'll have no trouble from anyone in town. Count on it." He stood a moment and listened to the wind. "Goodwillow," he said, as if to himself.

"You can't go back out into that storm," Molly said. "I'll make up a bed on the couch. I absolutely insist. Besides, we have to decide when it will be best to go into the forest."

He was going to accept, she saw, but shyly.

"Goodwillow," he said again. "That old man is making a powerful fight."

Raymond Goodwillow sat in his chair. He had returned indoors once the immediate danger was pushed back. Storm Man still threw wave after wave of wind, but Goodwillow cut the wind and threw it aside. Storm Man thundered in the hills, and Raymond Goodwillow knew that only the appearance of Storm Man's old enemy would bring such fury. Man-Among-Wolves walked or ran somewhere tonight.

Goodwillow met Storm Man's fury with a spirit of power and calm. Not even Storm Man could control the tides. All Goodwillow had to do was divide the storm until the tide began to run. It would be a terrible night's work, even for one who was young and able; and Goodwillow was no longer young.

Sleeping nearby, Pam muttered words from the old language. Her words gave him strength, even if he was not sure that she knew their meaning. Raymond Goodwillow sat before his fire and fought his old mentor.

He plumbed his memories for visions of eagle and raven, imagining how they turned and banked in the sky. He sent water to rush off in the directions they took. He listened as memory brought back the growls of bear and wounded cougar. He let the roar of water and wind merge with those growls, then he quieted them. His body had grown terribly cold with the effort sapped from each cell, but he ignored that. He was not sad, and he was not glad. He only knew that he must fight.

Chapter 22

GRAY DAWN BROKE OVER A RESTLESS SEA, AND HIGH SURF TOSSED logs as easily as kindling. Residents of Surfbreak woke to a town where sewers backed up to spread foul-smelling water along Breakers Avenue. Electricity was out, and households with only furnaces awoke cold. Wood smoke rose in small plumes as people opened long-closed fireplaces. The Aowl Museum stood black against the gray sky, and gray-black stains from smoke were like a curse laid on top of a curse.

The residents of Surfbreak met at Logger's Bar. They could not get a hot breakfast, but the bar owned a small emergency generator. The bar owner made coffee. He didn't figure to make much money, but announced that it was worth the trouble to see so many good church-going people hanging out in his joint.

Sheriff Mulling behaved modestly. The fire at the museum had restored his reputation, and he wore his torn leather jacket as demonstration that he had, pretty much single-handedly, saved the museum. He collected a free cup of coffee and a round of thanks, then headed back to the station.

By nine AM, he had received three reports of a body on the beach and two reports of a wolf pack. A local trucker walked in and asked for a Breathalyzer to prove he was sober, and then reported a pack of Indian ghosts in the forest just outside of town. The trucker then headed for Logger's.

By ten, Mulling contacted Tess Fiddert by long distance. Since

Fiddert had heard no stories of Mulling's bravery, she was unimpressed. When he mentioned fire at the museum, though, she began shooting off questions.

Mulling stood holding the phone back from his ear, and thinking. He took his time answering. Hysteria over a lot of hundred-year-old hand-me-downs was not Tess's style. There was nothing in that museum she should panic over. Only one thing would make Tess this nervous, he concluded—money. She must have a stash in the museum. Mulling grinned, grunted, and explained that the damage was minor.

"I'm flying back tonight," Tess said. "If there are going to be workmen doing repairs, then I have to protect the exhibits. I'll put all of the valuable papers in the bank's vault. You arrange for space in the vault."

Mulling agreed, and tried to keep from laughing. Ordinarily, Tess would have blown her top at being interrupted on vacation, which meant she must have quite a bit stashed somewhere in that museum. He didn't mind if she thought that she was running the show. "Valuable papers," Mulling muttered, as if he was taking notes. "Arrange for space in the bank's vault."

"It's that damned college kid," Tess said, trying to recover her composure. "She left a cigarette burning."

"It was lightning," Mulling said, then reconsidered. If Tess wanted to spread a rumor, it was okay by him. If Tess saw to it that Molly Snow caught blame for the fire, then nothing Molly Snow said would be believed. "Maybe she did," he admitted. "But, folks think it was lightning." He left it at that, confident that Tess would return to town and fill in the blanks.

No sooner was he off the phone than the door slapped open to reveal Surfbreak's mayor, Hal Bozman. Bozman advanced across the office, stabbing a finger at the air. The preservationists were already after the mayor to do something about the missionary church—throw a temporary roof over the stone tower, or something. The preservationists were howling about damage to the Aowl Museum. The damned electricity wouldn't go on, and the sewers were still backed up. Three doctors claimed that unless the streets were flushed, there would be epidemics of everything from cholera to hepatitis. Trees were down all over, and two had crashed through houses. Members of the volunteer fire department were attending to their own problems, the mayor said, and Mulling had damned well better get all this straightened out instead of sitting on his fanny behind a desk.

To which Mulling replied that he had his own problems, and the mayor could take a whiz up a flagpole. Mulling didn't know yet how many problems he had.

By eleven AM the wolf pack was reported in the forest three miles north of town. A group of men left the bar and headed out with rifles. Mulling didn't need a bunch of drunks shooting at anything that moved, but he was too busy to head them off. When the electricity came back on, storm damage caused a short circuit and a minor fire at the school. By noon, word came back from the forest. One hunter had shot and wounded another. A third hunter lay dead, his throat ripped wide open from an attack. By a wolf.

On that gray morning Molly Snow came fully awake realizing that she was alone. Before opening the bedroom door, she listened for sounds from the front room. Al was already gone, leaving a faint scent of the forest behind him on the blankets and sheets carefully folded on the couch. The woodstove already warmed the roof, and a kettle of hot water steamed.

Solitude felt less depressing today. It was a good morning for work. She would take the time to cross reference information from Aowl's diary that contradicted historical accounts. Al would come by after twelve, he'd said, and they'd go to the forest.

From the distance surf pounded, and the ocean sent a continuing roar across the rumpled dunes. Through the window she could see large branches that had been ripped from trees. In spite of the temptation to take a walk along the tide line, she got caught up in her work. Insights and solutions arrived with quick clarity, her thoughts more confident than in a long, long time. Of course, she recalled, she had not felt truly safe for a long, long time. Thoughts of Al tugged, bringing the memory of his strong arms around her. She had better get busy, she told herself, or she could lose several hours to daydreaming.

By eleven o'clock, her notes finished, she shrugged into her jacket and stepped outside. As she walked through the dunes she thought about Raymond Goodwillow. Al had said that Goodwillow was making a powerful fight, but had not explained. Now Molly sensed, without understanding, that her research wasn't quite practical. Goodwillow and Al talked of mysterious forces, as if they were living close to them. If they were right, she mused, it meant that she too lived near such powers.

Goodwillow was an old, old man. She did not see how he could be powerful, yet she sensed that he was. Al was that old, and yet he too seemed to have knowledge that did not fit with anything she knew. Molly stood in a dead calm after the storm and felt shock. She had come to research history, but in a way she couldn't explain, what she was learning was not history. Forces that felt older than time were happening right now. They whispered in the museum's walls, in Goodwillow's words, in the wind and the ocean.

Cresting the dunes, Molly looked up and down the beach. About two miles to the south, several people walked along the tide line, beachcombing. To the north, perhaps a mile away, a slight figure—a man or woman, perhaps a child—stood at the top of a dune. The rest of the beach lay deserted.

She had expected the storm's aftermath to be exciting, maybe even a little romantic, but had not expected to feel fear. Walking among the storm-smashed wreckage, she stifled a shudder. Flotsam lay all around, the most frightening among it the broken stem board from a workboat. Face up just beyond the reach of waves, the stem board was painted green, the paint new and smooth. White lettering announced, SEA SPRAY, HOODSPORT, OREGON.

She wanted to believe that it had been a boat adrift, unpiloted and torn apart by waves. Good sense told her that could not be true. No boat would have drifted from moorage in Oregon to first find the sea, then find this beach so far north. The storm at sea must have swept across shipping like a curse. The curse had been too strong for this small workboat. This boat recently contained living men, and they had died when this boat died.

Molly stood frozen, gazing at gray, crashing waves. She wanted to run. Soon, soon, her imagination insisted, a wave would lift a fisherman's corpse from the sea and fling it toward her. She backed away from the wreckage. It would have to be reported. Then she thought of Sheriff Mulling, and her mind balked.

This walk was not the adventure she'd counted on. From the south, the beachcombers slowly made their way toward her, still nearly two miles away. Northward, the slim figure still stood on the crest of a dune. Now less than a mile away, that silhouette seemed somehow familiar. Molly began to walk slowly in that direction. She thought of waves overwhelming the workboat, and of men thrown into the cold sea. There was nothing that could be done for the men who had once sailed the Sea Spray out of Hoodsport.

Death littered the beach. Flocks of gulls squawked and rose, then dove, then rose above dead fish and dead birds. Tree branches lay crisscrossed in huge tangles. Fir, spruce, and pine still carried some fresh needles, but the needles themselves were scraped and broken. Far ahead a bulky shape that looked like the body of a seal or sea lion huddled just beyond the reach of the surf. Gray light gave only the suggestion of colors, an echo of red, a touch of tan . . .

Terror froze her in place. She had feared that the waves would deliver a dead man. The bulky shape ahead lay unmoving. Whatever it was, it could not possibly be alive. She began heading east toward the dunes, skirting the shore near the body. The beachcombers, coming steadily from the south, would discover it. To the north, the slim shape still stood on the foremost dune.

She got halfway to the dunes before she stopped. There was not one chance in a thousand that the body on the beach was alive, but one chance was enough to turn her toward the surf again. If that tangle of flesh and flotsam actually was human, and if that human still breathed, she would never get over the guilt of not trying to help.

She approached as quickly as possible, fighting the drag of soft sand above the tide line. The mound resolved into a shape—arms, legs, a face. It was human, or had been. A man.

He lay on his back, torn face staring at sky through blinded eyes. Flesh fell away as if scraped by teeth or claws, and seawater had washed the corpse so that cheekbones lay exposed, white and unblooded. Pale flesh of the face lay drained of blood, but heavy bruises on the hands and arms showed that the man had made a strong fight. The bruises looked like black badges pinned on flesh now bloodless as wood. The man had been dead for hours. His clothing barely covered him. Even his boots were cut as if by razor teeth. She numbly backed away, wondering if this was what a man looked like after being attacked by sharks.

Even as she realized she was screaming, she had begun to run. She stumbled, fell, climbed back to her feet, and ran toward the dunes. The vision of the corpse followed, the features of that face imprinted like those on a familiar photograph. Her mind studied it, making a cold appraisal. When she fell a second time she stayed down to catch her breath, and then finally admitted what she already knew.

That corpse had the face of Sheriff Mulling. The black leather jacket was shredded to ribbons. Even the empty pistol holster had been torn and ripped like thin cotton. The man who had assaulted her, attempted to rape her, lay lifeless on the beach. The savagery of the dog that attacked him last night was so great that, even now, Molly could remember its slashing teeth, its terrible growl. Yet, no dog could possibly do that.

When she got herself under control she rose and walked slowly toward the slim figure standing on the seaward dune. She looked over her shoulder only once. A clot of torn tree branches blocked the mound of the body. From the forest, and close enough to be alarming, came the cracking sounds of gunshots. The sound of surf quickly swallowed them.

As Molly reached the lowest dunes, the standing figure grew recognizable. Pam stood looking seaward. Yet her stance seemed somehow different this morning. She did not appear to notice Molly's approach. With the beach as flat as a table, it was impossible that Pam did not see her. Molly stepped slowly and quietly, unsure whether to call out. If Pam did not see her, or chose to ignore her, then there had to be a reason. Terrible things were happening, unexplainable things. The reason might not make sense in the modern world, but it must make sense in some world that Pam and Goodwillow and Al knew about.

She climbed the dune, suddenly aware of a flash of color in the pinewoods behind Pam's silhouette. People were moving around up there. Maybe the body had already been reported. Maybe help was on its way. Pam still stared to seaward, but she did not seem to concentrate on anything. Her gaze looked endlessly outward, accepting the sea, the sky, the long expanse of beach. If Molly could put a word to the look, she would have described Pam as spiritual. She approached and stood beside Pam, but made herself wait for the girl to speak.

More sharp cracks, definitely gunshots, sounded from the pinewoods. The movement was no more than fifty yards off. Men yelled and whooped as if they were joking, perhaps drunk. A slurred cry—"Woofies"—hung momentarily in the air. Startled, Pam lowered her gaze from the sea and looked at the sand beneath her feet. She seemed to collect herself.

"Slide down on the north side of the dune." Pam spoke quietly. "Don't ask why. Do it now." The words carried authority that Molly hardly expected. Always before, Pam had sounded like a young girl, and a slightly confused one at that. "Move," Pam whispered. She slowly turned as if still not entirely in command of her movements.

Molly shifted sideways just as a blast of rifleshot cracked. Twenty yards to seaward a splatter of sand erupted. The next shot shattered a driftwood branch. A third blast came, a whack-crack echo of itself as more sand flew. Molly slid behind the dune just before Pam leaped down beside her.

"They do that sometimes," Pam said remotely, her mind still elsewhere. "They never shoot to hit, just shoot to scare. When they're drinking, though, anything can happen."

"They're deliberately shooting at us?"

"They're having fun. They're scaring Woofies." Pam's voice, empty of anger or fear, sounded as dispassionate as the surf.

Molly lay with her face pressed into the sand and realized that on this chilly day she was suddenly sweating. An adrenalin rush wanted her to run. But running would be stupid. Exposed, she would offer a target. Her eyes seemed to see more clearly, and her ears picked up every rustle of sound from breeze and sea and human movement. *Men in combat must feel this way*, she realized.

From the tree line came a sudden flurry of yells and shots. A man screamed as more shots sounded. Pam reached to take her hand. "Lie still. We don't want to be blamed for this."

Now snarls came from the tree line, and a second scream rose like a gull hovering in the wind, only to be choked off in midpoint. More shots came. A voice screamed, "God damn you, I'm hit."

Voices hollered in confusion.

"Shoot, shoot. That big sumbitch is getting away."

"My God, he's dying. Stop the blood."

Another voice, not screaming, but tense. "Artery in the throat. Ain't no way to stop it. Get the hell out. That thing might come back."

Sounds told of men in rapid retreat. One moaned and moved with a scuffle of heavy weight, as if being dragged. Molly got to her knees and looked at Pam. The young woman appeared neither kind nor happy. She did not look like she even liked Molly.

"You must come and see my grandfather," Pam said, "but not today. He is very weak, but I am stronger. You come tomorrow."

"He's ill?" It made no sense for Pam to speak so formally.

"He is very old, and now he is tired. You are not to blame, but if you were not here these things would not be so. Man-Among-Wolves would not run through the forest. The white people would not die. The Wolvine would not hide from the anger of Storm Man."

Molly felt defensive. "I don't understand. Why are you angry?" First the townspeople had been against her, and now it seemed that Pam was against her. Only Al remained a friend.

"I am not angry," Pam said, "and I would like to be your friend. Someday. Maybe pretty soon. You come see my grandfather tomorrow."

Molly stood cautiously and brushed sand from her jeans. "I don't mean to hurt anybody. I don't understand. All I did was go for a walk on the beach . . ." Then she remembered. "There's a dead man on the beach. It's Sheriff Mulling."

"There is no dead man on the beach." Pam turned to walk away, then paused. "Maybe someday The Great Changer will make a dead man on the beach. Maybe you saw what might happen, and maybe it will not happen. You come see my grandfather tomorrow." She walked quickly away.

Molly stood on the dune and looked up and down the beach. The shore lay flat and open. Even the beachcombers had disappeared. The view from the high dune was perfect, but the shore lay empty of any corpse.

Chapter 23

THE FOREST IN MIDAFTERNOON SEEMED STRIPPED OF LIFE. No birds called, and the rumble of surf diminished as Molly followed Al along a game trail. Not four miles from town, they entered a dense maze of green.

Within a hundred paces, all hint of civilization passed. Molly could not hear sounds from the road, and she saw no sign to suggest that human beings had ever walked among these immense, moss-furred tree trunks. Al whispered that this game trail was used mostly by deer.

Her thick wool sweater beneath a down jacket made her feel dressed for Alaska, not the western Washington forests. Beneath the canopy of trees she expected to feel protected and too warmly dressed. Now a chill rolled from the hills and spread among the trees. She was glad Al had insisted on the extra layers. Ferns, each larger than a broad dinner table, spread fronds covered by frost.

They had walked no more than a quarter mile, but she was totally lost. Alone, she might wander until she dropped, dead of hunger or exposure within a hundred yards of a house or a road. She would never know that the house or road was there.

"This is all second-growth timber," Al said quietly over his shoulder. "It can be difficult to imagine how it looked back when there were big trees. We have to walk for another fifteen or twenty minutes, but it's worth it."

These trees seemed quite big enough. They towered into gray

sky, their trunks so broad that three people with outstretched arms might possibly encircle them.

"Logged off a hundred years ago," Al said. "At the time, these trees were too small for the sawmills of those days. As trees go, these are youngsters, maybe a hundred and forty years. I'm taking you to see a real graybeard." He moved steadily along the trail, his long hair tucked beneath the collar of his jacket like a scarf.

From time to time she sensed movement in the forest, as if they were accompanied by fleeting shadows. Al's dogs must be roving, she guessed, then remembered that dogs would bark and romp. These presences seemed to form a vanguard.

She assumed they were near their destination when Al stopped and held up his hand for silence. The hushed forest grew darker, as if the sky had suddenly closed down under an overreaching shadow. The shadow moved across the tops of brush and between the tree trunks. The forest seemed to be falling into night.

"Cougar," Al whispered. "Down from the hills." He stood easily and his eyes searched the forest. "I figured you'd show up," he said with quiet calm. He seemed to be talking to the forest itself, or to something in the forest. "If you're looking for another go-around, you've come to the right place." The calmness in his voice made Molly shiver inside her warm jacket.

"Indian business," Al said at last. "There was once a medicine man named Storm Man. His tamahnous animal was cougar. Goodwillow might say that when you talk to the animal, you also talk to the spirit of the man."

He moved quietly along the game trail, and Molly followed. "This is wolf country," he said softly. "Deer country. Beaver. Elk. No place for cougar, unless cougar likes to be treed for the rest of his days."

She wanted to say that she had read about Storm Man in Alford Aowl's diary, but fear silenced her. The forest had grown darker under one great shadow. Only enough light remained to outline the crystalline frost edging the fern leaves. Along here, the trees were getting bigger, some probably hundreds of years old. Light sleet began slanting through the trees.

"Should we go back?" Her voice, even to her, sounded timid.

"Storm Man has power in the hills," Al said inexplicably. "His power in the forest has the strength of a mewling baby." The words did not seem addressed to Molly, but spoken as a challenge to the forest. "We're nearly there." He turned to Molly. "The trail leads around this hill. On a clear day you could see the high branches from here."

As they climbed a slight rise, an enormous Douglas fir emerged to hover over a hillside. Molly gasped, looked up, and realized that from where she stood she could not see the top.

Great lateral limbs crossed the sky like beams, and from the limbs other limbs rose, bigger than second-growth trees. It filled the darkened sky like a cathedral. Even the older trees resembled stunted striplings beside it. This trunk covered more ground than the cottage where she lived. This tree was a monument.

"I wanted you to see this for more than one reason," Al said.

Molly gazed upward into the dark sky as sleet changed to snow and a light wind began to blow.

"You wanted to see how things used to be. A hundred years ago this land was dotted with trees that had stood for centuries. We—I mean people—lived beside those trees in the same way they lived beside their grandfathers." His voice tried to conceal anger and loss and sadness. "You wanted to know how people used to live."

"What saved this tree?" Being in the presence of the tree felt nearly religious, and Molly found herself whispering.

Al pointed to the hillside which was already turning white with snow. Here and there along it dark circles marked the mouths of caves. "It's state forest now," he said, "but Wolf saved it. That was a denning area. I think maybe the loggers found safer places to log. Old stories say that there is one wolf that can't be killed. Wolf saved this tree." He looked upward to where thickening snow now brightened the sky. "This is no place for Cougar," Al said to the forest, his voice matter-of-fact. "If Cougar doesn't leave, wolf will begin to run."

A flicker of darkness, a rapidly moving shadow, crossed the hillside. Other shadows followed. Molly watched in disbelief, telling herself that it was a trick of the dark day and the snow. She lived at the end of the twentieth century, not the end of the nineteenth. No wolf packs ran in these forests. Wolf packs belonged in Canada and Siberia.

Yet the movement was as smooth as music, and it was the movement of wolves. Their running looked so natural, and they leapt past with such animal ferocity that the ferocity seemed normal. The shadows ran seriously.

Molly remembered that first night on the beach. This time there were no yips or yelps or barks. Not even a lion could stand before the onrush of that pack. The wolf pack running across the side of that hill seemed an inexorable, natural force. Molly heard her own small shriek as she jumped toward Al and gripped his arm. His other arm encircled her. "Nothing to be afraid of," he said. "I expect cougar is about to leave."

This was the second time he had held her, and this time his touch was familiar and comforting. His arms felt as if, in some almost remembered and mysterious past, Al had held her many times; had protected her on strange nights when storms walked the hills. Somehow she knew this man intimately. They had lain side by side, had made love, had even made plans for the future. Somehow, with his touch, she felt, not married, but wedded.

"There was another reason why you should see the tree," Al whispered. He watched the wolves disappear into the forest. "I wanted you to feel how much time a living thing might have. It might be possible to live forever."

There was too much mystery here, Molly told herself firmly. If anyone else said what Al was saying, she would fear for his sanity. Yet here she was, alone in the forest with a man who talked of living forever as if he knew it personally.

Before she could ask what he meant, the forest silence was shocked by a snarl. Darkness deepened. Snarling rose through the trees. It hissed, a giant cat at bay. The snarling of wolves answered. The hissing stopped, choked with a catlike scream. A flash of brown flickered momentarily between the trees. It dashed toward the hills. The wolves did not pursue.

"Cougar is a little baby," Al said to the forest. "Wolf has power here." He pulled her close, then reluctantly released her. "I wanted you to see the tree. I hope you will think about time." He seemed his normal self, all thought of wolves and cougars forgotten.

Molly stood staring after the fleeing shadows and collected her thoughts. She wanted two things, she realized, and she did not apologize for either of them. She wanted to be back in the cottage, in a world that seemed warm and normal and civilized. She wanted something else even more. She wanted the memory of him, the familiarity of him. She wanted him to hold her and make love to her as he had in the past. Molly shook her head and knew that she was making no sense at all. "Let's go home," she said, reaching for his hand.

"Yes, we should get back." He stood looking at the forest, his gaze puzzled. "There is a new power in this forest," he said. "Either that, or there is a new person with old power. Ray Goodwillow will know what is happening." He curled his arm over her shoulder as they turned back toward the trail.

Raymond Goodwillow sat before the stove as afternoon light faded toward darkness. Pam would be home soon, but for now she walked in the forest. Goodwillow could feel her presence out there, a young presence, and new. It carried its power awkwardly. The Great Changer had made things different again, but this time the changes were not so bad.

Goodwillow looked around at the familiar room. The great drum stood like the controlled voice of power. In the war that was coming, the war between Storm Man and the Wolvine, between Storm Man and Man-Among-Wolves, the drum would speak with the voices of forest and mountains and surf.

Man-Among-Wolves was trapped, Goodwillow recognized. Man-Among-Wolves had not been a bad man, but he had meddled in Storm Man's business. The meddling had brought sorrow to the white man, and to the Wolvine. It could only end in war.

This was going to be a terrible war, but Goodwillow sat filled with praise and contentment because it would be the last war he would see. This war depended not on him, a man too old for a final battle alone, but on the power of Pam and the presence of Birch— except that in this war Birch was named Molly Snow.

Goodwillow sensed Pam's presence in the forest, and found it strong. Pam was not confused, but power was new to her. He must live long enough for Pam to gain control. When that happened, he would be free to go.

Chapter 24

THE CHATTER OF SNAPPING TWIGS began to issue from the woodstove. In the kitchen, Molly put on the coffee. Al had gotten the fire going. The familiar twang of a couch spring announced his weight settling onto it. It felt natural to slide onto the couch beside him and stare with him into the fire.

Flames held races along the lines of cedar kindling, licking toward the larger logs to darken their crusts of bark. Outside, the rain lessened.

Nothing she knew felt like any help right now. In movies, she had seen plenty of seduction scenes, but in movies moments like this were false, chilled by the perfect faces and pretty colors magnified on the screen. Those kisses felt drained of the heat that already flickered at the base of her spine. Anyway, seductive actresses tossed coy glances over cocktail glasses, not over chipped coffee mugs. They wore revealing gowns, not jeans and flannel shirts and an awkward-to-remove turtleneck.

That settled it, Molly decided. She was damned if she was going to try some relax-while-I-slip-into-something-comfortable line. Al deserved better than trickery. She was not going to try to entice him into anything. Which meant that technically, she supposed, this might not even qualify as a seduction.

Small tongues of blue flame edged along the underside of two logs. From the kitchen came the slight rattle of the coffeepot gearing up to perk. After one more breath she would break the silence. Then Al made it easy.

"I heard somewhere that a long time ago they thought fire was one of the elements. One of those things that lasted forever."

"The Greeks believed that," Molly said, and realized at once how fatuous she must sound. This was no time for graduate school chatter.

"Indians know. Some things last forever. Spirits of wind. Spirits of fire. Even human spirits sometimes."

"I felt that today," she managed. This conversation was turning too somber for the urging she felt. She let the words carry her along anyway. "Out in the woods, it felt like something even more ancient than that tree." She thought of how she had wanted to be part of the life which that raw world promised, a life lived in the wilderness, almost as if she were one of those animals racing across the hillside. Her hand ached to touch him, as if by that touch alone she could enter the mysterious, wild world he seemed to understand.

A large log caught, sizzling when the flames hit a pocket of sap. Flames quickly encircled the log, embracing it in a red-yellow glow.

"Goodwillow would say that the way to understand ancient ways is to want to be part of them," Al said.

"Do you ever feel that?"

"Always."

His voice was deep and mellow. Molly paused to hear the words echo in her mind. Could he be asking what she too was asking? Was he talking, in his own shy way, about this longing she felt? Slowly, almost as if against his will, he turned and met her gaze. The look lasted only an instant before he quickly turned to study the fire again, but in that instant she seemed to see as much softness and longing as a man's eyes could hold. She knew she saw something else too, something lost and aching.

Molly tried to think of anything to say. They sat talking of ancient things, but this yearning to press her body close to his was even more ancient, the desire of flesh to touch flesh and somehow merge into the mystery of his life.

She pulled her gaze back from the fire. His forearm lay easily along the couch cushion, the fine hairs on the back of his hand curling like the leading edge of a wave.

"Maybe Goodwillow is right." In the instant of speaking she knew how to tell of her need. "When I was out there, I wanted to run with those wolves on the hillside."

The muscles in his arms stirred slightly, a tendon tightening beneath the skin.

Molly forced herself to go on. "I wanted to feel the wind on my skin. I wanted to lose myself in the smells. I wanted—" She paused, searching for any word that was more than a mere animal sound. No human word could equal the aching desire to let her body fall toward his, to be done with it.

"I wanted," she said at last.

From the woodstove, resin popped and light flared like a small flashbulb. It illuminated a tracing of red along his arm, a crimson line sweeping from wrist toward elbow. Before thought could hold her back, her hand reached to touch the line.

He did not flinch as her finger pressed lightly on the scratch. He turned toward her and firelight danced over his cheekbones.

"Branch caught me. Nothing much."

Incapable of resisting, she smoothed the pad of her finger up the line of the cut. The warmth of his skin traveled upward long her arm, igniting her nerves like fire racing up a twig. She pulled her hand away, but the connection would not break.

He reached across his body to place his own hand where hers had lingered. His palm closed over his skin as if trying to smooth down the finely woven hairs, to still the shiver that pulsed a cord in his neck.

"I too have known that wanting," he said at last, his voice so quiet she strained to hear it over the crackling of the fire. That low whisper went on. "This human life is much more lonely than the lives of those beasts. We feel everything they do, and more. The same loves, but deeper fears. They love each other, as well as animals can. We fear to love each other at all."

There was no shame in wanting him now, she realized. It was the answer she needed. She reached to place her hand over his own, feeling the hard edges of his knuckles, then the strength of his fingers as they closed around hers. He turned her hand and smoothed his own along her arm. The first touch was a gentle stroking, then it grew more urgent. His strong fingers kneaded her skin, inflaming it with pleasure each place he touched. At last his hands found her shoulders, gripping her and pulling her into him. Falling toward him, she breathed in the scent of him, his flesh, his hair, and her lips found the soft skin of his neck.

He drew her forward across his body until she was nearly turned away from him. Molly let her weight fold backward, sensing the nearness of his chest and letting her languor settle into it. He had taken her other hand and drawn her inward, sealing their bodies together as his lips brushed the back of her head.

His face nudged alongside, then he leaned to smooth his lips down the side of her neck. At the corner of her vision, firelight caught on the tangle of her own black hair interweaving with silver strands of his.

Strong arms closed around her and his fingers cupped her breasts, their touch warm and sensitive. She let her head hang back, her eyes closing. In her mind's eye she could see his hands smoothing the lower edge of her shirt upward, skimming beneath the sweater. His chest pressed firmly along her back, an unyielding pressure that drew her into him. Soft breath warmed her neck and his lips kissed there once, then again and again.

She let him fold her body under his, rearing back when his hands pulled at her clothes, wishing he could go faster and set her free of all human restraint. At last his hands tugged her shoulders downward. They pulled her into him, the soft fur on his belly burnishing her skin, and she lost herself in his smell and his softness and the wild darkness of his soft, guttural breathing. She felt herself tumbling toward a world of freedom, some primal, savage land where human thoughts and human words and even these cries scraping loose from her throat were fading memories, the remnants of a doomed and distant civilization.

Chapter 25

OVERNIGHT THE TEMPERATURE DROPPED, AND GRAY DAWN brought mist swirling light spits of snow. October faded to November. At the Surfbreak Cafe early risers huddled over coffee cups. On a normal morning the men would read newspapers, talk logging and football, and a few would sit dazed and mute with hangovers.

On this morning, the men's voices were heavier and the talk was not casual. The men were confused, and so they spoke too loudly. Smells of coffee and bacon were cut with the sharp scent of cleaner swabbed through the bores of rifles.

"Wolf pack."

"I laughed and called Mulling a damned fool when he blew his windshield out. Now, who's the damn fool, I ask?"

"A wolf killed Sims. At least they say it was a wolf."

"I was there. It was a wolf."

"This time there's no boozing," one man said. He was tall and thin, his knuckles skinned and enlarged from hard work. "No more mixing rifles and juice."

"It's the damn Woofies cause this," another man said. "Woofies are wolf-happy."

"Put a lid on that." The tall man leveled his gaze toward the speaker. "Start talking like that, and somebody might start listening." He raised his voice so everyone could hear. "If anybody's thinking Woofie, count me out."

"Maybe so," another man said, "but I wouldn't put it past the sonsabitches." He looked at the tall man. "You know so much about it, then lay out a plan for hunting. We don't want any more guys getting in the line of fire."

"We'll do it this way," the man said and began to lay out a plan of encirclement, one that would drive the wolf pack to the beach. "And we'd better get moving now, before Mulling shows up and stops us."

On this morning Mulling wouldn't have minded a cup of coffee, or several, and his usual stack of pancakes. Those pleasures would have to wait because he had important personal business. The patrol car was parked a quarter mile from the Aowl Museum. Now he sat in the museum's darkened office and waited for Tess Fiddert. She had flown into Portland from California late last night. She would rent a car. He figured Tess would bustle in here any minute, but he doubted she would come straight into the office. He'd gone over it with a fine-toothed comb. There was nothing hidden here.

If Tess Fiddert had a stash of money, she would check it right away. The first few minutes after she came in the door would be crucial. He'd find that money then, or likely never find it.

Daylight lay beyond the windows, but the light did not do much to illuminate the museum. Mulling glanced at shadowed display cases. Old photos, brown and blurry, hovered in frames and behind glass. They showed early loggers standing in groups before the stumps of giant trees. The men were dwarfed by the high stumps. Pictures showed early steam engines, logging trains, mule-drawn wagons, steam donkeys used for loading trees on flatcars, and the faces of workmen and bankers and politicians. These were the faces of men who had set out to conquer a wilderness. Proud faces.

Pictures also showed early makeshift taverns, rooming houses, and rickety churches. It seemed to Mulling that, for a moment, the large downstairs was filled with whispers of dead voices. From upstairs, sounds of beasts lived just on the edge of hearing—snarls, howls, the cries of ancient battles. Mulling sat upright, and his hand went to his holster. Workmen would be showing up soon to repair the damaged turret. He could use the company.

Only money, he guessed, could keep Tess working in a place as crappy as this. Tess had spent a lifetime here, arranging exhibits and stashing cash. He was willing to bet she had laid back a fortune. Mulling thought of Molly Snow, who was going to have to pay for playing little girl games with him. She worked in this place, too, although she didn't seem to like it much. Mulling leaned back and thought it through. He'd wait until Fiddert spread the rumor that Molly Snow had started the fire. Then he might pay a visit to that young woman. She was going to start behaving like a Woofie, and not like a fancy college girl. Beyond the office window, a car entered the parking lot.

Mulling knew every car in the county, and he did not recognize this one. It had to be a rental. Mulling stood easily, and walked toward a shadowed corner where he could see, but Tess could not see him.

Tess hurried in and closed the door quickly. She stood for a moment to catch her breath, then immediately went into the cloakroom. Muffled sounds came from inside—something being dragged, a small thump. Silence. Then the dragging sound resumed, and another small thump. Tess emerged and went to her office. Passing him unaware in the dark, she walked without haste. Completely relaxed now, she took off her coat and hung it on a chair.

Mulling let his breath out silently. He had just scored so easily, he could not believe it. Sure as the world, Fiddert had not gone into the cloakroom to hang up her coat. The money was somewhere in the cloakroom, under the floor, or under a trapdoor. Now she sat at her desk, writing and looking up from time to time at one or another of the display cases. Mulling figured she was listing the records that would have to be stored since damp air was getting into the museum from the burned-out turret. He also figured Tess really didn't care about protecting the museum records from mildew. Storing stuff in the bank vault was just an excuse to keep Molly Snow away from the museum.

Mulling remained in the shadows. The workmen would show up soon, and Fiddert would go to the turret with them. He could slip out quietly while they were up there. He would wait and take his own sweet time committing the perfect crime. Tess Fiddert was not about to report the theft of stolen money. His career in law enforcement was about to pay some dividends.

Molly woke to warm memories of being held, of lying beside Al, of falling into sleep with his hand touching her hair. She kept her eyes closed for a few moments, hoping he still lay beside her, but knowing somehow that he did not. He was obviously an early riser, and he had probably returned to the forest. When she did open her eyes, it was to find gray light filling the windows and soft snow melting against them. The room was warm. Al had built a fire before he left.

Today she had to visit Goodwillow. She sipped coffee and watched the swirling snowflakes, unsure whether she wanted to go anywhere near the Wolvine reservation. Pam had acted strangely yesterday. Once more Molly felt that she was not studying history, but walking through history.

Yet no scholar worth her salt would miss an opportunity to question Raymond Goodwillow. Molly made a quick breakfast, dressed warmly, and headed for her car. It was time to start acting like the historian she was, and not like a frightened kid.

When she reached the turnoff, she parked and walked along the unpaved road where puddles had turned to small pockets of ice. Smoke rose from wood fires in the shacks, but no faces appeared at windows. The forest felt unfriendly and remote today, and it seemed, almost, as if the Wolvine were in hiding.

Then she remembered Pam's words. The Wolvine were hiding from Storm Man. In the forest yesterday, Al had also mentioned Storm Man. But Storm Man had been dead for nearly eighty years. She had read the records.

When she stepped beneath the roofed shelter, she once again savored the sense of returning home.

"It is good that you came," Pam said, opening the door. "My grandfather is stronger, but still not so strong."

"I can come back another day."

Pam stepped backward, motioning Molly inside. Even today,

away from the madmen shooting at her on the beach, Pam did not seem friendly. Nor did she seem unfriendly. Overnight, she had somehow grown older, a girl changed into full womanhood. Her voice was quiet, but no longer shy or timid. "I think maybe it is good that you are here today."

Molly obeyed Pam's gesture to take a chair facing Goodwillow, and noted that the great drum no longer stood beside the wall. At the end of the room, the entry to a passage, or a cellar, or a cave, was no longer covered. It stood open but lightless, like the mouth of a den.

She was certain, when she looked at Goodwillow, that she saw a dying man. Thinning gray hair framed high cheekbones covered by flesh as thin as paper. His shoulders slumped, and his large hands seemed smaller, more fragile. Only the man's clear eyes looked fully alive with energy and strength. Molly started to speak, then stopped, feeling subdued.

When she looked past that withered face and into the eyes, she felt that she might fall into a great depth. It was not a depth of darkness, but one of mystery and power and change. Nothing, those eyes said, was fixed and permanent. Always, there would be flow. Always, there would be change. Molly Snow thought she might be changing even as she studied him.

"Birch," he said, his voice surprisingly strong. "When Birch returns, Man-Among-Wolves must walk. When Birch returns, Storm Man rides to war. I will tell about these things."

Raymond Goodwillow spoke simply, as though instructing a child. He leaned back in his chair, knitting his fingers on his lap, and began telling a story, or a history.

A woman named Birch, who had surely been Molly's grandmother, had been kidnapped long ago. She was married to Storm Man, but Man-Among-Wolves stole her away. Storm Man changed them both to wolves. Then Birch returned and was changed back to a woman, but Man-Among-Wolves remained a wolf. "He is ageless," Goodwillow announced calmly.

Heat from the woodstove grew as wind increased the draft. Molly moved her chair backward a few inches, but leaned forward to watch Goodwillow's eyes. They were without guile. Goodwillow told the truth as he understood it. Pam had taken a spot to the right of her grandfather's chair.

Goodwillow continued the story. When Storm Man died, the woman named Birch said chants and performed the ceremony to make the wolf into a man again. Goodwillow should have helped, but he did not, and now he was sorry. The ceremony did not work well enough. Now Man-Among-Wolves could walk as a man. When he did, great trouble came to the Wolvine and to the white people. For most of Goodwillow's life, Man-Among-Wolves had remained a wolf. Now he walked as a man. This happened because Birch had returned. There must be a war between Wolf and Cougar, between Man-Among-Wolves and Storm Man.

Molly sat stilled, believing Goodwillow even as her rational mind chased in a frenzy to find an escape. Her rational mind knew that men could not change to wolves, or wolves to men. And Storm Man was dead, buried, gone forever.

Yet Goodwillow spoke of cougar and wolf. Yesterday, in the forest, Al had talked of those same animals. Yesterday, she had seen wolves. Goodwillow and Al must have spoken the truth, her rational mind insisted.

She thought of Al, and of his strong arms around her. She wished Al were here, and sensed instinctively that he would expect her to trust Goodwillow. She knew enough about history to know that the modern world had lost at least as much knowledge as it had gained. Matters that were now branded as superstition, or occult, had once carried power among people who understood them.

"War? You mean with guns and fighting?" She studied Goodwillow. He seemed exhausted, and even more frail.

Pam answered for him. "Maybe worse," she said quietly. "A different war than the ones you talk about when you say 'history.' The next storm will be different than the last." She placed a slim hand on her grandfather's shoulder. "My grandfather is tired, and you must go. You will come back here pretty soon. When the storm begins, you come here right away."

Beyond the little house, wind swept the tops of the forest, and small branches fell as litter to the ground. "How will I know?" Molly asked. "It seems that it's always ready to storm around here."

"The wind will blow white. You come when the wind blows white." Pam's voice sounded much friendlier now. She picked up

Molly's parka and led her to the door. The two women stepped outside to stand beneath the roofed shelter.

In the forest, distant yells and whoops sounded. It sounded as if a great many men were moving slowly toward the beach. Molly felt momentarily afraid.

"They're not looking for us," Pam said quietly. "They hunt for Wolf, but Wolf is fast and clever." She motioned toward the house. "My grandfather is old. He used much of his strength in the last storm. He must not work so hard again."

"I don't understand what this means," Molly said. "I didn't want to tire him."

"You are Birch," Pam said simply. "That was the reason for the story. Your grandmother was Birch, and when you came here things changed. You are Birch."

Molly stood, stunned, no longer an observer. "You mean I'm in the middle of this."

"You are the middle of this."

"Should I go away? Then things will change back?" She heard the reluctance in her voice. She was terrified of the forces these people understood so well, but she did not want to leave.

"It would be too dangerous. I think there is only one place in the world where you might be safe. That place is right here." Pam pointed to the cabin, then to the ground at her feet. "There is plenty of power here."

Pam's eyes showed sorrow, and she spoke as a woman who was sad because her sister was threatened. "There is no protection for Man-Among-Wolves, except his own strength. Man-Among-Wolves is trapped." Pam turned back toward the door. "You come when the wind is white. When that happens, you hurry. Don't think of anything else. Just come here right away." The door closed, shutting out the small light which glowed from inside.

Molly walked toward her car, stepping carefully along the trail. As she walked, wind moved from the sea, sweeping the dunes and battering into the forest. From the distance, out there among the dunes, gunshots echoed. It sounded as if a small war had already started.

Chapter 26

Wind swept across the flat beach as men stood on the tops of dunes. The men shook their heads in embarrassment. They looked toward the tide line, wishing the tide would hurry in to swallow their mistakes.

The beach lay littered with dead dogs. They looked like torn brown and black rags—a spaniel, a golden retriever, some mixed breeds, and a shepherd that had been the leader. The bodies lay still and small and unthreatening.

Blood stained the sand.

"So much for the big bad wolf hunt."

"We're heroes, okay. What the hell was a pack of dogs doing in the forest?"

"Wait until the town hears this. We went gunning for wolves, and nailed some cockapoos and spaniels. Mulling is gonna laugh his fat fanny off."

One man, more ashamed than the rest, turned to shake his fist at the forest. "A wolf killed Sims. A wolf. We'll get you next time, you four-legged Woofie-loving sonsabitches."

"Put a sock in it," a man said. "We're all hunters. We know you don't score on every hunt. We try again tomorrow."

Molly returned to the Aowl cottage just before noon. The visit to Goodwillow's left her so unsettled that even the familiar cottage offered little comfort. She told herself that she should at least record Goodwillow's story, and record her own impressions before they slipped from memory. She wondered vaguely what a white wind would look like, and if a "white wind" was part of Wolvine mythology. To discover the truth about that, she would have to go to the museum.

She had not been there since two nights ago, the night when Sheriff Mulling tried to force himself on her. So much had happened since then. Pam had changed, and there was a body on the beach; except that there had been no body. She had gone to the forest with Al, and they had made love. Now Goodwillow predicted a war of storms, and Pam spoke of a white wind.

Crossing the dunes, she could see, even from a fair distance, that something was wrong at the museum. Trucks stood in what should be an abandoned parking lot. High up on one of the turrets, a man walked the slanted roof. He leaned backward in a harness, like a mountain climber leaning to catch leverage from a rope. The tower looked stained with a different shade of black. Molly gasped. Workmen were repairing the turret.

The front door stood open. When she stepped inside, the first thing she saw was Tess Fiddert standing over a display case. Fiddert wore a pink house dress sprinkled with yellow flowers. She was wrapping one of the Aowl manuscripts in waxed paper, then packing it in a carton. She saw Molly and did not smile.

"Back to the scene of the crime?" Tess asked. Her voice sounded almost cheerful, but the cheer was false and cruel.

"What happened? What do you mean?" Molly paused. "I thought you went to California."

"And came back from California," Tess said grimly. "Because a college chickie left a cigarette burning." She looked at Molly, and then looked around the museum. "This place isn't much," she said quietly, "but it's what I've got. It's mine, and you can get the hell out. Now."

Molly felt herself wilt before the attack, and then told herself to stop feeling intimidated.

"You are very wrong," she said quietly, surprised at the force of her voice. "I'm a professional, the same as you. I came here to do a piece of work. And I don't smoke. Now tell me what happened."

Surprised, Tess paused in her wrapping of a manuscript. She eyed Molly as if gauging her strength.

"There was a fire. All records and photographs are going to the bank vault. The rest of the stuff is mostly reproduction." Tess smiled a tight little smile. "Even if you had nothing to do with it, chickie, all you can do around here is scratch sand. You sure can't do any research. The museum is closed until next summer."

"You can't do this."

"It's done," Tess said. "Watch me do it."

"These records are publicly owned. They belong to the state."

"And the state will thank me for protecting them," Tess said grimly. "If you don't like it, trot on down and speak to the governor."

"I may do that." Molly tried to control her anger. "I'll have to do it unless you can answer a question." She paused. "Why are you so angry? I've never done a thing to you. I took care of this place as well as you did."

Clearly Tess was protecting something. Her eyes narrowed, and when she spoke, she seemed pleased with herself.

"See that drawer, fourth down on the left? Bottom of the stack. Look at it." A note of triumph sang in her voice. "Take a look at it, darlin', and then get the hell out."

When Molly opened the drawer she found folders containing old photographs. She lifted them out and pulled the bottom folder free. The label read: "Only photograph ever taken of Storm Man."

The picture was brown with time and stained with water. From inside its clear plastic cover three faces peered toward the camera. A young boy's face carried the guilelessness of youth. An old man stared, contemptuous, unsmiling, as he sat beside a young woman. Molly stifled a gasp. The image of the young woman was the image of herself.

Her hand trembled turning the picture over. On the back was written "Raymond Goodwillow, Shaman Storm Man, and Birch, of Wolvine tribe."

Tess Fiddert had stopped work and now leaned against the display case, taking time out to enjoy herself. Molly turned the picture back over. She studied the face, trying to find the least difference between herself and this woman who must have been her grandmother.

The other two faces came into focus. The boyish face of Raymond Goodwillow stared across time. In those days, having your picture taken was a big event, and Goodwillow seemed proud and serious.

The third face was Storm Man's. Folds of age and folds fat could not hide the power in that gaze. Storm Man sat dressed in ceremonial clothes, a great robe of skins hanging over his shoulders. The head of a cougar, mouth still wide in a snarl, crowned the hood on the cape. The cougar snarled above the harsh and open eyes of Storm Man, pitiless eyes that looked into the camera with subdued violence. Fat hands seemed violent even at rest. Storm Man was old, but his hair caught the light—jet-black, long and greasy. Molly shuddered, remembering a flash of brown in the forest and the yowl of a large cat. Cougar, she thought. Wolf. And war. She slipped the photograph back into the folder, determined to retain her composure so that Tess would not see the shock she felt. The image in the picture came at her as if from a dream, but a terrible dream it seemed she was living. She must not let Tess know that.

"I'm leaving now," she said, "but not for the reason you believe." Willing her hand to remain steady, she placed the folder in its correct place. "This is a picture of my grandmother," she told Tess. "She was from a northern tribe, and she was ten times the woman you will ever be. I feel sorry for you. It must be a very sad thing to know that you will never be anything but yourself." She walked to the door in silence, but as she stepped into the cold day she heard the hiss of a word.

"Woofie."

Outside, Molly stood in the chilly breeze, thankful for solid, cold reality. She fought to retain control. It was one thing to have Goodwillow say that she was Birch. It was another thing to accept the fact. It was still another thing to have seen that picture. No wonder Goodwillow said that she was Birch. Molly turned toward the cold wind, but the wind was not as cold as the wind that seemed to rise out of history. She thought of Birch. Then, because she had to, she thought of Tess Fiddert.

Molly wondered vaguely if her career was finished before it

was properly begun. Tess Fiddert made a good part of her living from what was left of the Wolvine, but she hated them. Tess would never let a Wolvine descendant work in the museum if she could help it. And now she could.

There was no way to stop Tess. If she tried, Tess would accuse her of causing the fire. The sheriff would say the same. That sort of scandal would wreck any academic career. Molly momentarily wanted to weep, and then thought better of it. Tears were not going to fix this.

She trudged toward the cottage, and with each step away from the museum, she felt better. After all, she had documentary proof that Aowl had drawn fake maps to protect denning areas. More importantly, she had the narrative of Raymond Goodwillow, a primary source. No one could question such evidence. While it would be better to finish researching the records, she already had more than enough for her thesis.

Besides, she told herself, she was onto something anthropologically important, even if it was not exactly history. Pam had definitely changed. Goodwillow spoke of war. No one even moderately sane would believe that a man could change into a wolf, or vice versa, but something was about to happen. She might be about to witness a ceremony that historians thought had vanished into the mists of the past.

Even more, it was now clear why Raymond Goodwillow attached such importance to her. Looking at the picture of Birch had been like looking in a mirror. Symbolically, at least, it seemed that Molly—a young woman—was the grandmother of Goodwillow—that old, old man. She smiled, but not with amusement. Only people who knew the ways of The Great Changer could really understand what was happening.

At least she would not have to go near that monstrosity a museum again. She would not have to deal with Tess Fiddert, or with Mulling either. She could begin work on her thesis today if she wanted. She imagined working through the winter in that small cottage, and her thoughts warmed. She pictured Al returning from the forest at night. His arms would close around her, encircling her in his strength and warmth and mysterious scents of the forest and sea. She could not honestly say that she was in love with this man. Maybe this was only an affair, but if it was, it was an affair she intended to make last.

Sheriff Mulling drove along the deserted beach, keeping to the hard-packed sand and scanning the dunes. There was a lot of work left to be done after the storm, but he figured the mayor could earn his pay for a change. Right now, Mulling needed a long drive and a quiet place to work out a plan.

With workmen repairing the museum, the next couple of days would be the perfect time to lift Tess Fiddert's stash. There were problems, though. Fiddert was a tough old bat, and she was vindictive. If she had the least suspicion that he'd taken the cash, Fiddert would find some way to make things hot for him. Of course, if Tess had laid back a major stash—and he figured she must have put away quite a sum over all these years—he hardly planned to hang around a crappy town doing a crappy job, anyway.

Maybe he should start by just checking the money. If there was a lot, the simple answer was to lift it and torch the museum. Fiddert would think the money was destroyed in the fire. Mulling hummed to himself, imagining high living along warm, California beaches.

A mile ahead, flocks of gulls rose, swooped, and dropped toward the tide line. There looked like hundreds of them, and Mulling wondered idly if a whale had beached. He upped his speed and closed the distance.

Along the tide line, and tumbling in the first reaches of surf, bodies of dogs lay stretched and bloodless beneath the squawk and feeding of gulls. Mulling slowed, counted the bodies, and grinned.

So the big and illegal wolf hunt had come to this—a bunch of scruffy mutts dead along a beach. He laughed out loud. Those big, tough wolf-hunters had done his work for him. No more worries about a dog pack.

Better yet, now the shoe was on the other foot. Those same punks had laughed at him for a blown-out windshield, and now it was his turn. He eased the car around, looking forward to a stop at the Surfbreak Cafe.

His tires spit sand, rousting a half-dozen gulls from where

they fed. They lifted off a larger body which lay stretched near the corpse of a Doberman. Mulling missed seeing it. They settled again, dug their talons in and began seriously pecking at the corpse of an overweight, middle-aged man, bloodless, with flesh opened to the bone as if ripped by furious claws and fangs.

Chapter 27

As Mulling drove to town and Molly Snow crossed the dunes toward her cabin, the tide turned and temperatures rose. Spits of snow turned to freezing rain. Molly entered the cabin and turned on all the lights, even though it was still daylight. She did not notice, at first, the pulsing beats of a drum. The sound was blown by wind, and it came from far away. Only after she started rearranging files did she feel the drum in the way one might respond to a subliminal suggestion.

To start on her thesis, it was important to see how much material was actually in hand. She began reorganizing notes and file cards, looking for a new arrangement. She had planned for everything to go differently, and restructuring it felt like tearing down a half-built building, then laying a different foundation.

The drumbeat muttered just on the edge of consciousness, dwelt among the rain swept trees like the distant echo of thunder. When she finally became fully aware of it, she made coffee, then went to the window to stare into the wet forest.

She listened, screening out the sounds of the surf and the wind. At first it had sounded like several drums, but the beats came too clearly and separately. There could be only one. The steady beating came from the Wolvine reservation. Probably only one drum on this whole coast could speak over such a great distance. That great drum in Goodwillow's house would not be given its voice over any small matter.

She remembered how, along these shores a hundred years ago, there were initiations and dancing. Dancers wore masks—raven, whale, eagle, cougar, and wolf. Among the flames of ceremonial fires Wolf was said to rise. There was one ceremony, requiring long preparation and calling people together for days, which served as a rite of passage or power. She felt ninety-nine percent certain that drumming like this could only signal the beginning of the Wolf ceremony, or what was left of it. Wolf and Wolvine, she reflected. Wolf and Man-Among-Wolves. And cougar. And war.

She wondered who set the hammered, steady beat. Goodwillow was too old. It had to be Pam. Molly looked into the forest, halfway expecting the wind to turn white. Instead, a gray shadow slid from among the trees. It ran easily, and she knew without doubt that it was a wolf.

At other times she would have frozen, immobile with fear. Now, somehow, she felt comforted. If wolves ran through the forest, they did not hunt for her.

The drum lived in the air, not as an annoyance, but a comfort. She continued working, oblivious to the daylight fading from the windows, oblivious to the moment when Al eased quietly through the doorway. She did not realize, until she looked up and saw him close the door at his back, just how much she had missed him.

He wore his usual faded denim. His long, silver hair looked tousled by the wind. A bramble, caught in it, dropped to the floor as he turned. He carried a skinned and gutted rabbit. Before he took off his coat, or even touched her hand, he put a large pot of water on the stove. He put the rabbit in and covered the pot.

"Let it work for an hour," Al said absentmindedly, "and then we'll throw in the rest." He pulled a couple of potatoes from his pocket, then some leaves which resembled spinach, and something that looked like roots. "It amounts to mulligan stew," he smiled, "but it won't be bad." His voice was gentle as he turned toward her.

When his hand came to rest on her shoulder, Molly momentarily wondered if the drumming had actually grown louder or if only the pounding of her heart swelled its volume. She closed her book and folded her hand over his. His hand stroked downward over her breast and toward her belly as he leaned to thread kisses along her neck. She stood slowly and led him into the bedroom.

As soon as they had settled onto the bed, he turned her again to close his arms around her from the back, pulling her tightly to him. Her heart pounded in her ears, yet before she gave in to the pull that wanted to draw her completely into the dense cave of his touch, she clung for an instant to the world outside that darkness a glimmer of sunlit lucidity that sparkled with questions.

Who was this man and how could he lure her into such shadowy depths of hunger and wanting? He always turned her away from him when he touched her, yet she could sense him completely—his smell, the tender murmur of his breath at her ear, the touch of his flesh and the soft fur of his belly. When her eyes closed, she could see him fully, not as he had stood in the doorway—a simple, quiet man—but as a wild and loving force that gripped her close and drew her hopelessly away from all that was familiar and human, all that she had once thought of as herself.

They tumbled over and over each other in pure animal play, and she let herself follow him deeper into the cave which seemed at once the center of a mountain and the dark hollow inside a pounding drum. Its pulse surrounded them—echoing the sound of her own heart, his heart pounding against her skin, the roar of wind and surf—capturing her with sweet smells of the sea and breath and earth.

At last he fell from her and sleep came to curl her close. The drumming faded into the soft rhythm of their bodies breathing together. She awoke once at the sound of a word, spoken perhaps in sleep. It was her name—Birch—and, half-awake, she nestled into him, content to remain in a dream where they ran like two animals side by side along a hill.

When Molly awoke, it was to the scent of simmering food. She opened her eyes and found Al watching her.

"That mulligan stew smells ready." He slipped from the bed, helped her stand, and began sorting out the clothing tumbled into the bedclothes.

He was silent as they ate, but not distant. Beyond the windows, the pulsing drumbeat dwelt like a familiar spirit in the darkness. Molly wondered if she was in love, and she also felt a little shy. If Al was slightly old-fashioned, it seemed that she was as well. She also felt a touch of fear. There were questions that had to be answered.

"I wonder how long Pam can keep it up," she said. "That drum has been going all afternoon."

"Hours and hours," Al said. "There's a kind of trance that comes with it. The drummer becomes one with the drum. I expect Pam will last until tomorrow morning. Someone else, maybe one of her sisters, will pick it up." The questions surged forward, wanting answers. Yet somewhere deep below them, as if in some cave of her mind where dreams and ancient chants made perfect sense, each question held its own answer.

Al took a forkful from his nearly empty plate, then set his fork along its edge. "Indian business," he said, reading the confusion in her look. "Serious business."

In the subdued light his long hair shone silver. He was not as relaxed as he appeared, and his movements were careful and accurate.

"Raymond Goodwillow told me a story," Molly said. "About Storm Man and somebody called Man-Among-Wolves. He said there would be a war."

"Did he tell you the name of Man-Among-Wolves?"

"No," she said automatically. Then she caught herself. Goodwillow had not spoken that name. Nor had Pam. Yet both knew it, and now, with a certainty as solid as the latch closing on a well-made door, she understood.

Alford Aowl had fought with Storm Man over the capture of Birch. He had taken Birch into the hills, hiding with her in the places of wolves, places only he knew. Storm Man's curse had changed them, if such a thing were possible. And it must be possible, Molly understood finally, because at this moment she stared into eyes which were both young and more than a century old.

All of these certainties raced through her mind in the instant of speaking that "No." They locked together before she could correct it. She felt as if she stood once again below the arching cathedral of that ancient Douglas fir. Al had been right. There were things in this world that were ageless.

"No," she said again, "Goodwillow did not tell me the name. But now I know."

Chapter 28

Molly stared into Alford Aowl's eyes, stunned with shock. The man himself sat across from her, but this man was also a wolf. Or could become one at any instant. It seemed impossible, and then the light in her mind shifted and it seemed so obvious, she could not believe she had not seen it before.

She remembered a dream when she had spoken Wolvine words, sacred words. The great, silver-maned wolf had been in it. She remembered the joy of tumbling with him, two animals at play, and a sudden ache gripped her thighs as her body remembered the thrill of making love only moments ago. The wild yearning she had felt for so long made sense now—if impossible madness could make sense. She was the granddaughter of Birch, and this man, this wolf loved her. Whatever of Birch remained inside of her loved him too, with a love that knew nothing about time or death.

Time seemed to bend sideways, then spread open like immense fan. She sat at a table feeling Birch's love, and in the reaching forests and hills she also felt The Great Changer dealing power and mystery. She momentarily understood the mind of the surrounding land, the minds of ancient trees. She felt the knowledge of salmon returning upstream, the knowledge of bears and cougars and wolves. She knew the world with the eyes of its beasts.

Then time snapped shut. The vision evaporated. *I do not understand these things*, Molly thought.

"Birch," Al said gently. "Birch is the center of the story."

His matter-of-fact tone carried no apology, not even a sense of wonder. "This seems unreal," he told her, "and I wish I could explain it."

She also wished he could explain. She wished that she could understand what had happened to her own mind, and to her own heart. So much change had come so quickly that she felt she could no longer even be stunned. Somehow, she was Birch. Yet, she still felt like Molly Snow. *And that means,* she told herself, *that I am still real; but real in a way that could never be understood in the world I know.* She looked at Al, who sat quietly. He was giving her time to absorb at least a little of what was happening. Then his gaze faded as if casting backward in his mind, collecting memories. "Missionaries used to come here and talk about predestination," he said. "I didn't believe that then, and don't believe it now. At the same time, this was something that had to happen."

Molly found she could not speak above a whisper. "How can this be?" she asked. It had been Al who commanded those wolves to drive the spirit of Storm Man from the hillside. Al, himself, while standing guard as a wolf, had attacked Mulling and driven him off. In the face of this truth, logic dissolved like fragile tissue in the wind.

"How can this be?" she repeated.

"Change happens around ceremonial fires," Al said. "There is power in the hills and forest. Sometimes I wish I'd never come to this coast. Sometimes, I'm glad. It turns out that I have some power of my own . . ." He stared downward at her hand, but did not reach to touch it. He waited, and it was obvious that he tried to keep her from fearing him.

". . . because I have become a monster," he said. He stood and walked to the doorway, stepped outside, and returned with more wood for the fire. "I don't mean a Frankenstein creature, or a werewolf or vampire"—he took a deep breath, then placed wood in the stove—"but, monster, nonetheless. A man-and-animal that ranges between two worlds."

Pain cut an edge beneath his matter-of-fact tone. With his back turned, he worked logs into the stove.

"What will happen? What?" Her voice was stronger now and she wondered momentarily if her voice also resembled Birch's voice. Probably so.

"The war is between me and Storm Man. Goodwillow and Pam will go to war. They fight to save the Wolvine and the white people. I fight to save me and protect you. Storm Man fights to reclaim you."

She tried to grasp what Al meant. Fear flickered a bright pulse. Did he want to protect her as he had protected Birch, to carry her away and hide her in the hills? Molly felt Birch's fear rise in her own veins, as solid as the memory of the night nearly a century ago when this white man had stolen her from Storm Man.

Al smiled sadly. "A futile monster," he said. "In my day, we considered whether what we did was good, or if it was evil. I am a man who wishes to be good, and a beast who is very good at being a beast . . . so, it isn't a question of good." He stopped, listening as the drum throbbed at the edge of hearing. There was rustling beyond the house, as if animals slipped almost silently through the forest. "It's a question of evil and ignorance, I expect. We're dealing with Storm Man and white people."

His eyes held more love than she had ever seen in the eyes of any human being. He moved quickly to pull on his jacket. "It's starting," he said. "There's a storm beginning to build in the hills. I have to leave. You will be safe here tonight, but go to Goodwillow's when the wind picks up." Startled at his sudden departure, Molly stood. She felt thankful he was not asking her to go with him. She held Al close, glad to sense his nearness in this simple way—real and solid and warm as any normal man. Some old, old part of her memory loved this man. Molly told herself that life was teaching a new lesson.

"The wind will get up quick when it starts," he said, releasing her. "Get to Goodwillow's right away. It only gets serious when the wind turns white."

Baffled, she pleaded to know more. "What is that? How can wind turn white?"

He met her gaze, his look clear and unwavering. She thought of the look Goodwillow had given when he expected her to know the sacred words. Al expected her to understand, but she did not.

"And how can I be Birch? And how can you be—" She paused, unwilling to say the impossible truth aloud. "How can you be both a man and—"

"You will know."

He turned to the doorway and disappeared into the night.

Chapter 29

As Mulling moved toward the cloakroom, the museum jumped to life before his flashlight. Shadows eddied, and low sobs dwelt among them. The name Aowl, Aowl, Aowl, was repeated, like the howling of wolves and, had Mulling listened, the voice might have sounded like the voice of Molly Snow.

Echoes and shadows and whispers hemmed him in. Mulling paused, mid-step, then forced himself forward. Only idiots believe in ghosts, he told himself. He'd read one of the brochures stacked by the museum door, several years back, and remembered what it said about ghosts in this place. Woofies and tourists might fall for that local color. They might even believe hard times were coming when bodies were seen on the beach. But he wasn't about to start believing any part of it. Wind made those sighing noises through the museum. Probably loose shingles in the burned turret.

Mulling figured on finding Tess Fiddert's stash in no more than ten minutes. After all, Tess had gone immediately to the hiding place. He cast the flashlight beam around the cloakroom, and over the floor. He looked for cracks that would reveal a trapdoor. Nothing showed up right away, but he felt unworried.

An hour later, with his flashlight dimming, Mulling began to worry. His watch read eight PM. He doubted that he had fresh batteries back at his office, and the grocery would close in an hour. It would take ten minutes to walk to his hidden patrol car, five to get downtown, five more to buy batteries, and five to get back; plus another ten minute walk.

Or, he could keep looking until the flashlight burned out. If he did not find Fiddert's stash, he could come back on another night.

The problem was that Fiddert might do the unexpected. With all of the workmen crawling about the building, she might move her money. He had better go for batteries.

As he left the museum, heading for the forest where the patrol car was parked, light wind brought the distant sound of a drum. Mulling told himself that if the damn Woofies didn't settle down, he'd have to drive to the reservation and settle them. He could already imagine the complaints he'd get when he checked the answering machine at the office. At least all the racket would give them something to report besides disappearing corpses. Surfbreak had more nuts, kooks, and crazies than any other town on earth. Mulling climbed in his patrol car, started it up, and turned on the lights.

Eyes of beasts stared from the forest, a semicircle of hostile gazes staring gold-metal above gray-blue muzzles. The eyes gazed unmoving, and Sheriff Mulling sat frozen, his hands gripping the cold steering wheel.

The wolf pack did not move forward, but it did not retreat. Mulling could pick up shadowy bodies in the darkness, but the eyes compelled him with their brilliance. He counted a dozen, and then counted fourteen, and then thirteen. The animals began to move, closing the circle. He hit the button for the emergency lights. They flared up instantly, pulsing into the dark forest.

A wolf stepped into full view. Mulling gasped. Red and blue light washed across the wolf so that it seemed spectral—the brilliant eyes turning to depths of metallic blue. Mulling had halfway convinced himself that the thing was dead, because he was sure he had shot it three times. Yet the silver-maned wolf from the beach, its teeth bared, stood waiting; standing easily, the leader of the pack. Other wolves began to close to the left. More moved on the right. Faint and far away, a drumbeat surged.

Tires spun, spitting gravel and twigs and mud. Mulling backed the car, turned, and got away just as the pack surged forward. His emergency lights still flashed, and in his mirrors he caught the faintest glimpse of the silver-maned wolf standing, mouth open as if laughing.

The wolves ran through the forest. Their fleeting shadows patrolled the perimeter of the reservation, covering ground in the easy lope that could carry the pack twenty or thirty miles between dusk and sunrise. The pack ran heedless of small night animals that fled into the forest, or large game that stood trembling behind cover. Deer melted into darkness, mice scurried, and house cats gone feral dived beneath logs.

The pack circled, carving new boundaries with each step. The perimeter grew, through the forest to the base of the hills, obliterating borders drawn around the Wolvine for nearly a century. They moved toward the town. Outside the Aowl Museum the pack stopped, and a silver-maned wolf raised a loud cry to the shadows within the museum. The wolves ran the road through town, and drivers shuddered and hit their accelerators as they told themselves they had been attacked by visions. The perimeter expanded onto the beaches where surf pounded.

As the wolves played along the tide line, high clouds rolled across an obscured moon. The wolves stopped to sniff, to dig, to make water against logs on one particular section of beach. They staked out territory around a spot from which frightened people had continually been reporting a corpse. The wolves did not linger, but melted into the forest again. As they ran, dark light gathered and gradually changed to spectral light. Silver glistenings tipped the mane of the pack leader. Silver flashes accompanied the pack as it ranged like a defending army around the sleeping tribe of Wolvine.

The drum had sounded in her sleep, and now, at five AM, Molly stood awake in her living room, holding a cup of milk and swaying to the drumbeat's rhythm. She had sat up late last night, stumbling into the bedroom after midnight to fall among blankets that still held the smells of Al's skin and hers.

At last she drifted off to sleep. She dreamed of Storm Man. He appeared first as a laughing cougar. Then he changed into a white wind that wrapped around her, carrying her through forest, over lakes, and into the high hills. She felt unclothed before the wind which throbbed, throbbed, throbbed, as if trying to overpower the beat of a drum. The wind fondled her with rough hands, and the wind laughed in vengeful and fearless tones.

She woke among tangled sheets at five AM and saw only the faint glow of the moon behind gathering clouds. Wiping perspiration from her neck, she listened for wind. It was quiet out there.

Beyond the window, the forest and the surf lay calm, but clouds boiled, scudded, rose high on the horizon. She went to the kitchen and heated a cup of milk.

In the complete stillness the drumbeat lay like a voice of ancient reason among the trees. Molly waited for the sliding figures of wolves to move through the forest, and she waited for the stillness of the night to be broken by the snarls of a giant cat. When nothing happened she stretched, tried to shake off memories of the dream, and finished her milk. She yawned, crawled back into bed, and returned to sleep. At least there was no wind. She hoped there would be none.

Several hundred yards up the beach, Sheriff Mulling stood before a deep closet in the cloakroom of the museum. Fatigue caused his shoulders to slump and his belly fell heavily over his belt. He told himself that it had been one hell of a night. But worth it.

A panel, made to look like a wall of the room, slid sideways. He had wasted time looking for a trapdoor, not expecting an entire wall to move. Now the beam of the flashlight played across Tess Fiddert's loot. Mulling had not figured on this much, or this much variety.

Four steamer trunks held the small bills she had skimmed from admissions—ones and fives and tens. He scratched his head, trying to estimate the total. What were twenty years of two-buck and five-buck offerings worth? It had to be a small fortune, and he wondered idly if even Tess had bothered counting.

The rest was even more difficult to put a dollar figure on. In a dozen large boxes holding glassine folders, pages of postage stamps lay protected from moisture. Mulling whistled under his breath. The museum did a lot of mailings, and Mulling could appreciate how Tess Fiddert had always added at least the cost of a few sheets of stamps to each. While he did not know a damned thing about stamps, he knew they were always at least worth face value. And some of these sheets were twenty years old. Stamp collectors would go dizzy at the sight of them. The stamps were probably worth even more than the cash.

The ugly part of Tess's investment for the future leered and grinned and snarled and laughed back at the flashlight beam. The deep closet held maybe thirty Wolvine masks—wolf, whale, cougar, and raven. These must be originals, definitely old, and not the reproductions that lined the museum's walls. And they must be worth a fortune if a man knew how to dispose of them. Mulling guessed a smart man could do a little legwork. He figured he was smart enough. He looked at the carved faces, the hollow eyes, the decorative skins and feathers. It would be a shame to put any scratches on these beauties, which meant this was going to be a big job. He'd better bring paper for packing.

Mulling smiled. At least he didn't have to worry about Tess Fiddert moving a stash this big. The operation would take too much time. He closed the panel and checked his watch. Dawn came late in winter, but he should get away before any early risers saw him. He stepped into the museum and let his flashlight beam play along the walls to find the most likely places where a fire might start and still look accidental. When he finally stepped out the front door, rustlings and whispers rose at his back.

Chapter 30

WHILE SHERIFF MULLING SLEPT OFF A LONG NIGHT'S WORK, DAWN rode the sound of a drum. Pillars of black clouds climbed above the hills like columns of smoke, and breezes played cold games of tag across the dunes. The gray sea rolled as methodically as a dirge. Men gathered at the Surfbreak Cafe, leaning rifles against the wall before they settled at the counter. The bulges of pistols showed beneath the coats of two or three.

"I have my doubts," one man said. "It looks like we're for dirty weather." He was wiry, with the rangy movements of a man who has spent his life outdoors. He stared through the windows at the gray morning. "Things could get ugly out that way in a little while."

"If that stinkin' drum keeps up," another said, "I'm gonna do something ugly to a bunch of sonsabitching Woofies."

"Count me out," the tall man snapped. "The Woofies didn't bring the wolves, and the Woofies didn't bring the weather. You guys are just looking for somebody to hate." He finished his coffee, placed coins on the counter, picked up his rifle and left.

"I always figured that guy was weak in the knees," another said. "You reckon that drum is telling us anything?"

"It's telling me to stay away from you guys," another man said. His face was weathered, and his knuckles enlarged from accidents with tools, or from fights. "I don't join lynch mobs." He finished his coffee, picked up his rifle, and left. Three others followed.

"That drum is telling me to pop off a few wolves," another man said. "Then maybe we'll make a little stop out there at the reservation."

A murmur of assent rippled along the counter.

When the first shock of thunder shook the cabin walls, Molly stepped quickly to the door, still dressed in her robe and holding her coffee mug. The sky looked blue and bruised, but no lightning creased it. Clouds scudded like great animals tumbling across the horizon. They curled upward in high altitude winds and rolled over each other as if rushing forward in time to the drum.

That drum, Molly was sure, had never missed a beat. Its sound still rolled from the forest, but it seemed different now. The voice was stronger, but the beat did not have the perfect intonation of last night. Molly figured one of Pam's sisters now sat before it, one who did not have Pam's skill. Pam was probably asleep. Molly studied the dark sky. There might be a storm, but the day looked like many other stormy days. She shivered and pulled her robe closer.

November chill ran its fingers through the thin material, and she remembered the curious, nearly savage feelings she felt making love with Al. For a few moments her mind had known ancient truths. Even now a kind of pagan music ran through her head, and her mind seemed to accept the sway and form of drumbeats.

As if in answer to her thoughts, the sky momentarily lightened, darkened, lightened, and the tops of trees were illuminated in flashes of white. Low thunder rumbled from the hills. Clouds above those hills must surely be bringing rain. Sheet lightning flickered like giant flashbulbs. The forest lay shadowed below, and the hills seemed capped with white. Molly turned and went in to dress in her warmest outdoor clothes. She had no way of predicting what would happen, and so it was best to be prepared.

Raymond Goodwillow listened to the low rumbling of thunder and to the hushed voices of the Wolvine gathered outside his shack. Beneath the roof of the open shelter, a fire blazed in the old fire pit. That fire would build a bed of coals through the passage of a stormy day, coals built to such depth that the fire would be like the sun. By nightfall it would be a center of light in the middle of total darkness. A fire like that would radiate enough heat that even an ice storm could not harm the Wolvine.

Goodwillow stood in the single room of his house while Pam slept nearby. The great drum sounded from beneath the shelter where Goodwillow's oldest granddaughter played and chanted. Many people stood around her, but they did not know what to do. A few carried masks, and a few—the younger ones with the strongest legs—clumsily tried to dance in the crouched-forward, foot-pounding movements that strained the calves and threw fatigue into the knees. The Wolvine had forgotten most of the old ways, but at least the people were making an attempt in the war against Storm Man. Goodwillow felt glad to be old, and glad to feel the power of his people return. The Wolvine had hidden for most of the twentieth century, but they were no longer hiding.

Only he and Pam were allowed to enter the cave at the back of his house, and Goodwillow went there now. In this cave Storm Man had danced and laid a curse. In this cave Birch had tried to change a wolf back into a man, and instead made him half-man and half-wolf. Now from this cave Wolvine power gathered to war with Storm Man. Goodwillow reminded himself that before many hours passed, very soon now, he would return here after the final moments of battle.

In old days the cave had been illuminated by a single torch, but now kerosene lamps glowed inside shining chimneys. Their oily scent mingled with the smells of moist earth and dampened charcoal. The air felt calm and cool, but its layers still held the separate smells of burning sage and animal musk, and of droplets of animal fat flaring up from fires now many years cold.

After a small passageway, the cave opened into a massive den. The earthen floor showed a hard-packed circle beaten smooth by dancing feet. Smoke from ancient torches streaked clay walls. Bentwood boxes held robes and the bones of Wolf, and small drums and tamahnous sticks sat beside the heavy mask of Wolf. On the back wall, where the ceiling began to arch, the great robe of wolf skins hung. The very edges of Wolf seemed to glow bluely from shadows. Raymond Goodwillow felt the strength of Wolf enter his mind and his old body. The wolf robe would be heavy, but Wolf was strong.

Power flowed in the cave, just as the power of The Great Changer flowed through the forest and above the hills. Goodwillow stood straighter as light tipped the edges of Wolf's robe with flashes of silver. Maybe Storm Man could turn the wind white, but Wolf could cut the wind with his silver teeth. For a moment Goodwillow thought about Man-Among-Wolves, and wondered what Man-Among-Wolves was going to do. Then he turned away, back to the great robe of Wolf. It was his work to defend the Wolvine, and in doing that defend the white people. Man-Among-Wolves must tend to his own business.

Throughout the morning and into early afternoon the streets of the town lay empty, although hammering sounds told of people boarding windows. The residents of Surfbreak were experienced with storms. They took no chances with this one.

There was a run on the hardware and grocery stores: oil to mix with gas for two-cycle pumps, generators, chain saws; bottled water, candles, kerosene. By 10 AM, the hardware ran out of tarp, canvas, rope. By noon, the grocery ran out of cereal, bread and canned soup, chili and beans.

The sound of the sea was constant in Surfbreak, yet early that afternoon its sound changed. Waves turned from the usual choppy break, break, break, and spread further apart, forming rollers so long and high that not even the oldest locals had seen such mighty water. The rollers broke further out and flooded further up the beach. Water spread like fingers to the broken boardwalk, even though the tide was not high.

People looked uneasy, joked in thin voices, then went about their business. There was a run on the gas pumps as people filled their tanks. "Just in case," one man said, while others tried to ignore him. "Just in case."

As rain began to fall in the hills, Tess Fiddert returned the shadowed Aowl Museum intending to spend the afternoon. She had already packed Aowl's papers and maps. They were safely stored in the vault of the bank on Breakers Avenue. There was really nothing left to do, but Tess did not want to leave.

For one thing, she consoled herself, there was no place go. Her house, closed for the winter, felt cold and empty. She knew every single soul in town, and didn't like a one of them. Besides, the weather looked too poor for visiting.

As the short day darkened toward late afternoon, she walked through the rooms that had been her domain for a working lifetime. She looked at the exhibits, mostly reproductions, and at the carved decorations on woodwork. She looked at worn stair treads where thousands of tourists' feet had passed, tourists whose money had helped build what she liked to call her "trust fund." As she climbed the steps she realized that her chest was tight from tension. She was tired.

Maybe it was time to cash in and get out. She could leave the history business to the Molly Snows of this world. Tess chuckled, thinking of the look on Snow's face when she saw that picture of Birch. The picture had been Tess's ace in the hole, and Tess told herself that she had played it perfectly. There was no more starch left in Molly Snow. That young lady would cause no further trouble.

The sounds of the Aowl Museum were so familiar that she had forgotten them. Now, as she climbed higher to check the work done on the turret, she sensed that the empty mansion actually was filled with voices. They were echoes and murmurs, whispers and sighs. Perhaps they only seemed louder today because she had been away a while.

Old timbers creaked, and the little-used steps leading to the fourth floor gave small squeals as they settled around hand-cut nails. Yes, Tess told herself, it was time to call it quits. She would move her trust fund out, a piece at a time, over the winter. When spring came to California, she would be there to greet it.

Shadows clustered as she arrived on the fourth floor. She walked through empty rooms, opened a door, and stepped into the damaged turret. From here she could see the ocean, the hills, the streets of Surfbreak. From this height she could see all the way to the Wolvine reservation, and she could see the road leading out of town. She could stand in the turret as if she were captain of a mighty ship; a black ship standing high above the gray sea and dark forests.

Sheets of rain cloaked the hills, and there was something going on along the road. Cars were lined up at the bridge. Fiddert blinked and looked again to where the dark band of a bridge should carry traffic across the Wolvine River. Cars were turning in tight circles there and heading back. It looked like one car had slid sideways into the yellow water.

The bridge had been swept away. Tess grinned. This town had it coming. Now no one could get into town, not unless they drove along the beach. Everybody knew how fast that river could rise. They should have been on the Highway Department's case years ago. This was sure going to raise hell with tourist season.

It would be a pleasure to be the first to give the news Mayor Bozman, Tess thought, and turned to leave the turret. Then she realized that someone would have told him by now. She nudged the door wider—the wind must have drawn it toward closing—and turned back to look at the ocean and the forest.

Even from this great height she could see that the rollers were taller than any she had ever known. Above them a faint glimmer of white floated, as if the sea were turning to milk. When she looked toward the forest, she saw faint echoes of white in the distance. The furthest trees seemed layered with white mists, like thin clouds riding the treetops. The white was still a long way from the reservation, but it crept slowly in that direction. Fiddert watched in fascination. Somewhere in Aowl's records, or in somebody's records, were entries about a white wind. Tess suddenly felt afraid and turned to check the door at her back.

Wind had swung it nearly closed. She firmly opened it again, resolved not to give into such foolishness. A white wind. Woofie business. Damned foolishness.

Tess looked down on nearly deserted streets which, even she watched, grew suddenly darker. She was conscious that the turret itself darkened. There was no sun to cast a shadow, and yet a giant shadow hovered like a dark kite above town. The shadow extended to the hills, seemed to flow from the hills. Gusts muttered in the stairwell at her back, echoing whispers that groaned like many voices straining with effort. In their sound, Tess thought she heard the sobs of a young woman. The sobs did not come from outside, but from the depths of the museum. There must be more damage than just the turret. Wind was working down there somewhere on the fourth floor.

It was time to go, time to get battened down for the storm. Tess turned for the door as the sobs seemed closer, more immediate. She stopped, frozen.

Only a crevice remained open, but that slice of the interior gave a view of solid and moving shadows. Shadows leaned, their edges blacker where they strained against the door's edge, and no one who knew Wolvine myth could mistake one of them. The shadow of a wolf crouched beside the shadow of a young woman. Sobs intermixed with the rumble of a growl, a growl low in the throat, warning, warning; the voice of attack.

Tess took a step backward, then caught her weight at the last instant. Four stories of empty air lay one step further. She reversed her weight and flung her body toward the closing door, aware even as she fell toward it that the crevice was narrowing. She threw her whole weight toward the slender opening only to meet the door's surface. The last inch of its closing slammed her backward.

The knob was like ice in her grasp, and it felt as unwilling to turn as if it had been welded into the lock. Tess went at it again, her palm burning with the strain. She tried fists against the black surface, then a shoulder. She paced back as far as she dared toward the far edge and managed three steps before ramming the door with her other shoulder. It held. The wind circled past, its hissing an echo saying, no use, no use. When she stepped back to stare at the flat black surface, she heard the voices.

They were rustlings and delighted whispers. They hissed from the other side like furious gossip. Amid that chorus, the sound of scratching began on the other side of the door, claws scrabbling on the wood as if they wanted to reach her. Terror surged beneath her breastbone. She backed away from the door and stood at the turret's edge, gripping the broken rail.

As Tess released her first scream to the wind, the shadow covered the museum. A gust picked up the scream and carried its red thread of pain out toward the surf. The boom of a crashing wave squelched it, but another scream followed. Tendrils of white encircled the sound, and white breezes toyed with it. Small wisps of white reached through chinks of the turret to surround her. She tried to bat them away, but they returned and others joined them. Tess screamed toward the empty gray band of road that marked the center of town. Wind took that scream too, lashing it around her like a whip before carrying it out to sea. After that, in each silence before she gave in and screamed again, the voices beyond the door swelled higher in waves of excitement.

Chapter 31

SHERIFF MULLING FIGURED HE COULD NOT HAVE BETTER WEATHER if he had ordered it. The approaching storm would close the town like a tomb. He drove through deserted streets on his way to the museum and chuckled because the big bad wolf hunters had not yet returned. It looked like those boys were going to get rained on, snowed on, blown out by wind, and then they would show up for a belt of whiskey at a bar that was already closed. They would not even find a lone can of beer.

When he entered the museum, a light burned in Tess's office. Mulling climbed to the second floor, shouted for her, and was answered only by what sounded like the echo of a scream. He climbed to the third floor. Nothing. He yelled into the fourth-floor stairwell. No one. Fiddert was gone, and she had obviously forgotten to turn off the light. Sheriff Mulling whistled tunelessly, then returned to his patrol car for flattened paper boxes. He told himself that he could have Fiddert's entire stash packed and loaded in not much over an hour.

In rapidly diminishing light, Molly Snow looked around the inside of the Aowl cottage and wondered if it was time to leave. During the short afternoon the weather had deteriorated, but in no single way. Instead, it seemed that small messages of bad weather dwelt everywhere. Thunder muttered, but did not boom;

and snow was replaced with rain, then with sleet. The forest continually blinked beneath sheet lightning. The northwest coast had the most unpredictable weather in the nation; but at least it usually settled down and did something. This day seemed undecided about what it wanted to be.

Twice she went to stand high on the dunes and watch the sea. Thoughts of history ran in her mind as the long waves grasped toward the dunes. The Victorians who had settled this area were fascinated with death, with the graves of departed ships, and with lonely beaches where dead voices murmured of happier times. Molly thought of the last storm, and of the stem board of that workboat, the Sea Spray. A true Victorian, she supposed, would imagine the Sea Spray out there making heavy way as its crew tried to keep it from coming ashore. The image was enough to send her hurrying back to the cabin.

In declining light she followed a hunch, packing all of her research into plastic bags before locking it in the trunk of her car. Al had once said the cottage was safe, but he had been talking about a different storm. This day felt too ominous to trust the safety of any building. As she closed the trunk the first strike of bolt lightning turned the sky to bright day. Molly screamed. She blinked, blinded by the afterimage of white light. She had seen a reddish-brown shape moving across the dunes, the movement liquid, flowing; the stretched-forward run of a giant cat. In the sudden flash it turned from brown to white, and then became brown again.

Storm Man. She waited for wind. Even as her rational mind told her that Storm Man was dead, and insisted that she was crazy to be outside when a wild animal roamed the dunes, she disbelieved its wisdom. That animal, which was much longer than a man was tall, could only be Storm Man. Molly rapidly got in her car and started the engine.

Now bolt lightning walked across the top of the forest on brilliant and crooked legs. Beside the cottage a large tree exploded as she watched; and a rain of branches thumped onto the hood. Molly numbly remembered it was a huge fir, a tree that had surely stood for more than a hundred years. Half of the tree tipped slowly, gathered momentum, fell, nearly striking the cottage. Smoke rose from the shattered hulk of tree still standing, but fire did not rise from the green wood.

Molly Snow backed away. She pointed the car to the road and headed toward town, wary of every tree lining the cabin road. When she reached the first buildings, she pulled to the edge and stopped. She couldn't see everything that was happening, but she could see a lot.

Sheets of lightning glazed the sky. High above the town there must be wind. She could almost feel it blowing up there, even though not a blade of grass stirred beside the road. She opened the window. Mixed with the long roar of surf was the low roar of an awful wind, a hurricane wind. It rode high above town where flashes of lightning forked across the hills. Thunder followed, louder than the voices of booming guns.

Molly felt suddenly small, vulnerable, and as afraid as she had ever been in her life. She looked down the road toward Surfbreak. At least in town she would not be alone. The people there might not like her, but they were people. A cannonade of thunder rolled from the hills, chased by a shock wave of vibration strong enough to wobble the car on its springs. Molly pulled into the middle of the empty road and forced herself to drive slowly. Another one like that could push her from the road.

Around the outskirts of Surfbreak, lightning struck into the forest, but the town sat in the center of the storm like an abandoned movie set. The streets were empty and boards covered many store windows. The only life she saw was a house cat. It sat in the middle of the street, licking its paw and grooming itself; a small brown cat sitting in a windless afternoon filled with thunder.

Molly took a deep breath. It was a house cat, nothing more. She eased the car forward and the cat glanced up, bored. It put its tail in the air and walked into the weeds of a vacant lot.

Lightning snaked along a hilltop. The wallop of thunder followed, shaking the road like an earthquake. Molly automatically hit the brake. Her chest and head flopped forward like a rag doll's, and through the upper edge of the windshield she glimpsed a puff of dust exploding. Or smoke. In the split second of its burst, the red metal awning which ran the half-block length of the hardware store snapped free of its accordion folds. It swung outward. Molly threw her body back in time to see the huge metal sheet, one strut dangling crazily, snap flat and sail toward the hood. It slapped there once, then flipped wildly past the windshield, over the top to rattle madly on the roof.

Molly ducked instinctively. When she looked again, that flailing red wagon was snapping back the way it had come, sprung toward the building by the strain of the two remaining struts. It planed at eye level, driving straight for the broad plate glass window. Boards partially covered the glass; but when the awning hit, the dust from old mortar puffed in slow motion, like white smoke in the lightning struck day. The window collapsed in a cascade of glittering swords. Molly sat immobile, trying to decide what to do. The hardware store stood exposed now. Glass lay in rubble, and the raw boards which formerly covered the window lay like wreckage cast onto a beach. A red lawn mower sat beside a green wheelbarrow. Something bounced from the hood of the car. The car trembled as if it were running at high speed.

Thunder did not kill people, she thought. Wind did not kill. But buildings could fly apart and launch wood and glass missiles, and those killed. Molly accelerated down the empty street. The only safe place was in a car that stood on open highway; but if hurricane wind descended into Surfbreak, even an open highway wasn't safe. Smoke rose from chimneys above the passing houses, but no one there would be glad to see her. No one would invite her in, or protect her from the storm.

Chapter 32

MOLLY ACCELERATED, KEEPING TO THE CENTERLINE. AHEAD, sheets of lightning licked in the distance. In the rearview mirror, clouds boiled over the receding, empty town. Then red and blue lights came up in the mirror, their pinpoints growing larger. A patrol car pulled from the road which led to the Aowl Museum. It looked like Mulling's car, but she could not believe the sheriff was driving it. Since seeing—or imagining—his corpse on the beach, she'd thought of Mulling as dead.

Molly's heart sank. It was Mulling approaching, she knew it. If Pam had said there was no corpse, Pam must be right.

The lights closed rapidly. Sheriff Mulling would see that she was alone. He would hurt her. He could do anything he wished. And he would. Pulling to the side, Molly fumbled the door locks shut, and told herself that nothing in the world would get her to step out of the car.

As the patrol car approached, it seemed surrounded by flashes of lightning. They concentrated where it passed, and all at once she realized that thunder had stopped rolling from the hills. The world was changing, changing, and now the flashes brought a horror even more unnatural than the horror of rape. Rape she almost understood. These flashes were beyond understanding.

Volley after volley of lightning streaked into the forest. It was impossible. Where there was lightning, there had to be thunder. Molly watched the approaching lights and wondered for an instant if she could have gone deaf. Lightning sliced the sky, yet there was no sound except for her gasping sobs.

A siren opened into the silence as Mulling approached, but his car did not slow. It swung to the other lane and blew past. The car continued to wail, and then the siren cut off, but the lights did not.

Molly sat in silence as the interior of her car turned white with lightning. The sheriff was going somewhere. Flashing past, his face seemed beyond tension, slack like the face of a corpse, white-lipped and hideous. Inside the patrol car, the back seat was piled high with paper bags and cartons. He was not interested in raping anyone, at least not now. Her relief was so great that she nearly forgot that she sat on an exposed road in the middle of what felt like a silent movie.

The Aowl Museum rose above the forest to spread a dark stain against the brilliant sky. "Someday that place will come down," Al had said. Now those words felt like a prophecy. She watched with fascination as the building began to pass out of history.

A flicker of fire glowed red in one of the turrets. A wisp of black smoke swirled away in a cloud of white that capped the mansion the way ice and mist cap the tallest mountains. A second flicker of red, this time taller, seemed sucked upward from the building. As smoke swirled, Molly saw, and could not believe, that wind blew up there from four directions. Winds converged on the tower to form an upward column of moving air, a suction drawing flames from the bowels of the structure; flames that rapidly mounted until the turret looked like a small volcano. Fire lighted the tall windows of all four floors. It threw sparks, flames, and smoke from a half dozen towers and turrets. Fire climbed rapidly into other turrets until the building looked like a gigantic firework.

No power on earth could save that building. Molly watched in fascination as fire spread beneath dark smoke that disappeared into the white cloud.

"The shadows will be freed," Al had said. "They will glad to be freed."

Now, from the smoke, the first shadows emerged. They flowed upward, strands of darkness blacker than the smoke, rising through the fire and whiteness. Shadows so intermixed that she could not see definite shapes; shapes of wolves and trees and cougars; shapes of men and women and children; or shapes of dying things cast along the rolling dunes and miles of beach.

On the damaged fourth-floor turret which had already seen fire once, something more substantial than a shadow wavered briefly. The smoke pulsed there, as if to magnify a flicker of color like the colors of a housedress. They wavered amid tongues of flame. The scream of Mulling's siren was receding, but now a shriek echoed in her ears, too loud and too close. A darker shadow, as ghastly as that dying shriek, turned and turned with its arms flailing wide. Then other shadows rose to swallow it. They fled upward so quickly that even the cloud of white became dimmed and gray.

Molly sat frozen in horror. Her skin grew clammy from the inside as if she had just witnessed a real human death, a flaring up of flesh more real than the shadows. The vision held her, and only dimly did she sense that the land was going dark and lightning ceased to cover the sky. When a jolt suddenly rocked the car, she snapped her gaze back from the pyre. The car had been hit by a huge breath of wind, and the wind was white. She fumbled for the ignition, then threw the car in gear. From every side, white flowed in a thin, milky stream, a rapidly blowing mist closing around her windows. Even as she watched, the world began to turn opaque.

Chapter 33

IF THINGS WERE GOING TO GO TO HELL IN A HANDBASKET, SHERIFF Mulling figured at least the weather was on his side. He passed the parked car of the skinny Molly Snow and caught a quick look at her face. She sat frozen in terror behind the steering wheel. That was just fine with Mulling. The little Woofie bitch had caused enough trouble in this town. She could sit on that road and rot as far as he was concerned.

His plans were falling together perfectly. Any number of pretexts could explain this trip out of town—police business, hunting the wolf hunters, or telling the Woofies to pack in their drum. He planned to go further than the reservation. When he reached the next town, he would rent a motel room, stash his profits, then return to Surfbreak. By then the museum would be gone. Mayor Bozman would be going nuts, and it would be a great time for the sheriff to take over and run things. Mulling supposed he would qualify as a hero for quite a while.

Only the thought of Tess Fiddert haunted him. As he set fire to the museum, the echoes of sound in that building, those muffled screams and murmurs and whispers, had all made him think of Tess's voice. At least, he wouldn't have to hear that voice much longer. Wherever she was today, she no longer had a museum and stolen money. She'd probably leave town soon.

Mulling glanced at the seat beside him. An Indian mask stared back, hollow-eyed. It jiggled on the seat, a mask made to look like a dog or a wolf. The entire car was filled with those masks, a good haul.

Things were certainly falling out right. The only inconvenience was having to take the beach route. Thanks to the Highway Department's radio bulletin, he had avoided taking the turn off that would only lead to a washed-out bridge.

Mulling slowed to turn onto a beach access road. He stopped for a moment, looking back at Surfbreak. Even from here, he could see the museum, furiously afire. The fire had taken hold almost too quickly to be believed. There was a lot of wind back there, and thin layers of white blew across the town and the road. The bitchy Miss Snow's car still sat in the road, and fingers of white reached toward it. Mulling rolled down his window. Maybe there was wind in Surfbreak, but there was no wind here. Lightning lit the access road, so constant that he did not need headlights.

Driving between the dunes, Mulling was vaguely aware that shadows crowded beneath the continual flashes of lightning. The shadows were slightly dimmed by the light. At first the shadows seemed both weird and threatening. Then he reminded himself that he had made it through almost a whole night with supposed Woofie ghosts inside the Aowl Museum. This was nothing. The lightning was playing some fancy games with the clouds, maybe reflecting from them. At the entrance to the beach, he stopped and figured his chances. The tide, coming in, rushed toward the access road faster than usual.

He was not going to make it. At least not for a couple hours until the tide turned. Black waves spread into the dunes like clutching hands. If the tide did not change soon, waves would come over the dunes and spread into the forest. There was not a scrap of solid sand down there. The entire beach flowed, changed, surged forward. Mulling watched as a breaking wave rushed toward the entry road.

It licked at the mouth of the road, the dark water nearly touching the car. The sea was black. Not green, not gray, but black.

He had to hide out somewhere for a couple of hours until the tide backed off. He remembered Molly Snow. He had some unfinished business with that young lady. He could turn back, drive to the Aowl cottage and be waiting for her when she came back home. Thanks to Tess Fiddert's gossip, not a soul in town would believe a word that Miss Snow said. If—Mulling chuckled—if she was in any mood to complain afterward.

The access road was narrow, and a rear wheel slipping over the edge would sink into soft sand. Mulling cut his wheel, backed and pulled forward, so intent on maneuvering that he did not see the shadows emerging from the dunes. Lightning did not fade these shadows. If anything, it made them darker. Mulling did not see the form of a man come from the dunes, a man carrying a dark burden in his arms. Before, and around, and behind the man ranged a pack of wolves.

The black sea broke behind the turning patrol car, and the entire world seemed without color. There was only black water and white surf. The whole world seemed muffled beneath an overpowering shadow, and Sheriff Mulling realized that even the lightning was being silently absorbed into that shadow. His turn complete, he flicked on his headlights.

A row of men stood not ten feet from his hood. They blocked the access road, and he automatically reached to turn on the emergency lights. His hand stopped before it touched the switch. He did not want to see more than he already saw. Mulling sat in his car, and waves of horror pressed him into his seat. He choked back a scream, tried to take a deep breath, and his chest constricted. His throat ached for air that would not come.

The wolf hunting party stood before him. He recognized the faces, but no flash of life quickened their eyes. Spectral. Ghastly, but only because they still stood upright. Mulling had seen his share of corpses, even grown used to them, but now he looked at the blank eyes of men he knew. These were men he had kidded with, or thrown in the cooler to sleep off a heavy drunk. He stared at men who were dead, but upright. Eyes were dull white globes in blackened faces, and the men swayed as if they stood in a mighty wind; but no wind blew and the only movement was the restless beat of pure black sea behind pure white surf.

Mulling stared at the line of hunters, and his hand shook so hard that he could not even make a small movement to put the car in gear. Those dull eyes watched, mouths still stretched wide in some final terror. Clothing hung in tatters. A low growl sounded inside the silent patrol car. Had he not been nearly insane with fear, Mulling would have sworn it did not come from the mask of a wolf. He was conscious that on each side of the car shadows deepened, congregating, a great assembly of shadows rising out of time and darkness and fear.

Then, at last, a human shape moved among the shadows and the men. A tall man with long, silver hair knelt gently on the sheltered side of a dune. He softly placed a burden on the sand. He murmured to it and stroked it. Mulling saw a yearling wolf. Gutshot, he thought automatically. It lay panting, unable to lick its wound. The beast lay like its own shadow on the dark dune.

The tall man stood, and behind him the assembled shadows gathered closer to hover near the wounded wolf. Barely audible through the half open window, murmurs and whispers intermixed with the long roll of surf. The man ignored the standing row of hunters. He walked to the patrol car.

Mulling sat frozen as the car's interior filled with the sounds of snarls. He feared getting out of the car, and he feared staying in. His hand fumbled for his pistol, but he trembled so hard that he could not work the slide. The silver-haired man opened the door. Reached in. He took the pistol from Mulling's hand so firmly that Mulling felt relief wash over him. This man was real. This was not a ghost.

"There's been enough killing," the man said, "or at least nearly enough. Your boys can shoot. We've got one wolf dead and one wounded." He looked at the line of hunters. "Damn this war," he whispered. "Damn all wars." There was sorrow in his tone, but his voice was not merciful. "Get out of the car," he said quietly. "Either get out or get pulled out."

Mulling tried to move and could not. He stared helplessly upward into the tall man's face.

"Because I don't have time to mess with this," the man said. "I have to fetch that yearling to Raymond Goodwillow. Maybe Goodwillow can save her." He opened the rear door of the patrol car, and his hand fell on Mulling's shoulder. The man seemed sad. "Get on out of there. You ran the race and lost." He looked into the car, where Indian masks rode cushioned by packages of money. "Trust to the sea," he said to the interior of the car, then he tugged at Mulling's jacket.

The sheriff moved slowly. He grasped the open door. He stumbled as he stood. Behind him, in the car, whispers sounded. Shadows moved closer, and one of them might have been a shadow once cast by Tess Fiddert.

"We were a pretty rough lot in my day," the tall man said quietly, "but we were men. We didn't go around assaulting women." He turned to the wolf pack. Small barks, growls, snuffling. Two wolves bounced like pups at play.

"I just told them to take their time," the tall man said. "They'll make a game of it." He walked to the wounded wolf and stooped to lift her. "It's not all bad for you," he told Mulling. "The longer they keep you alive, the longer the shadows have to wait." He gently lifted the dying wolf and strode away into the dunes.

White mist rolled across the sand as the wolves played. They leapt, snapped teeth together, waited for Mulling to stand each time he fell. They gradually unclothed him, claws and fangs stripping the leather jacket and rendering his boots to shreds. The wolves ran ahead of him as he stumbled in loose sand, and as lightning flashed across dunes and the silent sky.

His screams turned to sobs, and his sobs turned to desperate gasping. Claws raked his face, his arms, his chest and back. In the confusion of mortal fear he had some idea of escaping into the sea, so he staggered among dying waves. The waves probed cold fingers into his wounds.

The wolves played. They ran in circles, bumped against him, yelped and leaped. A claw ripped his face. He staggered in the surf, heading deeper. Wolves splashed about him like a pack of dogs playing around people on a sunlit beach.

Long before Mulling's last breath, black water rolled over the dunes. The sea entered the patrol car, floating Indian masks and flushing cash. Money tossed in the surf, bills that would wash up and down the beach, bills to be picked up by delighted beachcombers on some day when there might be sun. And long before Mulling's last breath, the Indian masks were borne on the reaching fingers of waves to be deposited in the forest. The masks lay beneath the trunks of scrub pine, and in thickets of blackberry. They gave life to the deathlike forest, and they accepted life as well. While Mulling died, the masks faded into darkness, and new life rose to run beneath the trees. The forest stirred with change. Shadows fled or rejoiced or took legs and walked. Other shadows hovered near Mulling as he staggered in the sea.

Night found bodies tumbled in the surf as the hunting party fell before giant waves. The bodies were bleached whiter by the sea. The sea took all but one; a middle-aged, overweight man in a rib-boned khaki uniform. He remained spread-eagled on the beach, staring blindly into the moonrise.

Chapter 34

WHEN THE WORLD BEGAN TO TURN, WHITE, MOLLY DROVE WITH fear, and with great determination. No other cars were on the road, so her speed did not matter. The car ran easily at sixty, but the speed could not last. White wind blew across the dunes carrying sand and dead grasses. It whipped the side of the car, and she dropped her speed.

She was not outrunning the wind, but the whiteness diminished as she fled further from town. In her mirrors, as if the town had floated into the white wind, Surfbreak disappeared. Here and there above the fading buildings, flagpoles and dish antennas still rode the top of the cloud. The whiteness rose higher, moving behind her like a stalking animal. It seemed trying to herd her back toward the Aowl cottage.

The reservation was the only safe place. If Storm Man became too powerful, even the reservation was not safe. Molly told herself to be sensible. This was a twentieth century road and she was driving a car through the real, three-dimensional world. This was just a storm, a bad storm. Not Storm Man. Storm Man was dead. There were no such things as curses.

Her logic faltered, and in a way she was glad. The fight between logic and old beliefs had been going on too long. Something awful was happening. Storm Man made this white wind surround her. Maybe in the equally true world of Indian legend and myth, death held more power than life. Old songs, songs she had never heard, blew in the wind. As the sky darkened into cold night, the lights of ceremonial fires burned in her memory. She felt that two people lived in her mind. She thought of her grandmother, Birch. She tried to listen to what Birch would know.

The wind carried echoes, whispers, shouts; the speech was in language she had never heard but somehow understood. Changing. Changing. She did not realize at first how rapidly her mind changed. The steering wheel suddenly felt alien. It was like touching a totally new and strange object. Her body remembered enough to step on the brake, to slow the car, to get it stopped. Logic told her that she must still be a mile from the reservation boundary, but in the face of the old knowledge welling up, logic trailed off. She had moved through some window of change. Logic gave only limited help.

Molly felt entombed in a steel box. She could vaguely remember how she had come to be here, but memory offered no way out of this huge metal shell. It took minutes to discover the snap of a cold door handle. She stepped out into the wind.

Memories stirred faintly, memories of a road, and a machine moving along the road. All around her lay encroaching dunes and encroaching forest. At her back, the car seemed a vaguely familiar object, like a closed carriage. Yet no horses stood near it as they should, and the thing had no shafts between which horses could be harnessed. Wind swept across the dunes, and old knowledge promised shelter in the dark forest. Her steps pointed toward the Wolvine, toward Goodwillow and Pam. Her steps carried her away from Storm Man.

Beneath a rising moon, white wind rolled over the dunes. Tendrils of white reached toward her. Storm Man's white grasp was slow and steady. He seemed contemptuous because of his power. He could take his time.

Now, balls of lightning rolled above the dunes like gigantic balloons. The balls were alive with electricity. She stood transfixed as parades of ball lightning shone bluely within the white wind. The balloons rose, fell, and occasionally one touched the earth, flashed, and disappeared. The balloons of light were great globes of power. Molly tried to move, willed herself to move, yet stood watching. A scrub pine clung to the lee side of a dune. A ball of lightning rolled toward it, touched, and the tree exploded. Molly screamed, but the explosion got her moving.

Loose sand slowed her. With each step she felt herself slipping further and further through the window of change. Wind took a new direction. It blew from the hills and tried to press her upright. She leaned forward and fought as its strength increased. The howl of wind dropped to the low roar of hurricane, and wisps of white flashed overhead and obscured the moon. When she stumbled and fell, she was nearly grateful to the wind. It was easier to crawl than to walk. Her knees registered the jabbing pain of small rocks and twigs. She crawled like a wounded animal into the sheltering forest.

A few feet inside the forest's edge, ancient trees rose into moonlight. Giant firs and cedars with trunks as wide as her cottage lifted branches high into the storm. Bolt lightning struck their tops, and a shower of twigs fell to scatter around her. Huge branches dropped, but the trees stood as strong as towering cathedrals.

It seemed to her, when she stood, that she entered a moonlit glade in which no other person had ever walked. She stood catching her breath, and wondering if she was still Molly Snow, or Birch. She surely stood in the late nineteenth century, and not in the late twentieth. Yet her memory remained, or at least some of it. Her memory lived beside the memory of another woman, the woman who had been her grandmother.

Wind roared across the dunes, and lightning mixed with moonlight. Shadows played back and forth across the glade, but the shadows did not threaten. Storm Man was powerful, but Storm Man had a weakness. Birch knew all of his ways. Now, memory said that Storm Man liked his power too much. Storm Man played with power, and while he played, others could escape, or plan against him. Her grandmother said that cougar could always be tricked by wolf, and that a woman with two memories had power as well. A woman with two memories could fight a war with cougar. When ice began to fall, blown from a cloudless sky by a white wind, her grandmother said it was time to leave. Storm Man would play tricks. Storm Man liked to play.

On the edge of hearing, as if from another world, the faint sound of a drum flowed among the ancient trees. Molly began walking toward its thundering pulses.

As she walked, the temperature plummeted and ice fell beneath lightning and moonlight. Flakes of ice stuck to her jacket. The constancy of its fall cast a screen, and on that whiteness visions of a mighty people stretched before her; people praising the salmon in the fish ceremony; people of the wolf, and Wolf himself rising from the smoke of ceremonial fires. Storm Man played with power. He sent the yowl and scream of a giant cat. Church bells tolled, and missionaries raised hands in supplication or disapproval. Beside the path dead men showed that the world was filled with plenty of war. Houses of white men burned and longhouses of Indians burned. Flames rose into the storm of ice, and the ice fell in places as rain, but it was ice again when it hit the ground. The footing became slick. She trembled with chill. Ancient memory reminded her to cross her arms and tuck her hands in her armpits. Maybe, her memory said, Storm Man could not freeze her chest that way. Maybe Storm Man could not break her fingers. The world seemed crisscrossed, and she bowed her head beneath the falling ice as she slowly walked toward the sound of the drum. Her memory folded over and over like the twisted and tumbled sheets of a bed which enclosed nightmares. In the moonlit ice, she saw visions of women taken against their will. The cruel face of Storm Man leered from the clearing behind her.

Molly felt him there, and she did not want to see him. Storm Man stalked her as the cougar stalked game. He wanted her to run. Storm Man was playing, her memory said. It was maybe a good thing to turn around. Storm Man must learn that she did not fear him.

Molly stood in a small cloud of ice between enormous trees whose height disappeared into a white wind. The ice wind danced, enveloping her face like a cloud of gnats. White wind obscured her legs and feet. She listened to memory's voice and recognized the voice of Birch. Birch's voice was her own, inflecting the soft syllables of an ancient tongue. She must allow nothing to startle her, it said now. No matter how ugly Storm Man looked, she must not show that she cared. And now she must look.

He rose into the forest, a giant creature, half-man and half-cougar. Red fire lighted his immensity. His arms rose toward her, and they were the gigantic arms of a man, but with the paws and claws of a cat. Electricity played around him in flat flashes and in jagged flashes. In his enormous face, his eyes seemed tiny, and they shone with cruelty and lust. His eyes said that he wanted her and that he would have her. His eyes did not speak of fondness, only of conquest. He would use her body, and from her body would be born a new clan of cougar. Cougar would walk the world, omnipotent.

"I think maybe Cougar comes to scare little children," Molly heard her voice say. She could not believe what she said. Surely this would anger Storm Man. At her back the drum pulsed, pulsed, and its voice swelled with ancient wisdom. "I think maybe Storm Man better get back to the hills before Wolf starts to run."

She had threatened him. Molly could not believe that she was being this stupid. Then she knew that it was not she but her grandmother who spoke. "Yea waa te ya wea."

The huge floating face bulged with anger. Electricity flashed blue in the white wind that gathered about his shoulders and began to blow toward her. A crash boomed in the night as electricity flashed into a giant tree. The tree leaned, and the stench of burning resin filled the wind. Electricity flashed again, then again. The tree tilted wildly and began its downward slide. It crashed into the darkness of the forest.

Wind struck her face, and Molly knew instantly that she would be found in this place. She would be frozen, silent as a statue. Storm Man's face bulged above his heavy body, a caricature of a nightmarish cat. Slick lips parted to show curved white knives of teeth. The white wind doubled its strength and whiteness. "Yea waa te ya wea," she said. "Storm Man better look out for Wolf. This is Wolvine land. Wolf is going to run." The soft nasality of her grandmother's words found new, low tones in Molly's own voice. "I think maybe Wolf is here already."

The drumbeat changed rhythm. Now the beat brought rapid volleys, like the reports of rifles firing through the wind. Molly turned, and the wind turned with her. She staggered in the direction of the drum. Wind hit in white bursts, shocking with coldness and ice. She bent into it and tried to concentrate only on the drum. As wind struck her face with the flat of its white hand, she realized she could no longer see in the cold darkness and colder white. Yet her grandmother chuckled. "Cougar came for a woman, and Cougar found Wolf. I think maybe Cougar's going to need a missionary pretty quick."

The drumbeats changed to flashes of silver, and each beat cut across the wind like silver teeth. In the dark forest, silver cut into white, thrust aside ice, and silver flashes assaulted wind. At last the wind ceased to press her backward.

Molly raised her head and glanced around. She could see that wind still blew all around her. Ice still fell, but it did not fall on her. A stream of silver flashes, vivid as migrating salmon, flowed through the forest. The strong voice of the drum carried them. As silver teeth cut the wind she saw fire in the near distance. This was not the spectral fire of Storm Man. This was not the fire of Cougar. The ceremonial fire of the Wolvine rose among the trees, and the silver teeth of Wolf cleared a stream, a stream that she might follow to safety, but a stream that also led to Wolf.

Chapter 35

As Raymond Goodwillow stood watching the exhausted figure of Molly Snow stumble from the forest, storms marched. Storms bred in the Bering Sea, storms rose from the Gulf of Alaska, and rain-laden clouds raced above the Japanese current. Arctic winds curled along the Canadian Rockies. Goodwillow watched Molly move toward the fire and he knew that if Birch were not with Molly Snow, then Molly Snow would be lost. He, Goodwillow, would have held back his strength for the main battle. He would not have sent the silver teeth of Wolf slashing into the wind. He ignored Molly as she collapsed beneath the sheltering roof. One of Pam's sisters could take care of her. Goodwillow held his full attention on Storm Man. Already Storm Man played dangerous games with the white people.

Goodwillow concentrated on Surfbreak, diving deeper into the feelings of that place. He felt the fear of people who were afraid to stay in their houses, and who were more afraid to step into the white wind. Their streets were once more covered with rushing water. The black museum building had burned, its curse devoured by fire and wind. Shadows of dead things blew through the town, through the forest, and along the beaches. Shadows stalked the streets. The shadows caused no harm, but they caused fear. The people huddled, isolated and miserable, while seawater licked at the foundations of houses. No help could reach them. They could not even help each other.

Goodwillow told himself that soon the ground would shake with new thunder. Lightning would attack the reservation, and the white wind would drive like a spear at the heart of Wolvine land. Volleys of fire and volleys of ice would attack the forest. If the ice succeeded, trees would crack with its weight. The river would freeze, and animals would cower and die. Winds strong enough to carry water from the sea would spread salt ice through the forest, poisoning every plant. Flood would not come from the sea, but from the hills; and flood would bring boulders and great trees crashing from the hillside. Wolf must win, Goodwillow told himself, or the entire land would become shadows.

He did not believe that Storm Man could shake fire from the earth and raise a mountain over them, but Storm May would try. Goodwillow cast his mind toward the north, reaching into the far Arctic night. He praised his power. The silver teeth of Wolf could defend the Wolvine from where Goodwillow stood, and it could attack Storm Man from northward.

The fire burned on its deep bed of coals. Beyond the fire, giant trees rose. As Goodwillow studied them, he looked closer, then paused and looked again.

The Great Changer had made things different again. The forest stood as it did when Goodwillow was a boy. The Great Changer placed paths of time across the battle scene, and sometimes the time was now, and sometimes the time was long ago. Shadows of dead things rose and took form. Masks of wolf and wolverine, of fox and cougar, came to life in the forest. Shadows of other dead things were captured by Storm Man, and when the attack came those shadows would fly through the forest, shrieking.

The Great Changer did not make Goodwillow young again, but a pathway of time ran beneath his old body. He felt the great weight of the wolf robe on his shoulders, and the weight seemed no more than the weight of a leaf. The heavy mask of Wolf felt no heavier than a scrap of paper. The greatest change now emerged from between the trees. It glided into the clearing in the shape of a man, but its long silver hair, the swift padding of its steps and, most of all, its scent told its true species. It knelt quietly beside the fire. Firelight sketched bright flickers around the hollows in its face. Many years had passed since Goodwillow saw that face.

Goodwillow wondered why The Great Changer had brought Man-Among-Wolves to this place. Man-Among-Wolves had his own war to fight, and Goodwillow thought that Man-Among-Wolves had better get started pretty quick. Instead, he knelt beside the fire as people chanted. The wounded body of a young wolf eased to the ground before Man-Among-Wolves's hands drew back.

The fur of the young wolf carried a hint of silver, or maybe the long, silver hair of the man made it look that way. The young wolf panted, very near to becoming a shadow. It would be the worst bad luck to have a wolf die just when the power of Wolf was supposed to run. Goodwillow gave thanks for the power of the ceremonial fire, and he gave thanks for Pam. Her shape separated itself from darkness and knelt beside the young wolf. Her lips moved, and her fingers touched the wound. The wolf panted, but its eyes glowed blue in the firelight. The shadows of death began to leave them.

Goodwillow curled the wolf robe closer against his neck. He tested his final strength and knew that it would last long enough. He looked at Pam, at the wounded wolf, at Man-Among-Wolves, and finally at Birch. Then he concentrated on the storms.

The radiant heat of the fire reached across twenty feet of ground and warmed Molly's face. She sat on a log, dazed and shaking, magnetized by the fire.

She had thought it would be tall. Instead, this fire was deep. It rose from a bed of coals where blue light was stronger than red. The heat spread so evenly that twenty feet from the fire was not too far. It might be a little too close. She became aware of a woman leaning above her to place a blanket around her shoulders.

"I'm Sara," a voice said, "Pam's oldest sister." The woman looked into the night forest. "Sit quiet," she said. "Don't move until you're told." She snugged the blanket around Molly's shoulders like a mother tucking in a child. "Trust my grandfather, because I don't think the rest of us know what the hell we're doing."

If the woman was joking, the joke felt grim. "Birch," she said, her voice filled with wonder. "At least Pam listened to the old man's stories." She patted Molly's shoulder, then moved away to stand waiting.

Shadows ranged from the forest where it seemed that no light dwelled. Molly's teeth chattered from the cold flight through the forest, but beyond her discomfort she could sense that something very old and very strong was being borne from the mists of time. No historian had ever seen this. She must remember it.

The great drum muttered a steady beat. It did not roar throb with silver flashes through the forest. The drum seemed to hold a private conversation with itself. The woman kneeling by it, probably Pam's other sister, struck its head with a short, rounded club, but the strokes did not originate from the woman. She seemed in a trance, allowing the drum to say what it wished. The woman was flat-faced and looked nearly Oriental. Long hair with beginning strands of silver fell over her shoulders and swung against her back at each stroke. Her blouse and jeans came from a dry goods store. Her fingernails were red from polish bought at a dime store.

Yet it seemed that the woman might as well be masked and robed in ceremonial clothes. The power of the drum transformed her. Her arm moved, obedient to the demands of the drum. The movement was as direct and unthinking as the response of an attacking animal.

Old memories stirred, and Molly could not tell whether they were her memories or the memories of Birch. Shadows of dancers moved before the fire. It seemed there were more shadows than dancers. The dancers stepped rhythmically, as if each dancer searched for a separate spirit to bring to the fire. A man wearing the mask of raven seemed to float on wind, yet his steps were as firm as the others. A fox brought trickery, and a bear brought strength. Molly told herself that she saw nothing except a small and isolated band of people dancing around a fire in a mighty forest. Even as the thought arrived, she knew it was not true.

Among the shadows on the far side of the fire, other people watched and waited. A flash of silver moved against the background of dark forest. Molly watched, and then her heart raced.

Al was here, Alford Aowl. Man-Among-Wolves made that larger shadow near the fire. Firelight inscribed lines of tension in his face as he stared down at a dark bundle near his feet. Someone knelt over the bundle. Molly saw that it must be Pam. Then Al smiled and turned to the forest. There, a pack of wolves emerged into the clearing, sliding across the ground like gray liquid.

Wolves stood or sat around Al, twenty or twenty-five of them. Some were enormous, their long bodies dwarfing those of the dancers, and some of their faces were masklike. A couple of dancers momentarily stumbled at the sight of them. The drum began to beat faster.

Molly's heart roared so hard, she thought her chest would explode. She loved this man. She loved him more than she had ever loved any other man, or any other thing. She loved him with passion, but even more, with savagery. A low rumble sounded from her throat. This was her mate, and with this man she could run through the night, or sleep curled beside him. Her love knew nothing of politeness, or of right and wrong. The drumbeat quickened. Molly started to stand.

"Do not move," her grandmother's voice commanded. "Stay where you are."

Her grandmother's voice echoed her own furious love, sobbing with its power. Her grandmother said that a woman with two memories had plenty of power, but she could also make plenty of mistakes.

Al reached in his pocket and pulled out a clasp knife. His deep voice carried across the clearing. "Silver of Wolf," he said. "Wolf goes to war." He swung his long hair to the front of his shirt, where it hung like a silver cape. The knife hacked at strands of the hair until they broke free. He moved among the wolves, weaving strands of silver hair in their manes. Silver came alive. The pack stood marked with silver arrows. Al turned to Goodwillow.

"Maybe you can do this alone, my old friend," he said, "but we come to help."

Al knelt to stroke the wounded wolf, then glanced up at Pam. "Strong medicine," he said to her. "Your power is big." When he rose and turned again toward the forest, the wolf pack closed around his steps. They moved slowly but without pause into the screen of trees. Within seconds, they seemed only a flash of silver in the night.

Molly sat poised, ready to act as soon as it was time. Some

part of her understood what was happening, but that part must belong to her grandmother. She no longer feared Storm Man. If he were here, right now, she would attack. Her grandmother's voice said that what Molly knew was right. Pretty quick now it would be time. Her grandmother's memory unfurled a vision of a nighttime forest, a forest filled with flashes. It seemed now that she too ran alongside the wolves, ran as Birch had once run, feeling the hot wind of their breath breaking over her. Then a rumble sounded nearby, moving toward the fire like an express train. The memory broke off. The ground began to shake. Molly tried to stand and felt herself thrown to the dirt. The ground rose, and fell, and rose. The rumble drove through the clearing, and even the drum fell momentarily silent.

Raymond Goodwillow motioned to the dancers. He picked up a heavy wooden staff. He slid the huge wolf mask over his face, and turned to the fire from which the spirit of Wolf must rise.

Chapter 36

THE WOLF PACK RAN THROUGH THE FOREST, CIRCLING WESTWARD toward the sea. It ran heedless of the screams of shadows that assaulted the forest, shadows that tumbled and flew before white wind. The captive legions of Storm Man howled and twisted. The faces of men and women long dead mixed among the howling heads of animals. Shadows of owls rode the wind above living owls that crouched on the ground, brought to earth by wind. A white wave of wind cloaked the forest so that stars and moon and lightning were swallowed in whiteness as thick as milk. As the wolf pack approached the dunes, it split, one group circling north, one south. The wolves cut silver streaks through the white wind.

Thunder rolled across the land and shook the hills. Here and there a house staggered, was hit again, and collapsed into rubble of stone and brick and wood. The town of Surfbreak rattled and danced beneath cannon blasts of thunder. In the sheriff's office, windows exploded. Concrete blocks tumbled after them. Across town, shadows of the dead flew weeping through the streets. People huddled in their houses and swore to each other that they did not hear what they were hearing; the tormented voices of people they knew, voices of people who everyone thought were still alive—the sheriff, the curator of the museum, and hunters. Surfbreak counted its dead by listening to their screams.

Lightning assaulted the forest; balls of lightning rolled from the dunes and struck among pines. Bolt lightning cut the white wind, topping old trees, splitting ancient ones. Lightning increased as ice swept from the north, and as the sea cast windblown spume that turned to salt ice. Temperatures dropped so quickly that younger trees' thin layers of bark could not protect them. Sap froze. The trees exploded as animals began to die. Mice curled in their burrows as coldness drove into the soil. Deer huddled together, stiffened, blind eyes staring blankly into ice and wind.

Screams of cougar flew on the wind, rising above the tormented screams of shadows. The power of Cougar gathered the wind, concentrating its currents so that they narrowed to a white spear pointing at the heart of the reservation.

The silver flashes of wolves met the spear, and some wolves tumbled and died. Wolves bit silver teeth across the spear, divided it, and the wind shifted, lost direction, fell into uncertain gusts from every quarter. Wolves circled on the beach, and there were not so many of them now. The screams of cougar rose among the shore pines as Storm Man moved toward the reservation. The wolves spread through the forest behind him. They followed, awaiting a time to strike, waiting for Raymond Goodwillow to strike.

Goodwillow danced as Wolf, and he felt the strength of Wolf enter his legs. He danced strongly, but even Wolf could not make a young man of an old one. Goodwillow had expected Storm Man to be strong, but not this strong. He remembered his old mentor, but then told himself to think only of Wolf.

Wolf lived in the fire, and Goodwillow felt Wolf moving in the flames. Yet Wolf did not rise. Something was not right. No ice yet touched the dancers, but ice fell nearby in the forest. Goodwillow listened to demonic cries growing louder as they clustered in the forest. Beyond the clearing, Storm Man's white wind clawed its way into the reservation. Goodwillow danced and asked the drum why it was not fighting hard enough. One of his granddaughters knelt before that drum, but she was not one who knew the old stories. The drum began to sound uncertain.

Maybe the wolf did not rise because the voice of the drum did not call strongly enough. Goodwillow thought of Pam, and then he thought of Birch. Pam had a lot of old knowledge, but it was mixed with new knowledge. Only Birch knew the old ways. Birch was not going to be fooled. Goodwillow did not know what Molly Snow was capable of, but he knew she carried Birch inside of her. He trusted Birch. His mind called out. Birch should take the drum.

Goodwillow watched Molly Snow rise to her feet. She stared from side to side, confused. Thunder rolled out of the hills from the east. This thunder said that boulders were rolling, that the forest would be struck over and over by boulders. Mudslides would follow, and the slides would fill the river so that the salmon could not return. No beaver could live, and bears would go away. The river would become a dead place. Goodwillow watched Molly Snow and urged Birch forward. At last her gaze came to rest on the drum and it was no longer confused. She moved quickly to kneel beside the drum, shouldering the other woman aside.

Once more the ground shook as screams of Cougar filled the forest. Feathers of ice began to fall at the edge of the clearing. Bolts of lightning appeared through the white wind, and a tree fell at the clearing's edge. Storm Man was getting too strong. Goodwillow said to Birch that she had better hurry.

Molly had held back from standing for as long as she could, but her grandmother's voice was too strong. Birch wanted her to walk to the drum, to bend her spirit to its power. Storm Man knew what he was doing, her grandmother said. Storm Man changed his attack. He was either going directly at the drum, or directly at Birch and Molly Snow.

The scream of the cougar sliced across the pounding of the drum, and its beat faltered. Pam's sister, her lips bitten white with concentration, strained to recover the rhythm that could call Wolf forth from the fire. Molly looked at Pam and Goodwillow. Goodwillow's body rose and fell with the dance, the great wolf robe swirling, but his legs were old. His eyes called to Birch, but seemed not to see Molly Snow.

Molly willed her body to cross the clearing. She remembered Al and knew now with certainty that she could not save him. Aowl was no longer a man. He could not live as one, but she could save these others. Molly felt the spirit of Birch flow like an ink over her consciousness. The last sensation she remembered was the weight against her shoulder as she pushed Pam's sister aside.

The instant she knelt before the drum, curtains of ice concentrated on the far side of the clearing. Tormented figures moved within the ice. The figures showed what kind of punishment she could expect; what punishments all Wolvine women could expect. What was threatened went far beyond rape, because it was that coupled with slavery. She would never be free, and what was going to happen would continue to happen, over and over.

Ferocity rose in her. She became claws and teeth, and she became remorseless. Her body felt like ice. Her soul felt stripped.

She looked at Goodwillow, and she gasped as the old man stumbled before the first blast of white wind. Wind touched the fire, fanning it from blue to red; black smoke swirling. She concentrated only on the drum.

Strokes of the drum cast shafts of silver into the forest, and the curtain of ice became thin. It faded as the drumbeats flew like arrows among the trees. The ice did not disappear. Then it once more began to build, and she began to chant. "Yea waa te ya wea nanee." The drum drove each sound into the forest, and Goodwillow joined the chant. Once more, the fire turned blue.

The forces were in balance. Thunder crashed from the hills, but the wind did not advance, nor did the ice. Her wrist felt pain from striking the drum, but she knew that soon flesh would merge the pain with the drumbeats and that would be all right. Her mind clawed toward the forest, its fury absolute, but not blind. It knew tricks and estimated the enemy. Storm Man was strong, but his strength was the strength of Cougar. Without that force, Storm Man was only a spirit. Storm Man had tricked Cougar into doing his work.

The drum began to speak to the forest, and it said that Cougar was plenty strong. Cougar was one of the great and brave beings. Cougar had the respect of Wolf, because Wolf did not go to Cougar's hills. Cougar never failed, but maybe Cougar could be deceived.

Goodwillow continued to chant, but his steps slowed as the drum spoke of Cougar. Then his steps gathered speed as he began to understand why Birch talked to Cougar.

The drum said that Storm Man turned the world to shadows. Our brothers were becoming shadows. Deer, and even shrews and mice were dying. How would Cougar stay strong when the world was shadows? Could Cougar's young grow fat and strong by eating shadows? The drum said that Cougar was being betrayed.

Snarls rose from the forest. The screams of great cats echoed through the trees, and an even greater scream came from where Storm Man advanced. The white wind increased and Storm Man rose beyond the clearing, a giant figure among the trees. Electricity sheeted around him, but it did not flash toward the clearing. The world became silent as thunder ceased. Snarls of Cougar sounded farther away as Cougar took his power back to the hills and Storm Man stood alone.

Raymond Goodwillow raised his voice in chant, calling Wolf to rise from the fire.

Chapter 37

At first that ancient spirit was only a face—silver muzzled, gigantic, like a mask carved from a slab of ancient cedar. The fire cast blue light across the silver of Wolf, and Wolf began to stand. Wolf rose to his legs. He stood in blue flame, taller than a man and howling defiance. At first Wolf was spectral, but he quickly became as strong as the fire in which he stood. Goodwillow turned to the forest. The power of Wolf turned with him.

Flashes of silver rose from the north where the midnight sun slept and northern lights lived. Aurora borealis arced like a silver rainbow across the black sky. Silver flooded about the tops of trees and fell through their branches. Silver fell across the face of Storm Man.

He screamed. Storm Man threw white wind, and the wind was cut to breezes. Storm Man threw bolts of electricity, and the bolts struck falling silver streams.

Savagery swelled each beat of the drum. Storm Man would run, and Wolf would chase. Defeat was not enough. Only destruction would end this. The drum fired silver bolts into the forest as Storm Man turned. He stood with his back to the clearing, and he was not so solid now. He seemed more like a spirit screaming in hate and fear.

A wolf pack stood across the trail. There were wolves with faces like masks, and wolves with faces like wolves. The large silver-maned leader crouched, ready to spring.

The pack advanced and Storm Man retreated. Each backward step brought him closer to the glowing fire. Wolf stood in it, snarling.

A shower of sparks erupted and singed a stain down Storm Man's back. A white mist rose and extinguished it. His power was ebbing, but it was not gone. Storm Man faced the silver-maned wolf, and he chanted even as he backed away. He ignored Goodwillow and Birch and Pam. He ignored the other wolves. He concentrated only on the silver-maned wolf, and his curse sounded firm even as the circle of wolves closed. That circle forced Storm Man backward, stumbling, flailing until he fell like a giant tree; falling into the fire, into the fiery maw of Wolf. In rising clouds of blue fire, the great figure fell under the claws and teeth of Wolf.

Wolf cut him, bit into him, tore open his throat. Fury rose in the blue flame as the giant figures struggled. Sounds flew in the night, and some of the sounds told of the death of Storm Man, but some sounds said that Storm Man's captives were free. The night filled with the rush of shadows that no longer howled, but only faded quickly into the blackness. Even as fury sounded in the snarls of Wolf, and death sounded in the screams of Storm Man, sighs of peace covered the clearing as shadows disappeared.

At first the body of Storm Man flamed with red fire, but the fire grew hotter as that shape became more insubstantial than a spirit. The body turned to a small cyclone of white wind, but the wind was drawn down into blue fire. Storm Man became nothing but a scream, and then the blue fire devoured the scream.

Molly Snow sensed where she was with perfect clarity, and she could remember all that happened. Yet the eyes which had seen those memories were different eyes. Her grandmother said that everything was okay. Wolf stood in blue flame, and then Wolf settled on his haunches as the night turned silver. No wind blew. Stars above the clearing glowed like scales along the silver sides of salmon. What happened was good, her grandmother said, and what was going to happen was not so bad. Her grandmother sounded hopeful, but sad, and Molly felt that sadness as her own. It seemed that Birch was about to follow the other shadows that fled to freedom.

Wolf returned to blue fire, sinking down, until only the mask of Wolf stared from the coals, staring at Raymond Goodwillow. Then Wolf was gone. The clearing returned to night, and the stars burned blue.

Goodwillow stumbled, faltered, went to his knees. The heavy mask of Wolf fell to the ground. His staff tilted into the fire and blazed red. Pam came quickly to his side, and her sisters joined her.

Around the fire the Wolvine stood motionless, waiting for Pam to tell them what to do. She helped Goodwillow into a sitting position, then turned to Molly. "My grandfather is weak, but he will see this to the end. Decide now. Pretty quick now, it will be too late."

Molly stood, or else her grandmother stood. Molly's confusion was a silent partner to Birch's rapid thoughts. Man-Among-Wolves would be a wolf forever. Storm Man's final curse had made it so. Not even Goodwillow, if he lived, could remove that curse.

Molly followed Pam's gaze and saw that on the far side of the fire the silver-maned wolf sat. The wolf pack waited around him. Firelight turned Man-Among-Wolves into a blue and silver sentinel that guarded the Wolvine, that would always guard the Wolvine. Molly touched the sadness which rose in her, and its meaning began to unfold. She felt the spirit of her grandmother drawing away. The threads that joined them stretched and began to fray.

"Yes," Birch said aloud, "this is what needs to happen. I choose this and I will never be sad for it." As she spoke, Molly felt a rush of savage love, and she found herself walking to the silver-maned wolf. She reached him and only then became aware of the shadow of a young woman stepping from the forest. The shadow moved with animal grace, and it met Molly as she stood before the silver-maned wolf.

She looked down. At her feet lay the yearling wolf, wounded, but not panting any longer. The young wolf struggled, then rose awkwardly to its feet. Then shadow and wolf merged, and Molly felt the last threads of her grandmother break from her. Molly Snow stood before a wolf pack, and the yearling wolf bounced, licked the face of the silver-maned wolf. The yearling moved as if she had never been wounded.

Molly looked into the face of the silver-maned wolf, this face of Man-Among-Wolves. She sought some recognition, some memory, but its gaze was alien, alien and unknowing. The wolf looked about the clearing where the Wolvine stood waiting. Then, as if satisfied that all was well, his great body turned and he led his pack into the forest, the yearling wolf trotting at his side.

Chapter 38

MORNING LIGHT FOUND THE STREETS OF SURFBREAK LITTERED with the aftermath of war. Along the main street, as Molly Snow pulled her car to the curb, a bulldozer chugged through light Northwest rain. It pushed debris from the lane toward the sidewalk. A few buildings still stood. Molly backed up and parked her car near a vacant lot where a huge Army tent stood. Smells of coffee and food came from the tent. A National Guard helicopter whipped above her, ferrying injured to a hospital after delivering supplies.

Molly climbed from her car and looked around. The bank windows were broken, but the building was protected by a man with a rifle. She breathed easier, knowing that the Aowl manuscripts were safe inside the bank's vault. She looked toward the museum.

Its blackened remains lay on high and tortured ground. Not even a stub of a brick chimney interrupted the sky. The fire had been so furious that nothing was left except a still-smoldering blackness, and that blackness spread along the sides of the hill as if making a last reach for Surfbreak. Molly shuddered. The town would be better off without the place, although the town would not believe that.

Around the Army tent, young children wearing brightly colored nylon jackets ran and played in the rain. Their schoolhouse was down, and no doubt their parents told each other that the town faced total ruin, but the children played. And in a sense, Molly told herself, *all* of the people, including Molly, were children. The

Wolvine, except for Pam, were children walking through a forest of darkness while not even knowing that the forest was there. Life and meaning had changed.

Out at the reservation, where she was not welcome this morning, the people buried Raymond Goodwillow. She had watched as Pam sat beside her grandfather and waited for the dawn. Pam's sisters worked in the house, and Pam had said that her grandfather would be buried in the cave at the back of the shack.

Molly Snow did not know how, or with what ceremony, but when the burial was over, she would be free to return to the reservation. She would be free to spend time with Pam if she wanted.

The problem was, she told herself, she did not know what she wanted. In the trunk of the car, safe in plastic bags, lay enough research for her thesis. She would have to finish that, not because she wanted to, but because it added to human knowledge. Today the small jealousies and smaller games of college life looked pathetically pale. And yet, being a historian was a very good thing. It was some of the world's oldest work and she must find ways to do it that would show the true sinew of history, and not its futile battles. Maybe she would spend the winter with Pam. Maybe when spring came she would know what to do. Maybe when spring came, and ice broke up north, she would find work among the tribes in Alaska.

A bulldozer puttered nearby, and she felt a hand touch her elbow. She looked up to see the concerned face of a young National Guardsman. She thought that, compared to him, she must look incredibly old.

"Ma'am? Are you all right?" His hand was gentle but firm as he steered her from the path of the bulldozer.

"I'm fine," she said softly, "or at least as well off as everyone else."

The boy tried to be encouraging. In fact, he tried so hard that he nearly sounded bubbly. He spoke of an engineering company that would soon arrive. In his young world, it must seem that things that were broken could always get fixed quickly. "I'll get you some coffee."

A cup of coffee would be nice, Molly thought. She remembered the night she had first made coffee for Al. She thought of their walk in the forest and of how she had felt when they first made love. She looked toward the museum, half expecting to see a silver shadow standing above the ruins.

Nothing was there, but it seemed as if gleams of silver creased the gray sky above it. She told herself that when the boy returned with coffee, she must remember to be polite and thank him very kindly.

Jack Cady (1932-2004) won *The Atlantic Monthly* "First" award in 1965 for his story, "The Burning." He continued writing and authored nearly a dozen novels, one book of critical analysis of American literature, and more than fifty short stories. Over the course of his literary career, he won the Iowa Prize for Short Fiction, the National Literary Anthology Award, the Washington State Governor's Award, the Nebula Award, the Bram Stoker Award, and the World Fantasy Award.

Prior to a lengthy career in education, Jack worked as a tree high climber, a Coast Guard seaman, an auctioneer, and a long-distance truck driver. He held teaching positions at the University of Washington, Clarion College, Knox College, the University of Alaska at Sitka, and Pacific Lutheran University. He spent many years living in Port Townsend, Washington.

Carol Orlock's second novel, *The Hedge, the Ribbon*, won the Western States Book award, and her first, *The Goddess Letters*, was honored with the Pacific Northwest Booksellers' Award and the Washington State Governor's Award. Her stories and poems have appeared in *Ms. Magazine*, *Calyx*, *Women of Darkness* and *Fine Madness*, among others.

For many years, Orlock taught fiction writing for the University of Washington Professional and Continuing Education Program. She has been awarded a Washington State Literary Fellowship and selected as a semi-finalist for the Iowa Short Fiction Award. Her nonfiction has appeared in numerous national magazines, and she has published two nonfiction books.

www.ingramcontent.com/pod-product-compliance
Lightning Source LLC
Chambersburg PA
CBHW031102020726
47495CB00007B/2006